Grimm Inscriptions

DANIELLE ACKLEY-MCPHAIL

JAMES CHAMBERS

GORDON LINZNER

BERNIE MOJZES

CHRISTINE NORRIS

CYNTHIA RADTHORNE

MICHELLE D. SONNIER

DAVID LEE SUMMERS

PATRICK THOMAS

JEFF YOUNG

Grimm Machinations: More Steampunk Faerie Tales

edited by
Danielle Ackley-McPhail
and Greg Schauer

eSpec Books
Pennsville, NJ

PUBLISHED BY
eSpec Books LLC
Danielle McPhail, Publisher
PO Box 242
Pennsville, New Jersey 08070
www.especbooks.com

ISBN: 978-1-956463-25-5
ISBN (ebook): 978-1-956463-24-8

Art Direction: Mike McPhail, McP Digital Graphics

Copyeditor: Greg Schauer
Cover and Interior Design: Danielle McPhail, McP Digital Graphics

Dedication

To Everyone Who Helped Make This Faerie Tale Happen.

Contents

The Souls of Misbehaved Boys

Based on The Adventures of Pinocchio

JAMES CHAMBERS

At the noise, a window opened and a lovely maiden looked out. She had azure hair and a face white as wax. Her eyes were closed and her hands crossed on her breast. With a voice so weak that it hardly could be heard, she whispered: "No one lives in this house. Everyone is dead."

"Won't you, at least, open the door for me?" cried Pinocchio in a beseeching voice.

"I also am dead." "Dead? What are you doing at the window, then?" "I am waiting for the coffin to take me away."

After these words, the little girl disappeared and the window closed without a sound. "Oh, Lovely Maiden with Azure Hair," cried Pinocchio, "open, I beg of you. Take pity on a poor boy who is being chased."

"When the dead weep, they are beginning to recover," said the Crow solemnly.

"I am sorry to contradict my famous friend and colleague," said the Owl, "but as far as I'm concerned, I think that when the dead weep, it means they do not want to die."

—Carlo Collodi
The Adventures of Pinocchio

A BOY IN ASHY RAGS AND SECONDHAND SHOES SHIVERED ON THE CORNER of Stratemeyer Alley. He blew into his cupped hands to warm his fingers, while he gazed the length of the alley, seeking. Despite his obvious destitution, he risked much venturing out after midnight in Appleton Corner. Criminals in this part of New Alexandria traded in more than money and contraband. Even an undernourished urchin offered potential riches in his pale flesh and brittle bones. The boy knew this, of course, and the tip-tap of passing footsteps sent him retreating into the nearest doorway's cloaking shadows. After the *pitter-patter* faded, the child returned to the curb, his rangy body a scarecrow in the quavering gaslight.

His wide, watery eyes scrutinized the gloom. Seconds produced minutes which accumulated, as they must, into an hour. The boy slumped to the cobbles, his back against the sooty brick of a tenement building. After a time, he tented his legs, rested his head on his knees, and sobbed in the posture of lost boys everywhere. Denied a lifeline in the midnight desert of stone and fog, he dozed, tumbling into an irresistible slumber born of fatigue of the heart as well as the body — a thin and shiftless sleep where he saw his mother's sad face in his dreams, defined forever by her pleading eyes, the only beauty he'd ever known.

The bray of a donkey echoing along the alley snapped the boy alert.

He bounced to his feet, eyes wide in wonder at a silver shimmer that repelled the night like a fallen moonbeam. The illumination tumbled shadows along the alley until they assumed the shapes of their material counterparts: a pack of twenty-four donkeys drawing a broad coach driven by a pale, plump man with a cherubic grin. The donkeys all wore leather children's shoes tied to their feet, so their hooves made little noise upon the cobblestones; straw bound by rags to the iron coach wheels muted their passage too. Only the beasts's snorting breaths and the Coachman's wheezing chuckle gave voice to the assembly, creating the impression that the coach sailed out of the night itself. Spirits lifted, the astonished boy whistled and waved.

Lamps dangled from hooks flanking the driver's seat. They bobbed and scintillated until settling as the coach stopped. The Coachman's doughy face glistened in the lamp glow. Produced by no ordinary oil, the light fringed everything it touched with a hazy glimmer. From the coach, a multitude of young eyes observed the boy, whose joy faltered upon seeing so many youths like him packed in tight. Though the crowded boys welcomed him with cheers, he saw no room at all left to join them.

"Hello, lad," the Coachman said. His voice whispered like a cat's hiss, like a mother's good night kiss, like a secret hurriedly breathed into one's ear. "Do you know where my coach goes?"

The boy nodded, too intimidated to speak.

"Excellent, yes, excellent. So there are no misunderstandings, let me hear you speak the place."

The boy parted his lips and blurted his answer: "The Land of Toys."

"Ah, correct, accurate, right you are."

His voice unlocked, the boy spoke more readily. "They say that in the Land of Toys every day but Sunday is a Saturday. Boys spend all day playing, and there are no teachers, no… *parents*. Is it true?"

"Most positively true, indeed. Now, young master, what is your name?"

"Bron, sir. Bron McMartin."

"Such a stout name! Well, Bron McMartin, do you wish to travel to the Land of Toys? Not every boy is meant to make the journey. Do you wish to leave behind your old life for that wonderful place with these other fine, young lads?"

Bron hesitated, awestruck by the donkeys, the coach, and the Coachman himself, but mostly by the crammed-in boys garbed in so many different styles of attire they formed a patchwork quilt of youth that seemed to hail from every part of the world.

He frowned. "There's no room! How can I ride with you?"

The Coachman chuckled, like bells dampened in felt, as if he didn't fully exist in Bron's world. "I always have room for one more. You shall ride right here with me." He patted the space beside him on the driver's bench. "But only if you really, truly wish to go to the most marvelous land in all the world. Is that your heart's honest desire?"

Bron nodded. "Yes, yes! It is."

"Climb on, then, Master Bron."

The Coachman offered his hand.

A faraway voice reached Bron's ears: *No, Bron, don't! Get down! Get away!* The unknown voice drifted to him from the far end of Stratemeyer Alley. *Run! The coach is not what you think. It's bad, Bron! Very bad!*

Bron glanced at the alley mouth, but the oily glow of the coach lamps bleached away everything beyond their reach. The driver's welcoming hand waited. The boys in the coach urged Bron to board. The impatient donkeys tamped their feet. Their eyes frightened Bron. They resembled the eyes of the old dock horses where his father worked the ports on Muhheakantuck Bay, sad, worn-out horses with their ribs showing on their last days before being sent to slaughter. Their eyes reminded him of hungry dogs that scavenged food in the gutters; of his mother's eyes on nights his father came home reeking of drink; of her eyes on the last night Bron saw her before she vanished, or ran away, or went home to her family in the South, or was kidnapped by pirates. He didn't know which of his father's explanations to believe, but none altered the sorrowful look on her face that pitied him in his dreams.

Get away, Bron! Run!

Footsteps joined the anonymous voice now.

"The Land of Toys is only for the cleverest boys." The Coachman lowered his hand, prelude to withdrawing it. "I won't take one who doesn't genuinely wish to go."

"Oh, but I want to go. I do! I do!"

Bron boosted himself onto the coach step, grabbed the driver's fleshy mitt, and hoisted himself onto the seat.

"Huzzah! An excellent choice made by an excellent bo—"

Interrupting the Coachman's words came a solid shadow caroming between him and Bron. It latched itself to the Coachman's shoulders then erupted into a flurry of thin arms and legs beating the man about the face and throat. The *thock-thock* of wood striking flesh filled Bron's ears as the shadow-shape pummeled the driver. Its torso clanked and spit blasts of wet air.

"You dare strike me?" the outraged Coachman cried.

He lashed back at the shadow-figure, his hands tangled briefly by the coach reins, but then he seized his attacker in his massive, pulpy grip. Held motionless in mid-air by the Coachman's outstretched arms, the shadow-fighter resolved into a most unexpected thing: a marionette! A carved, wooden head, arms, and legs sprouted from its iron-and-brass torso, which breathed steam from valves along its ribs. Bron knew marionettes from the street fairs his father took him to, leaving him alone for hours at the puppet theater while he drank in the beer garden, but he'd never seen one like this. It wore clothes like those of the Italian immigrant children Bron's father despised and seemed to act all on its own.

"Put me down!" the marionette said in a boyish voice. "You won't steal any more boys."

Bron searched for a puppeteer pulling strings and speaking for the effigy from a nearby rooftop or ledge but saw no one. With one hand, the marionette grasped its left ear, formed of brass rather than wood, and cranked it rapidly, sending its wooden nose jutting out to strike the Coachman square in the face. The more he cranked, the more the nose hammered the man until his expression crumpled with a pained grunt.

"Oh, you insolent pest," the Coachman cried. "I've had my fill of you. Stay out of my business!"

He hurled the artificial boy to the alley stones then lashed the reins and spurred on the donkey team. They trampled the poor marionette, snapping its joints, denting and cracking its iron-and-brass body, spilling gears and rods from within, and splintering its limbs beneath their hooves despite their soft shoes. The coach wheels trundled over it, further crushing it under their weight.

The pleading voice sounded again: *Jump, Bron! Before it's too late!*

As the coach accelerated, Bron saw a boy and a girl, a few years older than him, rushing after it. They waved their hands and yelled for him to flee. The vague shadow of an adult followed them. *Get off the coach! Don't go!*

The pleas planted seeds of doubt in Bron's head. They sprouted fast through the happy singing of the boy passengers and the feline humming of the Coachman. The coach rolled out of the alley onto the verge of a place Bron didn't know, a part of the city he'd never seen, or perhaps a space altogether different, one between New Alexandria and the Land of Toys. The warning voices, the snap of splintering wood, and the cracking of brass echoed in his head. A mournful donkey glanced at Bron, who thought of his dream mother. Menace writhed now in the Coachman's expression, devoid of its former warmth and welcome. The round-faced man curled his vermicular lips in a terrible grin of smug satisfaction.

"We're on our way now, boy," he said.

His altered face spoke of unknown dangers more than pleasures and filled Bron with the same chill his father's intoxicated eyes sent along his spine the nights he came home late from the pub. He wished to escape that fear. The chance that it might travel with him even to the Land of Toys proved too much to bear. Bron leapt. His body burned, as if the light of the coach lamps peeled itself from him, then he struck hard cobblestones and tumbled into the gutter.

The coach rolled on, its passengers belting out a happy child's song. The donkeys' braying faded. The Coachman laughed, then all of it—the boys, the donkeys, the Coachman, the coach, and its realm of glimmering light—blinked out of existence.

City bleakness returned. Bron sat up, rubbing his left arm, which had taken the brunt of his fall. Tears rolled from his eyes. Beside him lay the broken marionette. A yellow-haired, old man in a gray suit and fine leather shoes hurried, scooping up the remnants. His arms laden with broken wood, he smiled softly at Bron and said, "You made a wise choice. If something sounds too good to be true, it is. You pay a price for every pleasure. Say, boy, pick up that iron regulator? It's more than I can carry."

Bewildered, Bron hefted the indicated part from the cobbles.

"Ah, mille grazie," the old man said. "Follow me now."

The old man carried his burden to an ethereal woman in a diaphanous turquoise dress and silk cloak. Azure light dappled her hair, which wavered in a breeze that touched only her. She gazed at Bron with a motherly expression.

"Such a fine boy you found to lend you a hand, Geppetto," she said.

"Hey, who are you there?" an unknown voice called.

Looking over his shoulder, Bron locked eyes with Andy Parker, an older boy he knew from the streets. Beside him ran one of his regular pals, Gabriella Martini, and behind them came—oh, but Bron refused to believe his eyes, refused to believe New Alexandria's favorite son and genius inventor, Morris Garvey, founder of Morris Garvey's Steam Sweeps and Machinations Sundry, might care a whit for what happened to the likes of him.

"It's getting rather crowded in this alley," said Geppetto.

"It's time for us to go." A blue light, aqueous and vibrant, emanated from the lady to encompass Bron and Geppetto.

"Go where?" Bron said.

"You'll see soon enough. Just hold on tight to that regulator," Geppetto said.

As the lady's blue glow spread and brightened, Andy leapt, aiming to seize Bron and hold onto him. Despite his determination, he missed his target and succeeded only in knocking from Geppetto's arms one of the marionette's wooden hands, which had cracked loose at the wrist.

"Wait!" Andy shouted, grasping the broken hand from the ground.

Then—like the coach—Stratemeyer Alley, and all of Appleton Corner, the whole of New Alexandria itself for all Bron knew, vanished, taking away Andy, Gabriella, and the man who resembled Morris Garvey. When Bron's eyes recovered from the dazzling glow, he stood face to face with a mechanical monster: a cricket almost as tall as him, fashioned from iron and brass. Embers glowed behind its faceted eyes, and its gleaming, wire antenna twitched at Bron as it pried the marionette's regulator pump from his grasp.

"Thank you, boy. I'll take it from here." The iron insect spoke in hissing exhalations of steam. "We've got our work cut out for us tonight, we surely do!"

"Damnation," Morris Garvey spoke into the dead air of Stratemeyer Alley. "I hate magic. It doesn't make a lick of sense."

Andy Parker stared at the puppet hand cupped in his. "If only we'd gotten here sooner."

"We did our best," Gabriella said. "The wagon comes different places each time. It's a devil's task figuring out where it'll be soon enough for us to intervene."

"It's true, Mr. Garvey. The boys who hear about the wagon but don't resolve to join it sort of forget where it's going to appear, if you get what I mean. We must ask them at just the right time, or they can't tell us. Only the ones determined to go remember the location, and they don't like sharing it because rumors say the coach is always packed. It was a miracle Bron gave me any hint at all."

"Six boys — that we know of — gone in three months to this mysterious Coachman, yet you're telling me my Sundry Troubleshooters aren't up to the task of finding him once and for all? Shall I inform Inspector Matheson and the New Alexandria Police that my eyes and ears on the streets, who know this city inside and out, better even than them, can't predict where this Coachman will appear?" His expression softened, and his posture relaxed. "Well, it's certainly no easy task I assigned you, I'll grant you that."

"We almost saved Bron tonight, didn't we, sir?"

"Should I compliment you on a fine job *almost* done? Who knows where that odd couple took him? Who are this yellow-haired man and his blue lady? Have the streets whispered of them?"

Gabriella shook her head. "We never heard nor saw nothing of them before tonight, sir. Could it be they were after the same thing as us? Saving the boy from the Coachman?"

Garvey pursed his lips. "Hmmm, possible, I suppose, but I doubt it."

"So do I," a woman said. Garvey smiled at the dramatic entrance of Anna Rigel, Queen of New Alexandria's witches, who melted out of the alley shadows to the surprise of Andy and Gabriella. Anna approached Andy and held out an open hand. "I believe you have a bauble of interest to me?"

"Seeing as how we've been stumped, I called in some extra help tonight," Garvey said. "Andy, show the Madam Queen what you gathered."

"Yes, sir." From his pocket, Andy produced a bronze pocket watch — but when he opened the cover, it revealed no watch face, only a large opal set within and coruscating with light. He placed it in Anna's open hand. She shut her eyes, then circled her other hand over it. Light and shadow bent to her, making her waver as if observed through a heat mirage. Her body curved to the gravity of the bauble. Her tailored dress of celadon crushed velvet fringed with ivory lace swirled around her slender figure.

"What's she doing?" Gabriella said.

"That's a magic detector," Andy said. "Mr. Garvey invented it."

"This is a newer model," Garvey said. "It not only reveals the presence of magic but siphons off some of its emanations and stores them in the opal. Ms. Rigel is now scrying those remnants."

Anna groaned. Her head tilted forward, then snapped back. Light burst from the opal, filling the alley with a riot of color, heralding a shriek from Anna. When the flare passed, Garvey and the children stared at New Alexandria's Queen of Witches lying prone on the cobblestones, her eyes deathly closed.

"Anna!" cried Garvey.

The inventor fell to his knees beside the witch and felt her wrist for a pulse. He leaned close to her mouth in search of breath. Anna reached up, draped her arm around the back of Garvey's neck, and pressed her lips to his. Too surprised to resist, Garvey found himself engaged in a long kiss that brought a blush to the faces of the children.

"Mmmm," she said. "That's one way to awaken a sleeping witch."

"Sleeping?" Garvey raised an eyebrow.

"Close enough. I didn't anticipate the kinds of magic the opal absorbed. If I hadn't separated myself from it by entering a protective trance, it might've poisoned me. Your Sundry Troubleshooters are very lucky to be alive, Morris. They encountered some especially bad magics tonight."

Garvey stood then helped Anna onto her feet.

"What kind of magics, Anna?"

"Metamorphancy — and necromancy."

The words formed a cold cloud of sound in the air.

"My god, Anna, are you saying I sent these children on the trail of a necromancer?" Garvey said.

"What are those magics?" Gabriella said.

"Metamorphancy is magic that changes things, isn't it?" Andy said.

"Yes. And necromancy is magic that communes with or resurrects the dead, the darkest kind of magic. A necromancer's soul rots from the inside out." Garvey retrieved the blackened magic detector, studying the opal's burned-out surface and streaks of ash seared into the bronze setting. "Anna, did the necromantic energies come from the Coachman or the others?"

"Given the Coachman's reputation, I'd venture he's the source of the metamorphic energies."

"Which means young Bron has been whisked away by the worst kind of witch," Garvey said.

"Please, Morris, there are no bad witches, only bad intentions," Anna said.

"How do we find the boy?" Morris said.

"Sir? Madame Queen?" Andy offered up the broken marionette hand. "Would this help?"

Anna eyed the relic and gestured for it. "Hmmm, there's a chance. May I see it?"

Before Andy could surrender it, though, blue light returned to the alley as a turquoise sphere of heatless brilliance descended, encompassing Andy in its color as it lowered, intensifying and blotting out all but the broadest of shapes of the alley. It flared for a long moment, then winked out.

"My eyes can't take much more of this," Garvey said, blinking.

"I'm sorry about your eyes, Mr. Garvey," Gabriella said, "but where's Andy? He's gone!"

Turquoise light filled a ramshackle room on the second floor of an Appleton Corner flophouse.

Andy, who couldn't figure how he'd come here, pressed himself into a corner and struggled to keep fear from overwhelming him. The yellow-haired man shoved a dilapidated dresser against a wall. Next he moved a chair, a nightstand, and the bed, clearing the center of the floor. While he labored, the turquoise lady smiled, crooking her mouth. Blue light flowed from her, a color lush with mystery and power. It tickled Andy's skin and raised his hair on end.

"Arrange him now, Geppetto," the turquoise lady said. "Then bring the new receptacle."

Geppetto lifted a leather sack from the bed. He withdrew a length of splintered wood from it, then set it on the floor with care. He removed a second piece, then yet another, and many more, until he emptied the sack and arrayed the wooden remnants like skeletal remains disinterred decades after burial, minus a right hand. Tatters of an Italian boy's outfit clung to the pieces. A crumpled felt hat rested by the smashed-in head, which, with its half smile and open eyes, stared at nothing. After Geppetto emptied the sack, he opened the closet and released a terrified Bron McMartin locked inside what Andy took for a torture device: a sleeveless iron jacket mottled with rivets and gauges and clamped together at his shoulders and hips. Pipes prodded from its back and under his arms.

"Oh, master, you improve it every time," a voice said, a hiss trailed the words. "You work with iron and brass as well as you ever did with wood and string." The giant mechanical cricket strode into view. Its wire antenna quivered as it clanked around Bron until it spied the missing hand. "Ah! Unfinished, incomplete, not right, oh dear, oh dear."

"Don't worry. Our Blue Lady has brought us the missing piece." Geppetto approached Andy, still cowering in the corner. "You have one of my son's hands. Please give it to me."

Andy gaped at the man, whose eyes told stories Andy lacked the experience to understand.

"Give it over now, boy. It's not yours, is it?"

The mechanical cricket hopped around in agitation. Bron stood as if paralyzed within his iron shell. Blue light shimmered around them. It produced cold sparks where it touched the wood debris on the floor.

"Come now," Geppetto said.

"If he won't give you the hand, take it, you old fool," said the Blue Lady. "We can't restore your son without it."

"What are you doing to Bron?" Andy forced out the words, following Mr. Garvey's advice to always think fast and speak his mind.

"That's none of your concern," Geppetto said. "The hand, please."

"Are you going to hurt Bron?"

"Why do you care what happens to him? He doesn't care what happens to himself. You saw how he tried to board the coach for the Land of Toys. Do you know what happens to boys there? Sooner or later, every last one of them catches donkey fever and turns into a donkey for the Coachman to sell into hard labor or lash beneath his reins. It happened to my son. He's one of the only boys to ever recover. Do you think a boy who does that to himself is worth your worry?"

Andy's gaze darted between Geppetto and Bron. "You didn't know that, Bron, did you? Tell us why you wanted to go with the Coachman."

Bron trembled. His lips parted, but no words emerged.

"Go on! It's okay," Andy said.

"I only wanted to get away from my father," Bron said. "He hits me when he drinks."

"Bah!" Geppetto waved a dismissive hand. "What kind of boy abandons his father? What boy worth his blood runs away from home? Do you know how it pains a man to lose his son into the wide world, to spend his days searching, to find the boy only to go through it all again the next time he breaks his promises?" Geppetto stormed at Bron, his face aflame with rage as he shouted. "You don't deserve to have a father, whether he hits you or not!"

"Geppetto! Time is passing," the Blue Lady said. "Cricket, seize the boy."

The iron cricket rushed Andy. Before he could react, it sprang behind him and gripped him with four of its six legs, yanking his arms behind his back. Geppetto searched Andy's pockets until he found the missing hand.

"Be glad this is all I wanted from *you*, boy."

Geppetto placed the hand on the floor in its proper position amidst the marionette debris. He grabbed Bron and walked him to the center of the arrangement then forced him to lie down with his arms and legs overlapping those of the marionette. Runners of blue light flared and traced the parallel sets of limbs before concentrating over the heart of the iron jacket.

"Geppetto, stand back now," the Blue Lady said.

With reluctance, Geppetto retreated from the demolished marionette, one hand still reaching toward it as if to offer comfort.

"Best cover your eyes now," the cricket told Andy.

"How?" Andy said. "You're holding my arms."

"Well, close them then. You won't want to see this."

Andy ignored the suggestion. His hair bristled and a cold sensation formed in the depths of his gut. It welled to freezing dread and set his teeth chattering. Bron's mouth widened in a silent scream. Of pain or fear, Andy couldn't tell. The temperature drop bled his strength. It took all he had to stay on his feet and not look away. As much as he wished to close his eyes, he refused because Mr. Garvey would ask him later what happened, and he intended to give the most complete report he could.

A pounding came at the door. A man hollered to enter.

"Go away, leave us alone!" Geppetto shouted.

The knocking and hollering only grew more insistent.

"We can't be interrupted, Geppetto," the Blue Lady said.

"I know, I know," said Geppetto.

His shuffling footsteps marked his passage around the edge of the room.

Andy didn't understand how he could walk through the horrors that swam in the blue light that filled the air. In it, bones and skulls floated on a cosmic tide of decaying corpses whose eyes projected anguish and misery. Among them appeared glimpses into shadowed places like nowhere on Earth. On the far side of the room, Geppetto opened the door, then surged outward and threw a well-formed punch at a man in the hallway. His fist struck, but the man grabbed his arm and yanked Geppetto against him. Together they caromed off the corridor wall opposite the door, then fell to the ground. Geppetto gained the advantage over his challenger and raised his fist for a decisive blow. Before he struck, a woman in a celadon dress swept her fingers across his wrist, paralyzing him. Then the door swung shut, once again trapping Andy in the terrible blue mystery.

"Morris, are you hurt?" Anna said.

Garvey freed himself from Geppetto's grip, brushed himself off, then smoothed his suit. He stretched his left shoulder, where Geppetto's blow had landed.

"Not seriously, but I wager that'll bruise. He packs quite a haymaker for an old man. Good thing he didn't catch me on the jaw."

"Who is he?"

"Damned if I know. How long will your spell hold him, Anna?"

"Not long."

"Fine, then, let's see what he was so eager to keep hidden."

Garvey reached to open the shoddy door. Blue light seeped out from every crack in the wood, outlining the doorframe as he gripped the tarnished knob.

"No, please don't," Geppetto said. "You'll kill my son."

His voice escaped from between frozen lips, wheezing from deep within his throat.

Garvey hesitated as he read Anna's surprise. "Is he supposed to be talking?"

Anna shook her head. "No. His willpower must be immense. He's protecting something very important to him in that room."

"Is it safe to enter?"

"I've no idea, Morris."

Garvey knelt and met the old man's frozen stare. "Free him, Anna. Let's see if we can't get our answers straight from the source. And, old man? Don't try anything wild. You won't catch me by surprise again, and I've held my own against much tougher than you."

Anna gestured, then the old man dropped to the floor, completing his interrupted blow. He gasped before he rolled onto his back and eyed his captors with trepidation.

"Let's start with your name," Garvey said.

"Geppetto. I am a marionette maker." The man pulled himself to a sitting position. "If you open that door, my son will die."

"Is that true? What will happen if we don't open the door? We're looking for a boy named Andy Parker and another called Bron McMartin. Are they in there? Are they in danger?"

"They're there, yes. There's nothing you can do for Bron. If you leave things be, the boy, Andy, will be returned unharmed."

"That's not the answer I want to hear," Garvey said. "Let's start over. Tell me exactly what's going on inside that room."

The blue nightmare of death and decomposition swirled.

"The marionette's name," the cricket said into Andy's ear, "is Pinocchio. You know him?"

"No, why would I have heard of a marionette?"

The cricket leaned closer to Andy. Its antenna tickled the top of his head, and the heat of its steam exhalations drew perspiration from his neck and cheeks. "He is unique. Geppetto carved him out of a rare piece of wood and brought him to life."

"Isn't that what puppeteers do? Make inanimate things seem alive?"

"Yes, I suppose," the cricket said. "How odd it never occurred to me how similar are Geppetto and the Blue Lady in endowing life to the dead. Oh, you clever boy, the Blue Lady will enjoy you."

Andy disliked that notion. The neglected flophouse room contained a horrifying tableau of death and shadows, all spinning out from the Blue Lady as she wove her spell. Horrors of rotted flesh and miserable ghosts surrounded him. Relentless cold gripped him, tighter even than the cricket's iron hook-toes. Latched in his mechanical jacket, Bron suffered as if something clawed at his heart with cruel deliberation. Fringes of blue light locked him to the floor. His limbs combined with those of Pinocchio in funhouse mirror reflections compressed to a single looking glass. The boy's face paled. His cheeks sunk. His legs and arms thinned. The wood of the marionette stitched itself together, knitting splinters whole, filling gaps. The marionette head expanded to its original form. Its shattered eye reappeared. In tandem, Bron's face became gaunt and hollow.

"What's happening to him?" Andy said.

"She's resurrecting him." The cricket misunderstood Andy's question. "Pinocchio always wanted to be a real, live boy. As if he understood the value of life. Ha! Do you know he once killed me? Smashed me with a hammer! But the Blue Lady resurrected me as a ghost so I could serve her forever, and Geppetto built me this fine carapace."

"What will happen to Bron?"

"The moment he set foot on the Coachman's coach, he gave away his life for the taking. Thanks to you and your friend, the Coachman lost him, leaving him for the Blue Lady to claim."

"Claim? Like property? That's mad," Andy said.

"What do you know about it? Pinocchio survived so many dangerous adventures with help from me and the Blue Lady. I helped him even after he killed me!"

"I'll bet the Blue Lady made you help him," Andy said.

"What if she did? Why shouldn't I do what she asks? She brings the dead back to life. When she met Pinocchio, she found the key to defeating the Coachman, her oldest enemy. Years and years ago, so many years no one remembers exactly when, the Coachman took a boy special to her, turned him into a donkey, and sold him, never to be seen again. She's warred with him ever since. When the Coachman took Pinocchio and his friend, Lampwick, to the Land of Toys, they both caught donkey fever and turned into dumb animals—thus, she found her champion! Lampwick never recovered, but Pinocchio did with the Blue Lady's help, and he swore vengeance against the Coachman. He vowed to help the Blue Lady defeat him. In return, she made him a living boy. Then the unthinkable happened. The first time Pinocchio challenged him, the Coachman killed him."

On the floor, a nearly skeletal Bron lay superimposed over a nearly restored Pinocchio. As life faded from Bron's face, it emerged in

Pinocchio's. As Bron's face saddened, Pinocchio's grew joyful. A terrifying thing to see, human joy in a marionette's wooden face.

"Stop it! You're killing him," Andy said.

The Blue Lady paid no attention. She concentrated on the resurrection. No longer serene and beautiful, she appeared withered and haggard. A wicked grin bent her lips around her crooked teeth. Andy forced his limbs against the cold dread that permeated him and renewed his struggle against the cricket.

"Let me go!" he said.

"She won't allow it," the cricket said. "She won't release any of us until she kills the Coachman. But death means a different thing for a real, live boy than for a marionette. Geppetto pled for her to return her son to him, but the Blue Lady's powers have their limits. So they struck a deal. If Geppetto built a mechanical device to house Pinocchio's soul, she would resurrect him. This shell of mine came first, Geppetto's prototype, for in those days, I served as a phantom. They brought Pinocchio back, but the Coachman killed him again. He has killed him over and over, every time the Blue Lady sends him as her assassin, because Pinocchio rarely learns from his mistakes. Yet each time he dies, it grows harder to revive him. The Blue Lady must expend the soul of a misbehaved boy to return Pinocchio to life."

"You mean Bron's soul? He didn't misbehave," Andy said. "He fled a terrible father. What boy wouldn't leave a mean-drunk father for the Land of Toys?"

"You may be right, but the Blue Lady lives by her own rules."

Blue light deepened around Bron. While Pinocchio grew more vibrant and solid, he thinned and faded. Andy's limbs succumbed to the gravely cold and resumed shivering. Only one thing offered him any heat: his burning anger at having saved Bron from the Coachman only to doom him to a much worse fate.

"Dear god, you inhuman beast," Garvey said of Geppetto after the man finished his tale.

"Where would you draw the line for your son?" Geppetto said.

Garvey had no answer. He whirled away from Geppetto and gripped the doorknob.

"Prepare yourself, Anna," he said. "I'm afraid this will be unpleasant."

He thrust open the door. Blue light flooded out.

Garvey entered the room and froze. The watery glow bewildered him. Horrible shapes filled it, but they eluded focus, swimming around him like beams and flashes of light. At one side of the room stood a skeletal figure in a blue dress and cloak. Her face stretched tight as a drum skin over her skull. Hair like seared grass wriggled on her scalp. A blue glow radiated from her body, directed by her gnarled, knobby hands, waving like a conductor's. At the center of the room, Bron/Pinocchio jigged in the air as if hung to dance from invisible strings. Broken sticks, shattered hips, and wooden shards clung together within Bron's ghostly outline. The iron jacket pumped out puffs of steam as its soul-fuel gained heat. Even the Italian clothes had stitched themselves back together.

From across the room, Andy shouted, "Mr. Garvey!"

Anna pressed against Garvey, a reassuring contact. Her energy joined his, a protective aura against the forces rampant in the room.

"Let me deal with the necromancer. You free the boy," she said.

"Let's hope we're not too late," said Garvey.

Heedless of the swarming blue terrors, Garvey rushed to Bron/Pinocchio, his keen eye already assessing the mechanisms holding the iron jacket in place. Before he reached Bron, he held the multi-tool he always carried and shuffled through its implements to select the best one to remove the jacket.

The Blue Lady screeched at Anna. "Your magic cannot defeat mine!"

"Good thing I've got more than magic at my disposal," Anna said.

She stepped into a sudden punch and connected square in the Blue Lady's face. The blue light paled and flickered. For a moment, the freezing cold relented. Anna swung again, knocking the Blue Lady's hideous face sideways. Another wave of weakness churned the blue spell.

"Cricket, help!" the Blue Lady cried.

Distracted by his master's cry, the cricket released Andy and leapt across the room to menace Anna. The Blue Lady seemed reduced, as if the physical attack had drained some of her life. The cricket snatched Anna's hand in two of its legs, yanked her off balance, and toppled her to the floor, where it pinned her. Freed, Andy rushed to the side of Bron/Pinocchio. While Garvey worked at the clamps and connectors of the iron jacket, Andy took a different approach.

"Pinocchio!" he called. "Pinocchio! Why must you harm this good-hearted boy? How can you steal his life for yours? He has done nothing wrong." Some of the joy faded from the marionette's face. "Are you a protector of boys, Pinocchio? Or a thief of them?"

Geppetto lumbered in from the hallway and braced himself in the doorframe.

"No," he said. "My son, my son."

"What kind-hearted, real, live boy would steal life from another? Bron broke no promises to his father. He's tried to live up to his father's expectations and received only punishment and pain in return. He has grown up without a mother. Would you hurt him for your own selfishness?"

Bron/Pinocchio turned as if spun by a puppeteer. It gazed at Geppetto, questioning.

The Blue Lady screamed. The cricket held down Anna.

All of the seals and connectors of the iron jacket undone, Garvey resorted now to pounding on it. "It won't open," he said. "The damned magic holds it tight."

"Pinocchio, are you even a real, live boy trapped in iron, brass, and wood? Are you better off than Lampwick as a donkey while you're stuck in servitude to a witch?"

"No!" cried the Blue Lady.

Her magic flowed back to her, the power she'd released in waves cascading into her all at once. It filled her and lit her up. For a moment, it restored her beauty, then all the light winked out. The Blue Lady collapsed to the floor. The cricket released Anna to rush to its master's aid. Anna rolled away and clambered back to her feet. Geppetto hurried to Bron/Pinocchio, where the last shimmers of blue magic sparked cold and silent.

"Father." Tears rolled from Bron/Pinocchio's eyes. Andy didn't understand how a marionette could weep. "Father, I love you. I want to be a good boy."

"Pinocchio!" Geppetto cried out.

The iron jacket cracked open in Garvey's hands. He reached in and yanked out gears and rods until it ceased to function. Bron tumbled from the air, dead weight landing in Garvey's arms.

The fractured assemblage of the marionette lingered a moment before it succumbed to gravity. Andy held its right hand as it rained to the floor. The Blue Lady and her cricket withdrew into shadows and vanished. Garvey laid Bron down gently as the color returned to the boy's cheeks.

Bron breathed deeply then sat up.

"You're safe now," Garvey said.

As Garvey helped Bron onto his feet, Geppetto, sobbing, gathered up the pieces of his broken marionette and replaced them in his sack. After a moment's hesitation, Andy helped him.

The Fox and the Clockwork Bird

Based on The Wonderful Bird

JEFF YOUNG

WHISKERS TWITCHING IN RESPONSE TO THE MOTION OF THEIR LIPS, the clockwork mask the Fox wore concealed the owner's face as they lay on the edge of the rooftop. From here, they could see to the left the new cathedral rising above the houses of the merchants. A glance to right revealed the row of artificers' studios, where a single curl of smoke and flashes of light were visible from a high window. Dropping back to the center brought the palace into view, where the snapping of flags in the early morning breeze reminded the Fox of taskmasters goading on their charges. Perhaps it was time to begin the work they had agreed to.

It had all begun with three questions:

"Now, this is strictly between you and I because I have heard that you are most capable in resolving difficulties. As you know, I Horatiu, being one of the chief artificers to the queen, I must occasionally prove my expertise against other challengers by creating a work so unique that it stands as a testament to my abilities. My Spinning Cathedral, which turns ever so slowly throughout the hours of the day so that the sunlight pours through the stained glass of the windows, is a marvel and works like a charm. However, there are those that maintain that it is going too far and defeats the purpose of a cathedral because it is too gaudy. You are a wise seer, as I see by your most wonderfully constructed mask, and I ask you, what can I do to sway their opinions?"

"Now, this is strictly between you and I because I have heard that you are most capable in resolving difficulties. As you know, I Ciprian, being of the chief artificers to the queen, I must occasionally prove my expertise against other challengers by creating a work so unique that it stands as a testament to my abilities. I am a creator of fabulous clockwork animals. You have most certainly heard of the menagerie of the Queen, and I have created something that outshines all of my previous works. However, everyone that I have shown it to says that it is too much and that all of the jewels on my fabulous bird couldn't possibly be real, making it seem tawdry. You are a wise seer, as I see by your most wonderfully constructed mask, and I ask you, what can I do to sway their opinions?"

"Now, this is strictly between you and I because I have heard that you are most capable in resolving difficulties. As the Queen of this country, blessed with a great many capable artificers, good natured gentlefolk, and bounteous lands, it falls to me to ensure that the stewardship of all this comes to the proper hands. I was blessed with three sons before my dearest was taken from me, and in order to show equal favor among the three strongest lords of my lands, I sent each away to foster. Now that I am faced with determining which should be the most appropriate heir, I find that I know none of them well enough to choose. You are a wise seer, as I see by your most wonderfully constructed mask, and I ask you, what can I do to determine the best choice?"

After a moment of silence, the Fox carefully scratched at their chin under the Seer's mask and said to each, "I shall return in three days with an answer." Then the Fox moved on through the town visiting the market, the leather worker, and the smiths, gathering the requisites for their trade. Eventually, the Fox retired to their shop. As the Sun went down, they turned over the sign to indicate the location was closed and sat down at the worktable to think.

The sound of someone clearing their throat surprised the Fox.

Swinging about, they confronted a mask that was not familiar. It was an old woman's visage done in dark wood. The Fox could tell there was no clockwork inside to move the features as with modern masks, but rather a series of springs that cleverly responded to the flex of the facial muscles of the owner. She was low in the shoulder, but obviously taller in her youth. Her voice was rough and breathy, "I am sorry to have caused fear. I merely awaited your return. Sometimes I am easy to overlook."

"Hardly, madam. Not with such as a mask as this. It is a treasure. A marvel of execution. Might I look upon its workings?"

"You may, in time. I have a task for you, but first I must consider what I want. I will come to you when I am ready. If you are successful, you shall have all of the hours you desire to study my mask. But for now, it is unseemly for me to remove it. Do be patient and you will be rewarded."

"Patient I will be then. Is there anything I can help you with now?"

"No, I once again apologize for startling you. I will take my leave. Good day."

The Fox watched the woman with great curiosity as she left. What a delicious mystery. They were certain they knew everyone of consequence, having made all the finest masks in the kingdom, or so they thought. A delicious mystery, in deed.

Then, after assuring themself that no one else lurked in the shadows, they relocked the door. Around them hung the many cleverly carved masks that were the result of their dexterous hands. Bits of wire and gears were scattered about the table. The Fox picked up two small gears and a large one. Placing them down on the surface the Fox linked the teeth of the smaller ones into the big one. Moving them caused the larger to rotate. "That's the way they want it to be," the Fox commented. Then grasping another gear and dropping it in between all three, rotating it caused all of the gears to move. "This is the way it will be." Laughing, the Fox leaned back in the chair and looked up at the multitude of masks hanging above them.

The masks had originally risen as mere fashion taken up when the royals were struck by the pox. These allowed the nobility to present whichever face they wished to the common folk. Now as the industry of coal-burning and steam came round, the masks also served to filter out the smog that lay over the city. It continued to amaze the Fox that so many put such faith in whatever mask one presented. As the maker of such masks, the Fox had access to all of them. From family member to family member, a long chain of mask-makers reached back into history. But few were willing to use their talents as the Fox did. Reaching up, they pulled off the Seer's mask they wore and gazed upon it. The stars and symbols etched in gold complimented the lines carved into the face giving it a greater sense of age and wisdom, borrowed but briefly, and now set aside.

Opening a cabinet, they placed the Seer's mask within and drew forth the orange-furred visage with its long dark whiskers and pointed nose. Staring at it, the Fox frowned and peered closer. Something felt wrong, something felt out of place, yet the mask appeared in fine working order.

Never mind, they thought, *all is well now.* Settling it on their face, they gave a sigh of relief. The ideas began to come at once. Very shortly thereafter, the Fox had a plan.

To the creator of the Spinning Cathedral, the Seer gave the following advice:

"Your creation is most beautiful and has a most unique attribute in its ability to follow the Sun. However, people are used to other things. You must

show them that your work has the approval of the divine and of tradition. There is an old story about a King who commissioned a cathedral that continually fell to pieces. It was only after a divine bird of great beauty came to rest at its top that it was shown to be blessed and the work proceeded without hinderance. The King himself sent his sons out to find this bird. Consider this story and perhaps you will find a solution."

Since the words of seers and sages were often somewhat mystical in nature, the architect hastily thanked the Seer, paid them, and bid them on their way.

To the creator of the Beautiful Bird, the Seer gave the following advice:

"Your creation is most beautiful and has a most unique attribute in its glorious, bejeweled exterior. However, people are used to simple things. You must show them that you work has value and purpose beyond being something to look on. You must make it able to fly and then take it to the town square and set it free. There is an old story about a King who commissioned a cathedral that continually fell to pieces. It was only after a divine bird of great beauty came to rest at its top that it was shown to be blessed and the work proceeded without hinderance. The King himself sent his sons out to find this bird. Consider this story and perhaps you will find a solution."

Since the words of seers and sages were often somewhat mystical in nature, the artificer hastily thanked the Seer, paid them, and bid them on their way.

To the Queen the Seer gave the following advice:

Your children are each possessed of strengths that make them unique. You must determine which has the particular strength that will make them the best ruler. A task will test them and reveal their inner character. There is an old story about a King who commissioned a cathedral that continually fell to pieces. It was only after a divine bird of great beauty came to rest at its top that it was shown to be blessed and the work proceeded without hinderance. The King himself sent his sons out to find this bird. I have heard that there is a beautiful, bejeweled bird of strange and mystical beauty that has been seen in the kingdom even now. Consider this story and perhaps you will find a solution.

Since the words of seers and sages were often somewhat mystical in nature, the Queen hastily thanked the Seer, paid them, and bid them on their way.

The Fox lay on the roof and considered the morning. To the left, the cathedral spun ever so slowly in time with the rising of the sun. To the right, a door opened and a small man carrying a basket walked from the artificer's row toward the center of town. At the very center, near the top of the tallest tower of the Castle, a window opened, and a woman leaned out, long black hair spilling over the sill. Just as the first rays of sunlight fell onto the center of town, the artificer pulled the cover off of his basket and a gorgeous bird bejeweled with rubies rose like a flame into the air. Moments later, three young men rode out of the palace gates. The gears had begun to turn, now it was up to the Fox to spin them harder.

The oldest prince rode an iron horse whose front legs were modeled on those of a strong stallion and blued with the same process that made gun barrels robust. At its rear, two large, steel-banded wheels took the place of legs, and it towed a cart full of coal. In the beast's belly sat a burner lit with a hellish flame until smoke curled from each of its flared nostrils. Trailing ashes, it rolled with a great clatter through the streets and off into the wood bearing its master.

The middle prince rode a brass horse who had three legs in the front and three in the back, each pumping like great pistons. In its belly sat a fire lit by logs of wood. Strapped to its side hung a great shiny axe. This beast likewise trailed smoke and ashes in its passage until it bore its master into the trees.

The youngest prince rode an old nag, born not built, who fought him every step of the way. This beast looked as though it was not long for the world and in its passage, left the smell of the cow pasture and rotten cabbage as it broke wind from its noisome breakfast. The townsfolk that gathered at the commotion, were heartily glad when the nag slowly bore its royal master into the forest as well.

A cry came from the street and a hand pointed upward. As one the crowd lifted their gazes, as overhead flew a wondrous sight. A most beautiful bird with a long tail that curved and shone in the air. Its body shone in the light, a thousand winking red jewels glittering. The spectacle flew off above the trees. A glorious bird, three questing princes — what could it all mean?

Above them all, the Fox turned round and danced on the rooftops. What a merry game they had set afoot. Then they leapt from cornice to gutter over and over until the wall surrounding the city came into view. With a surge, the Fox flew over the top and disappeared into the forest. After scampering into the underbrush, they sat down and pulled out their bag. Aside they set the beautiful fox mask and from within then withdrew one envisaged like an old man. A quick change of clothes and an old woodsman stood in the same spot. After settling on a stout piece of wood for a staff, the Fox picked up their bag, assumed a hunched over shambling walk, and made their way deeper among the trees.

Later in the day, as the sun sank down to paint the hill ahead of them in golds and reds, the Fox heard a great clatter, and the acrid scent of smoke flavored the air. When they rounded the bend at the foot of the small rocky hill, they came upon the oldest prince in his iron armor. His steed had come upon the scree at the base of the hill and one of its great wheels was wedged between the edges of two large flat boulders. Try as he might, the prince could neither move his mount forward nor back for it was stuck like a fly in amber. In trying to lever apart the rocks, he had bent his great iron sword; and in attempting to break free, he had poured more and more coal into the belly of the iron beast until his supply dwindled. When the Fox found him, he was carrying water in his helm from the small stream nearby to refill the boiler and build up more steam.

"Well, there, old man. Your timing is excellent. You must go back to your village and summon help so that I can continue on my quest. If you are determined and set your pace well, I am certain that you will make it easily before the wolves come out tonight. Tell the villagers your prince, Bartolomeu has sent you and seeks their assistance."

The Fox considered him, considered the sky, considered the ground and once again the prince. "It is already too late for one such as I to make my way to the village before the wolves arrive. I am not much of a dinner for them. Rather, I fear for you, my lord. You would make them a fine meal. Bank the coals of your steed. There is a cave nearby. It is safe and warm, and a fire will keep all manner of wild things at bay. In the morning, I will lead you to the village and gain you the help you seek."

The prince considered the offer. His iron mask glowered in response to the clockwork following the muscles of the prince's face and the jutting iron beard swung back and forth as the prince worked his jaw. The Fox was particularly proud of the masks made for the royals. They could tell the prince was about to attempt to send them off again, so they crouched down even lower and looked more pitiful. Eventually, Bartolomeu relented as the Sun continued its way downward. Lighting a torch from the coals of his steed, he gestured his guide to lead onward. As they walked at the Fox's slow pace, the prince related his grand quest to obtain the beautiful bird.

"What will you do if you cannot find it?" asked the Fox as they neared the base of the hill.

"Why, I will take great quantities of gold from the treasury, go into the taverns, and spread the word that there is a bounty set on the creature. Surely, brave men there will join me in my quest and with their help, I will succeed."

While the plan had its merits, the Fox suspected that at the best, the woods would fill with drunken treasure seekers and at its worst, the prince would empty the funds of the kingdom for naught. Considering neither outcome favorable, they led the prince to the entrance of the cave and bade him enter. Bending over slightly, torch ahead of him, the prince stepped into the darkness. Reaching up, the Fox pulled at the vines concealing the great iron gate to the side of the cave entrance. Once clear, they grasped the edge of the gate and swung it closed. It slammed shut with a great clatter, locking with a click. Gathering up their staff, the Fox set off around the curve of the hill ignoring the threats and cries that issued from the cave. Even in the growing dark, they set their feet down with care, for they knew the woods and this place down to the last rock. Then, a waft of smoke caught their nose and their pace increased.

The prince in the brass armor sat at the base of the hillside. It was far too steep for anything to climb above him, and he had found a nice cul-de-sac to guard against any other entry. His fire blazed in the narrow entrance and behind him gleamed the bronze of his steed. A great pile of wood sat ready to feed not only his fire but also his transport. The Fox considered all of this before revealing themselves in the firelight. The camp site was well thought out and resourceful, perhaps good qualities, but with all things, it was best to be sure. When the prince rose to place a log on the fire, the Fox stepped into the light.

"Well there, old man, come forward. There is no need to skulk in the twilight. My fire is warm and for certain there will soon be wolves about."

"You are too kind," the Fox said and then joined him by the fire. The prince's mask was one of brass and the clockwork eyebrows were most expressive. Once again, the Fox was pleased at the measure of their work. Then the other related the tale of his quest for the beautiful bird.

"What will you do if you cannot find it?" asked the Fox.

"Why, it flew into the woods. If I have to, I will chop down every tree until I find it," he reached over and grasped his great axe. "Let no man say that Prince Grigore gives up easily. At the worst, I will set fire to the woods and burn it all down. The bird is made of jewels, it will not be harmed by fire."

The Fox stared solemnly into the fire and considered those words. This would not do. They loved the woods, their second home, and what was to stop such a fire from eventually catching the roofs of the townsfolk's dwellings? They put their hands on their knees and pushed themselves slowly to their feet. "I think you have done well in choosing your place, good Prince, but wolves are clever and many. Though your fire may cow them at first, they can still scramble up on top of these rocks. Bank the coals of your steed. There is a cave nearby. It is safe and warm, and a fire will keep all manner of wild things at bay."

With a little more convincing, the Fox led the second prince, carrying his great axe, around the curve of the hill to yet another cave. In short order, Grigore stood locked inside. Once again, the Fox stretched and then considered the remaining prince. Cracking their knuckles and then picking up the staff, they set off into the woods once more.

It took a little longer to find the final prince. No other scent of smoke lingered in the woods, and it was only after a great deal of listening that the Fox finally heard a thin voice singing in the distance. While the other princes had ended up near the hill, the last prince was right out in the middle of the woods. The Fox suspected that he had not made better time than the others on his broken-down nag, but rather kept riding until the horse simply stopped. At the base of the roots of a fallen tree, the Fox found the prince wrapped up in a threadbare blanket and shivering. His wavering song had faded but the scent of the flatulent mount brought the Fox the final few yards. This prince's mask was of leather, but it still bore several clockwork embellishments that allowed the features to draw themselves up in fear and surprise.

"Have no fear, your majesty, I am but a humble woodsman. Can I help you build a fire? It will keep away the wolves," suggested the Fox as they knelt and pulled out a tinder box. Expressions ran across the prince's mask—shock, concern, and then finally a smile.

"Of course, you are too kind. I fear I left my flint at home in my haste. My name is Simion. Your company is welcome."

"Give me a moment and we shall have a fire." The Fox knelt, struck sparks, and with a little work soon had a fine fire going.

"Will you share my meal?" Simion asked.

"With pleasure, your majesty, but let me add some herbs and vegetables I have gathered from the woods." The Fox drew forth their bag and together the two built a wondrous stew. Sitting around the fire, the flames crackling cheerfully, the nag tethered just inside the light, but down wind, they both relaxed. Eventually, Simion related the tale of his quest for the beautiful bird.

"What will you do if you cannot find it?" asked the Fox.

"Why shouldn't I?" responded the prince.

The Fox was a bit taken back by that amount of confidence. "What do you mean?"

"Well, it's obviously a clockwork bird created by an artificer. It flew in a straight line once it gained the air. It will continue flying until its clockwork runs down. I suspect it will fly over the entire woods and beyond that it will come to the desert. It is the calm season and little wind moves over the sand now. If I ride along its path, it will be sitting on the sands waiting for me."

The fire crackled some more before the Fox had anything to say. They were rather impressed with the logic of the prince's argument. They also did consider the state in which they found his majesty. Perhaps he was excellent at logic, but failed at common sense? Helping themselves to more stew, the Fox said, "If you don't mind my pace, I shall accompany you. I would very much like to see this beautiful bird."

Simion's mask smiled once again, "You are most welcome."

The beautiful, jeweled bird flying overhead on a tether, Prince Simion led his nag triumphantly through the city gates. At his side strode an old man leaning on their staff. A certain joy chased itself across the features of the elder as they considered the bird and occasionally, the prince. At the steps of the gate of the palace, the crowds of gathered villagers parted to let them approach. At the very top sat the queen on her chair, but oddly enough she faced away from everyone. The Fox looked at the prince and shrugged. In the time that it had taken to acquire the bird and to journey back, they had come to appreciate certain qualities in the prince. Only when they stood before her Majesty and she turned slowly about, revealing a remarkably familiar wooden mask, did the Fox realize they, themselves, had been outfoxed.

Taking a moment to consider both before her, the queen said, "Your bag," indicating the Fox's worn satchel. Loath to give it up, they glanced at the guards, the courtiers, and the crowds and finally accepted there was no alternative. Once she had it in hand, the queen spared a brief look within and her mask drew up in a smile, the wooden bits creaking slightly in protest, for perhaps this aspect had not often seen use. Then she turned and walked inside the palace, and both were left to follow. Simion reeled in the rope on the beautiful bird so that it fluttered above his shoulder as he walked.

None of the guards or others entered. The prince and the Fox walked behind the queen until she entered the throne room, seated herself, and then turned to consider them. She reached into the bag, pulled out the Fox's true mask and set it on the right arm of the throne. Then she reached up and removed her own, setting it on the left arm. The Fox had never seen her without a mask. She was beautiful. Her features strong and determined. But what struck them the most was the short length of her hair. She'd cut it so that it wouldn't give her away in her disguise. Noticing their attention, she ran a hand through the strands. "Much like yours, I imagine." Now the Fox quivered briefly in their boots. Clever, she was too clever by far. But her gaze had gone now to her son.

"Simion, you've done well. Congratulations."

But her attention returned once again to them, as she considered the Fox. She picked up the wooden mask holding it out to them. "You desired this? Well, I have a commission for you. I require two masks. They should be exactly alike. Each should be able to project dignity, trustworthiness, compassion, all the qualities of a good leader."

Looking at both of them now, she finished, "And they should fit each of you."

Simion's brow furrowed and the Fox's as well.

"Simion, your logic is impeccable. Fox, your cleverness is indomitable. But each of you are missing things when you are set to a task. Together, I suspect you will be formidable. The type of rulers I would have no worries about inheriting my kingdom."

"But, Mother, why make them look the same?"

"Every time someone looks at you, they will expect the same sort of response and offer you the same respect if they cannot tell the difference."

Simion's mask registered confusion, but when he looked over at the person beside him, there was no longer an old man, rather someone mimicking his same stance and confidence. The Fox's mask could not conceal their grin.

Standing, the queen then strode forward to them and despite their protests removed the mask from each until they looked upon one another. It was most certainly not love upon first sight. The Fox considered the prince and found his forehead slightly broader than the visage of the mask and his chin had a dimple that was missing as well. This was the real Prince, not the perfection offered by the mask. Of course, they… *she* wondered briefly what he thought of her high cheekbones and slightly larger than ordinary eyes.

"There," the queen said, hands upon hips. "No more lies, little vixen." Then reaching out for their hands and clasping them, she said. "You are well matched, and we can certainly consider another match later, but for the time being, I am content."

The Vixen looked askance a moment before asking, "And your other sons?"

"Oh, I think we shall give them another day to consider their circumstances before releasing them. We have a border to the East and border to the West. Perhaps a castle of iron to the East and castle of brass to the West. I think the sunset would reflect nicely on that. I think we even know an architect and an artificer who might accomplish such tasks. Don't we, Vixen?"

Dropping their hands, she looked up to consider the bird fluttering above them. "Before that however, there is one final challenge for you. The bird must be seen at the top of the cathedral. The people must have their stories. Don't forget that every tale grows from a seed of truth, even if we must plant it there ourselves. I am certain you are capable of accomplishing this." Then she reached up to the throne and grasped both of the masks there. Considering them, she turned and offered the wooden mask to the Fox and the vulpine one to Simion with a smile. "Best start getting used to thinking outside your comforts."

Three Days of the Cuckoo

Based on The Elves and the Servant Girl and The Elves and the Shoemaker

BERNIE MOJZES

I. Slave

THEY WOULD NEVER HAVE CALLED HER A SLAVE.

Never mind that she'd been bought and paid for, enough money to keep her mother and sisters from starving for a few more months. Never mind the drudgery, the bars on her window, the beatings when she ran away, the beatings when she didn't. Never mind the poor girl hobbling stiffly to the market every morning. Can't run far on broken feet.

No, never mind what everyone with eyes could see; this was a civilized country.

II. Contract

"You're a clever girl, Lucia," her mother had said, failing to hide the tears in her eyes. "And it's an opportunity. You'll see. You'll have a chance to learn a trade, and when the contract is up, you'll be able to find work anywhere. And it's only for a short time. Three years. It'll be over before you know, and you'll be free before your sixteenth birthday."

But it wasn't, and she wasn't. The fine print is hard to read when you don't know how, and before she was fourteen years old, Lucia had unknowingly violated so many clauses of the contract that she'd increased her indenture tenfold.

Lucia's master was a shoemaker, or so he claimed. He had the tools, and plenty of fine leather, and a stockroom full of shoes of impeccable quality, which he sold grudgingly and for a great deal of money. But she'd never seen him make a pair, and whenever shoes came in needing repair, he set Lucia to the work. Once, drunk to the point of slurring his words, he spun an incredible story of Elves — tiny naked Elves that came out only at night — having cobbled all these fine shoes. Of Elves having made his fortune.

"We were so grateful that we made them all little suits of clothes, so they wouldn't have to be so cold in the winter." Lucia's master scowled, then, and fingered Lucia's dress, threadbare to translucence. "Little bastards ran off that night. Never make *that* mistake again."

III. Clockwork

It turned out that the shoemaker had never been very good at his job, and only the accidental servitude of the Elves had altered his circumstances. He'd since tried his hand at some other trades, as he was rich enough to dabble—metalwork, woodcraft, clockmaking—but he was neither industrious nor meticulous in his habits. He'd also imagined himself an aspiring inventor and alchemist, but possessed neither insight nor curiosity. The workroom was filled with the castoffs of his ephemeral interests.

It was a misbehaving cuckoo clock that changed Lucia's fortunes. First, the minute hand came loose, dangling forever at the half-hour. The shoemaker was certain he could fix it. Over the course of three days he disassembled the device, machined several new gears, and reassembled it. Success! The minute hand worked.

Unfortunately, the new gears were ill-formed; the clock no longer kept time properly, and the bird insisted on waking the entire household by cuckooing incessantly throughout the night. On the third night, after two more attempts to fix it failed, his wife smashed the clock on the floor.

She cuffed Lucia on the side of the head. "Clean that mess up, you lazy girl."

Lucia gathered the shattered pieces. She'd always loved this clock, despite its inadequacy at measuring time. It had, since she'd first come here, reliably, accurately, and cheerfully described her masters—*cuckoo!*—and she had considered it her secret friend. She brought the splintered case, the gears and springs and weights, the bent hands, the shattered escapement, and laid them out on her bed. She placed the brightly painted cuckoo bird in the center and, for the first time in years, burst into tears.

How could she stand to live in this house without those bright moments to break the unending horror? No, she couldn't. Since escape had proved impossible, there were really only two choices.

She chose the harder path: she would fix it herself.

For weeks, in between chores, she labored in the workroom. That was safe, as long as her chores were complete and she kept a keen ear—her masters had no use of that room. Soon enough, she had rebuilt the clock, as good as new. But why stop there, when there were so many improvements to be made? The original escapement mechanism was both inefficient and inaccurate — she'd had to set the clock daily, before it was broken. The new escapement she created eliminated any backward motion of the wheel and nearly all friction. With a few other minor adjustments, the clock kept true time, within a few seconds a day.

That was enough to justify adding an additional hand to track those passing seconds, and while she was adding gears, it was hardly any trouble to add a smaller, inlaid clock face to count out the days and the months and the years. She set the date: July 14th, 1838. Six years, two months, eight days, 4 hours, and thirty-two minutes since her mother scratched her mark on a piece of paper.

But most importantly, she fixed the bird, making it what it should have been from the beginning. She endowed it with articulated mechanical joints and elaborated on its pipes and bellows. It no longer simply popped out and cuckooed; it walked out, fluttered its variegated wings, grey and brown and white with hints of lavender, lifted its beak, and *sang*.

IV. Little Helpers

Lucia's masters had steadfastly refused to have their home connected to the city steam system, claiming they preferred the "old ways" of doing things, which meant having Lucia do them.

"Steam is dangerous," Lucia's mistress said, despite having no qualms at speeding through town in her very own Cugnot roadster, which was far more likely to explode than a dishwasher. "I won't have it in my house."

The public steam system wasn't just good for heating the house in the winter, though that in itself would have been worth it, in Lucia's opinion. It also could be used to power timesaving appliances that washed dishes and clothes and heated kitchen stoves without wood or coal. Of course, the Metropolitan Steam & Heating Authority strongly recommended that installations and any *direct* application of steam be restricted to qualified professionals, and she had heard of the horrific burns suffered by those who thought themselves more skilled than they were.

It didn't take long for Lucia to realize that any motion that can generate the movement of a dial and control the actions of a tiny bird can also be used to generate other forms of movement, provided sufficient energy. With a little more power, she was sure, she could create clockworks that could ease her drudgery. Dishwashing would be a challenge, of course, and probably one best left to a steam-powered device, but clockworks capable of movement meant the ability to perform actions that were not tied to a steam pipe. Yes, she could already envision the construction of a clock that could sweep and mop floors, or carry the groceries from the market for her.

What she couldn't envision was a means to power all that motion. A pendulum-driven mechanism would need to be taller than the house, and any spring or coil strong enough to sweep out a single room would likely be impossible to wind. A miniaturized steam engine would still weigh a hundred pounds empty, more, with the boiler full, far too much for a delicate clockwork to support. Besides, it would fill the house with soot and steam, that she'd just have to clean up afterward.

The solution presented itself in the person of a Mr. Jeremy Playfair, natural philosopher extraordinaire and soon, he was quite adamant, to be invited into the Royal Society for his advancements in the realm of electrical induction, whatever that was. Mr. Playfair had taken up a stall at the market, between a greengrocer and a spice merchant, where he demonstrated a small device no larger and not terribly different from an eggbeater, other than a pair of wires dangling from one end.

Mr. Playfair's spiel, delivered in what he apparently believed to be a carnival barker's voice, faltered and wheezed, beset with a stutter and something of a lisp. He was, Lucia thought, not ugly, despite a slight harelip that twisted his smile. His suit was of as fine a make as her master's, though nearly as threadbare as her own dress (over which she wore a coarse, woolen shawl, even in the warmest weather, for modesty's sake).

As Lucia was the only person whose attention he had attracted, he sighed and gave her a weary smile.

"W-welcome, welcome, young Miss, to a m-m-miraculous world of the future, where you can hold the power of the gods in your hands!"

"Thank you, sir. That device, what does it do?"

Mr. Playfair launched into a torturous and largely content-free monologue that Lucia quickly interrupted.

"I'm sorry, sir. I haven't much time."

"Ah, yes, yes. To the p-point, then. It's a p-portable electrical generator, capable of producing an electric current, using the principles of induction."

"I'm terribly afraid, sir, that I don't know what that is."

"You've heard of B-b-benjamin Franklin's experiments, and Mr. Faraday's?"

Lucia shook her head. "Only if it's spoken of in the market, here."

A look of pity crossed the man's face. "T-truth is, nobody actually knows *what* it is, and barely how it works. The key components generate charge not through contact but through movement in p-proximity. But we can certainly see what it does! For example...." Handing the device to Lucia, he pulled a tray out from under the table. A dead frog lay limp in the center of it. He had her turn the crank, and he touched the tips of the two wires to the frog.

Lucia squeaked as it kicked itself forward. Then, cranking harder: "Do it again."

She considered the results thoughtfully, and then shook her head. "No, it's no use. Dead frogs will smell up the house something fierce."

Mr. Playfair almost successfully suppressed a smile. He fetched something else from under the table—a small cart, no bigger than her two hands side by side, with four tiny wagon wheels. On the bed of the cart lay a block of metal and tightly coiled copper wires. He clipped the wires to two posts on the metal block and then nodded to Lucia, who dutifully cranked the generator.

The cart rolled forward until it reached the length of the generator's wires. One of the clips popped off, the wire fell away, and the cart stopped.

"Ahh, rotational motion, now *that* would work," Lucia said, and Mr. Playfair leaned in toward her, excitement flushing his face. "Very well, in fact. And with better gear ratios—or even a stepped gear mechanism— you could have that turning quite quickly with hardly any extra effort. It's just.... walking about after them would become tiresome. If only there was a way to store the power, so they could be entirely independent."

"A battery, yes. There are, of course, Leyden j-jars, which, uh, uh, can store electricity from an external charge, but the discharge is, uh, abrupt. Some other forms of batteries actually produce a charge, but not for v-v-very long, and then they're permanently drained. If there was a battery that could be repeatedly charged and then discharge in a controlled manner? That, Miss, would change the world."

Lucia smiled, certain that if she understood the basic principles, actually constructing such a thing would be trivial. "Would you tell me about batteries, Mr. Playfair, if you please?"

"I th-thought you didn't have time."

"*Much* time, Mr. Playfair." She consulted her pocket watch, an intricate device of wood and metal and glass of her own construction. "Twenty-seven minutes, if I'm to finish my chores here and be back in time to cook dinner."

Twenty-five minutes later, Lucia was convinced that a rechargeable electrical battery was within reach. The shoemaker's dabbling in alchemy guaranteed she would have any requisite materials, from various metals to sulfuric acid.

"Thank you, Mr. Playfair, for an enlightening afternoon. I truly must be on my way, but first, I must ask, may I have one of your wonderful machines?"

"R-r-really?" His eyes widened. "You actually mean it. Of course! That would be, uh, uh, uh, £1 3s."

"You know I can't pay you, Mr. Playfair, but I'd like you to give me one anyway. In return, I will give you something I hope you would find pleasing."

Mr. Playfair's eyes flickered toward Lucia's watch, only briefly, and he blushed fiercely when he realized she had seen.

"This? This is just a trinket, Mr. Playfair. I will build you something much better than this." She would make him a clock, one that incorporated some means of employing his induction generator in its function. And when she perfected the rechargeable battery, she would bring it to him as well. With a sigh, she placed the watch on the table and slid it toward him, leaving it next to the dead frog. "Please, have this as well."

He picked it up and examined it. "I am speechless, Miss... Miss..."

"Lucia." She took the induction generator and placed it in her basket. After a moment's hesitation, she took the tiny cart, as well, and he didn't stop her. "Where shall I find you, Mr. Playfair, in a week or two?"

"Oh, I'll be right here, of course, p-p-probably have to fight the crowd to get close."

"Mr. Playfair, we both know you won't be here next week."

His shoulders sagged. Yes, she knew desperation well enough to know what she was seeing, and to know not to say anything more about it.

"So where shall I find you?"

He produced a card and handed it to her with a sigh. "As c-c-castles go, it's not much."

Lucia glanced at the meaningless characters on the slip of paper. She'd need to ask someone to read it to her. She hated that, but she hated the idea of admitting it to this hapless and hopeless man, whom she'd found also quite smart, and charming in his artless way. She placed it in her purse and, with a parting smile, hurried away home.

Soon. She would see him soon, and she analyzed the fact that that thought caught the breath in her lungs and quickened her pulse.

Proximity, indeed.

V. The Workshop

But she didn't see him that week, or the next, or anytime soon, at all. Her master had misplaced his favorite pipe, it seemed, and in the process of turning the house inside out, had ventured into the workshop.

"Girl!" he bellowed from the open doorway. "Girl! Where in the blazes are you, you wretch?"

Lucia had been at the washing, and she was still wiping the suds from her arms with a damp rag as she ran up, breathless. The front of her dress was wet and clung to her skin. She tried not to be obvious about how she held the rag in front of her chest, but for once, her master had no eyes for her.

Instead, they were on her clocks, the ones she had already completed, and the pieces of the clock she was making for Mr. Playfair, strewn (neatly) across the worktable.

"Explain." He gestured helplessly through the door. "Explain all this."

"I fixed the broken cuckoo clock, sir," she said, her voice hesitant, her gaze lowered. "Then I, I thought I could do better. It should be perfect, for you, to hang on the wall in your living room. It's not perfect, yet."

Her master's face was red, and he spluttered wordlessly at her.

Lucia swallowed her rage and tried to make herself small. "I only worked on it when my chores were done, I swear. I didn't mean to make you angry. I... I won't do it again."

"Like hell you won't," her master roared, dragging her bodily into the workshop and pushing her up to the worktable. "Go on, girl, show me what you've been shirking your duties for."

Nervously, Lucia set about machining the gears for the new clock. She hadn't yet figured out how to incorporate the electrical elements into the piece, but she knew that her master wouldn't be impressed if she just stood there, staring at the bits and pieces as she visualized a design in her head. No matter, she'd just build a regular clock, and Mr. Playfair would just have to wait an extra week. So, a few more gears, and the escapement, a delicate piece of work in itself, and she was ready to see how well the pieces fit.

She looked up only to realize that both her masters were now in the workshop, watching and muttering to each other. How long had it been? It was only when she was immersed in the geometries of the clockwork itself that she wasn't acutely aware of the passing of time. In those moments, there was only the work, as if the part of Lucia that observed herself as a self simply disappeared.

"What did I tell you?" her master said to his wife. "Who needs God-damned Elves?"

"The Elves were a gold mine," she replied.

"Diamonds are better than gold."

Too late, Lucia realized her mistake. Her contract no longer mattered. They were never going to let her go.

VI. The Letter

Cognizant of the new value of Lucia's labor, and unwilling to bring in a new servant who might discover the secret, Lucia's masters grudgingly took on her old chores, though with less diligence than they had demanded of Lucia, and with ill grace. Lucia, they locked in the workshop from morning 'til night.

Her master sold her clocks as his own work, mentioning them casually to his long-time patrons for shoes, after swearing them to secrecy.

"Only a select few deserve to own one of these masterpieces," he'd say, after boasting of their accuracy. "People like you. Tell no one."

So, of course, each of his customers told only a handful of their friends, and quickly, the demand for Lucia's clocks grew beyond her capacity to provide. Her masters woke her earlier and worked her late into the night. They brought her meals into the workshop, the better to keep her building. Her only respite came when prospective customers visited.

Locked in her bedroom as the shoemaker gave tours and showed off her latest creations, Lucia fumed at his incoherent and nonsensical explanations of the mechanics behind the machines. Not that she'd likely have done a better job; she had none of the language or the mathematics to describe the principles on which her work was based. Her methods were more direct. She could just see it, the sizes and ratios of the gears, the spacing of the cogs, and the relationship of all the pieces in their glorious geometries. She could feel in the weight, in the tensile strength of the materials, what movement would result in response to specific applications of force, whether that force come from a pendulum's swing or a wound coil.

She had, before she had been discovered, disassembled and re-assembled Mr. Playfair's electrical generator several times, and had begun to understand the nature of its working: the secret lay in two elements that exerted some force against each other by moving in proximity with each other, which seemed impossible until she realized that it was not too dissimilar from the interaction of the Earth and the Pendulum, which, without touching, together generated the force that made her clocks work. But now she had no time to investigate electricity further, either the generator or some way to store the charge that it created. Under nearly constant scrutiny, she hid the generator under her mattress, where the lump it made wasn't much bigger than the others.

One morning when Lucia was escorted to the workroom, she found a small envelope sitting on the table, addressed in a tight, neat hand. It was sealed with bright red wax imprinted with the image of a tiny bird. She was curious, of course, but, reasoning that if she hadn't made sufficient progress on the latest commission by the time her masters returned, they would withhold her breakfast, she put it aside and got to work. Besides, it's not like she could read it, anyway.

Though the shoemaker was immediately suspicious, when he arrived with a tepid bowl of lumpy porridge, he allowed her to eat while he interrogated her.

"Where did this come from?" "Who sent it?" "What's it say?" "Why is it addressed to you?"

It would be as tiresome for us to recite the interrogation as it was for Lucia to endure. She had answers to none of it, even when he shouted loud enough to bring his wife to the door.

"What's the fool girl done this time?" she said.

"She's got a letter."

"A letter? Liar! What's it say? Who's it from?"

The interrogation was even more tiresome the second time around, but Lucia answered honestly and dutifully, only once allowing a hint of her irritation to surface. Now that her labor could be converted to gold and silver, they weren't likely to harm her, but they could still make her life even more unpleasant.

The shoemaker's wife slapped her for her impudence and snatched the envelope away from her husband. She tore it open carelessly, ripping the letter within nearly in half. Holding the pieces together to read, her expression shifted from irritation to confusion to delight.

"It's the Elves," she announced. "One of the little bastards is about to be a father. Says one of our clocks would be the perfect gift for his son. They want us to present the gift ourselves in seven days, and three days later they'll bring us back with all the gold that will fit in our pockets."

This was, of course, not precisely what the letter said, but people see what they want to see, and they immediately set Lucia to building the most elegant, grandiose clock that would fit in the workshop. Lucia's mistress set about sewing a new suit for her husband, one that seemed to be made almost entirely of pockets, and a dress for herself, similarly constructed.

VII. The Elf

The Elf did not appear on the seventh day, or the seventeenth. He climbed through the bars of the workshop window almost two months later and hopped nimbly to the floor. He was smartly, if unusually, dressed in a multicolored suit, and wore a bright green bowler upon his head. Lucia found herself surprised that he wore sensible shoes, and not shoes with the pointed, curling toes she'd seen in illustrations. At full height, he stood barely above her knee.

He gave Lucia's masters each a polite nod, and turning, bowed deeply to Lucia.

He was grinning as he straightened. "Thank you for saying you'd come. Thank you thank you thank you!" Lucia was surprised at his accent, much like the Welsh girl who sold mutton at the market, only higher pitched.

The shoemaker cleared his throat. "Greetings, old friend. It's so good to see you again. As you can see..." gesturing at the monstrous clock that filled the middle of the room "...I've built for your son a clock fit for a king."

The Elf blinked at him. "How do you know it will be a boy? No, no, that'll never do. It would never fit into the Elfhopter, and besides, the clock has to be built in our land, in three days, from local materials.

Rules, you know. And, wait, did you say *you* built it?" The Elf burst into laughter. He took off his hat and slapped his knee while the shoemaker reddened. Turning to Lucia, he said, "You should have seen the shoes he made. No two the same!"

Lucia kept her face carefully neutral, though she could see in the set of her mistress's mouth that she would face retribution for this humiliation later.

"No, no," the Elf continued, "the builder must come, and only the builder. There's only space in the Elfhopter for one passenger your size."

Lucia's masters muttered to each other, until her mistress snapped suddenly at her husband. "No, you can't. You're the most useless man I've ever met. You can't even glue on a clock hand, much less build one from scratch. The girl has to go."

Abandoning modesty, she pulled her many-pocketed dress over her head and handed it to Lucia.

"Put this on, girl, and go with the Elf. Do well, and you'll have two days off a week, and a share of the gold."

Lucia knew these for lies, but she endeavored to comply. Try as she might, though, there was no way she could fit into her mistress's dress. When she had first arrived in this house, one month, three days, and seventeen hours shy of thirteen years old, her masters had both seemed huge and terrifying, and she'd never stopped thinking of them that way. But at nineteen, she stood nearly a head taller than her mistress, and was broader in both the shoulders and the hips. There was no way the dress would fit.

"I knew we fed you too much," her mistress snapped. "You'll have to wear my husband's suit."

Lucia was very nearly her master's height, and while the suit was tight in the chest and baggy in the crotch, and the fabric of trouser legs wrapped oddly around her thighs, it did, in some manner, fit. She gathered some tools, and a magnifying glass. She also pulled a watch from a drawer, the prototype for the watch she'd given Mr. Playfair. Not nearly as pretty, but just as functional.

The Elf instructed Lucia's master to remove the bars on the window, and then the two of them climbed out and up a rope ladder to the roof.

Perched upon skids that straddled the peak of the roof was an odd contraption. At its base was a boiler and accompanying engine, which apparently drove both a set of massive fan blades suspended horizontally above the machine, and a smaller set of blades in the rear of the machine, set on a vertical axis. Four large tanks were built into the chassis, one at each corner, attached by copper pipes to the boiler. A hopper full of coal sat within Elf-reach of the pilot's seat.

"Climb in!" the Elf shouted as he added coal to the boiler. "Just have to say one thing now, because we won't be able to talk once we're airborne. Keep your hands and head inside the passenger compartment at all times, or you'll make a terrible mess."

Once they were settled and the steam pressure built up, he engaged the engine, and the rotors began to spin.

Looking up at the blades, whirling fast enough to be nearly invisible, Lucia hugged her arms around her chest, determined that she would not, under any circumstances, make a mess.

VIII. Time...

The Elf had not lied about the noise, and Lucia's ears rang by the time the Elfhopter set down on a plateau that jutted like a granite stump above the foot of the Elves' mountain. Never mind her ears! She had flown! In the air!

"Have Elves always flown in these machines?" She was shouting, she realized, some part of her still experiencing the *thump-thump-thump* of the rotors and the whistle of escaping steam, though the machine had slowed to a full stop before the Elf would allow her to leave her seat.

"Of course not. We used to ride eagles, but they're terribly unpredictable, and many a traveling Elf was never seen again. Did the eagles abandon them in some distant and inaccessible land? Or did the eagles eat them? We will never know."

The Elfhopter had taken them due north, Lucia believed, though her sense of direction was not nearly as refined as her sense of time. But the Elf set their course to match the compass set into the control panel, and their path rarely deviated from needle's aim. She had spent the trip torn between desires — to watch in wonder as the London streets and the countryside beyond slipped away beneath them, or to examine the Elfhopter's controls and learn what each did, and how. They stopped twice to refill the water tanks, seeking out flat fields by running water, and Lucia had taken those opportunities to interrogate the Elf about her commission.

"We are an industrious people," he replied, "but terribly irresponsible. We lose everything: our hats, our hearts, our wallets, but most importantly, we lose time. We have a terrible sense of time, and we have never understood how it flows or how to measure it. Days and weeks and months pass without our knowing it. And now that your people are starting to catch up to our technology, understanding time will become critical to our survival."

"I don't understand," Lucia said.

"Do you have any idea how long my brothers and I labored in the shoemaker's workroom before we escaped?"

Lucia shook her head.

"Neither do we, but the three of us worked hard and long enough that we made him a fortune that we did not share in. You perhaps know what that is like. How do you think humans who would gladly exploit the labor of their fellows would treat Elves, if they could? Only our technological advantage keeps us from bondage, but that advantage is shrinking."

After that, she no longer paid heed to the Elfhopter's controls. She would have plenty of time to learn them later. Right now, she kept her eyes fixed on the Earth as it slipped below them, but she barely saw it. Instead, she visualized gears, and formulated a plan.

IX The Baby

The baby was no bigger than the runt of a litter of kittens, and would have fit in the palm of Lucia's hand had the Elves allowed her to hold it.

"Is it a boy or a girl?" Lucia asked. The green swaddling offered no hints as to gender.

The mother cocked her head in indignant confusion. "How should we know?"

"Hush, love, she's only Human, and doesn't know any better," her husband said. To Lucia, he said, "It'll decide that for itself when it's old enough to have an opinion on the matter. And before you ask its name, it will choose that for itself after it learns to speak."

Ah. So that was how the Elf had come to be named Choo-choo, and his wife Pony. Well, it was no stranger than anything else in the kingdom of the Elves. They had dug deep into the heart of the mountain, an elaborate warren of tunnels, most of which were too small for her, even if she crawled. The industrial areas were more comfortable, rooms and corridors designed to accommodate machines that rivaled and exceeded (to scale, of course), the grandest accomplishments of human endeavor.

It was in one such room that she had met Choo-choo's wife Pony and their nameless child, who chose that moment to start squalling.

Pony offered it a nipple, which it ignored. She held the baby out to Choo-choo. "I think it needs changed."

"Well, well!" Choo-choo turned to Lucia. "I should show you your workshop. Mustn't dawdle, you've only three days, after all!"

X. ...After Time

The workshop was as well-equipped as she could have hoped, but in miniature. Still, she could make do. Shooing Choo-choo from the room, she set out to implement her plan.

Quickly, she machined a set of small gears. Disassembling her watch, she replaced some of the gears and added others, changing the gear ratio and increasing the interval between movements. It set her teeth on edge every time her watch ticked another second passing — when it should have ticked roughly eight hundred fifty-two times in that interval! If Choo-choo told the truth about Elvish sense of time, she would have plenty of it to build a clock — she would simply need to recreate the error she had just introduced in the new clock, with precision. And then maybe she'd even get some other work done, too, while she was here. Maybe Choo-choo would be willing to teach her to read, or teach her Welsh.

She would have a reprieve from her contract, which she could blame on the Elves.

And if she was lucky, maybe she'd still be here when the baby chose a name for itself.

Smiling, she got to work.

XI. Gallows

"Fly safe!" Pony said, hugging and kissing Choo-choo to the point of embarrassment.

"I don't want you to go!" The child ran up to Lucia, wrapping arms around her leg, until Lucia crouched down.

"I have to, Cuckoo. My three days are up, and I have to go back to London. But you're a clever child, and I've no doubt you'll grow cleverer still. Remember how I showed you how to change the gears in your clock? Promise me you'll do that as soon as I leave? I put the new gears in an envelope for you."

She had also left a letter, explaining her deception and the purpose of the new gears, as well as the correct date — 14 August, 1846 — and how to set the correct time based on the positions of the stars. Choo-choo was right. The Elves were childlike in some ways, ripe for exploitation by people like her masters. But imagine if they could harness their cleverness and industry with even the faintest awareness of the passing of time! Humans would never catch up.

She climbed into the Elfhopter next to Choo-choo and put in her earplugs, then together they lifted into the sky. The compass, she had learned, did not point North. The ornate character was not an "N" but an "H," and always pointed Home. Now, it pointed directly behind them.

All the way back, Lucia fidgeted, picking at the skin around her fingernails. Her masters would be displeased at her seven-year absence. She only hoped the gold and gems the Elves had insisted she take would temper their anger. But when they reached London, her masters' house was gone, a ruin of blackened stone, still stinking of ash.

The streets were too narrow to risk landing, but Choo-choo saw a clear area in a nearby park to set down. People gathered about to gawk, but kept a healthy distance from the spinning blades. Lucia kissed Choo-choo on the cheek as the rotors slowed to a stop, and then dashed out of the Elfhopter, which spun up and lifted off as soon as she was clear of the blades.

Bound by contract, she should have immediately sought out her masters, given them their gold, and tried to bargain for her freedom. Perhaps now that she could read, she could find a loophole in the contract. How to find them was unclear. She could ask the neighbors; surely someone would know where they were staying.

On the other hand, it would be nice to have a *little* taste of freedom in London, and to see what had changed in the years she had been gone. She could sit in the park, read a newspaper, perhaps visit a restaurant and take a room in a hotel. Or perhaps she could look up Mr. Playfair. After seven years, what was one more day?

There was a boy on the corner hawking newspapers, but what she heard as she approached froze the blood in her veins.

"Murderess of electric generator inventor sentenced! Execution by electric chair tomorrow noon!"

Murdered? Mr. Playfair? Lucia's heart thudded dully in her throat as she purchased a newspaper. Yes, there it was: Rose Murphy, a girl of sixteen years, and faithful servant for seven of those, wickedly butchered her master. The electric generator, patented six years ago, greatest invention since the steam engine, *blah, blah, blah...* But wait. That wasn't a photograph of Mr. Playfair, underneath the fold. That was a far more familiar face.

She fumed. Her master had found Mr. Playfair's generator and taken it for his own. His type would never be satisfied with what they had. But now he was dead, and his wife with him. Who knew what horrors the poor girl had endured to drive her to this?

She spoke with police, the constabulary, and court clerks, shedding bits of gold from her many pockets along the way. It was disconcerting how many of them confused her for a young man, perhaps sweet on the convict; after seven years among the Elves, she had forgotten how important gender was here, and she wasn't prepared for how differently she was treated in a suit rather than a dress. More seriously, but also more aggressively combative.

The judge who had tried the case had retired for the evening and could not be bothered, but she caught him as he left his home in the morning, impressing upon him not the innocence of the girl, but of the extraordinary circumstances (which included a handsome diamond necklace for his wife), and of the value of mercy.

The gallows at the Tower of London consisted of a platform and scaffold, and had been modified for the occasion: a massive version of Mr. Playfair's egg-beater sat beside the platform, with a hookup to the city steam driving the rotation. A hideous wood-and-metal chair had been placed under the scaffold and connected with heavy cables to the generator. The girl was being strapped into it as Lucia and the constable with the judge's papers pushed through the crowd.

"Stop! Stop!" Lucia shouted. "She's been pardoned!"

"Commuted," the constable corrected, gasping. "Commuted to transportation for life." The crowd booed them both.

The executioner scowled as he unshackled Rose and passed her back to the guards. "Well, this is your lucky day, now, innit?"

The guards had cast her back in irons when Lucia got through to them. It took a fair bit of negotiating, and her pockets were somewhat lighter by the time the guards agreed to allow Lucia to handle the transportation.

"Careful with this one," a guard said, handing Lucia the girl's chains, and the key. "Looks harmless as a wet cat, but she's Irish, and you know how that lot are."

Lucia and the girl—Rose—stared at each other. Finally, Lucia sighed.

"I just have one more thing I need to do in London before we go to, to wherever we end up going."

XII. Mr. Playfair

Mr. Playfair's card placed him in an apartment—hardly a castle at all—on Thrawl Street, in Spitalfields. Lucia had no idea where that was, but Rose blanched.

"If you mean to be selling me as a whore, I'll be taking the scaffold, thank you very much."

"So, you *do* talk. No, neither of us need do anything we don't want, except leave the country."

The Spitalfields streets and alleys teemed with people of a dozen or more ethnicities, with skin that varied from as pale as Rose's to the dark brown of the Indian subcontinent. The scent of cooking from thousands of stoves filled the air with spice—curries and peppers, onions and garlic. Her own people were here, dark-haired and olive-skinned; she vaguely remembered the cadence of their speech from her childhood, a song from the Mediterranean.

It should have been glorious, but London, it seemed, poisoned everything. Desperation vied with hopelessness here, and predators moved brazenly through a fearful populace. Lucia walked ahead while Rose followed, watching for pickpockets.

Mr. Playfair, if he was still here, lived on the third floor of a filthy tenement. They climbed rickety stairs that smelled of mold and urine and knocked at the door. A girl of nearly Rose's age answered.

Lucia pasted on a smile she didn't feel. "We're looking for Mr. Playfair. Does he reside here?"

The girl scowled at her. "Mum! ''E's looking for Uncle Jeremy."

"He's at work. Come back later, sir, or if you're looking for a handout, don't come back at all."

Lucia craned her neck to look past the door. The woman sat propped up in one of two beds in the single room flat. A bandage on her right leg was stained, red and yellow.

"I'm afraid it's the other way 'round, ma'am. I made a promise to Mr. Playfair seven years ago that I was unable to keep. I'm here to rectify that."

"Let them in, Charlotte." The woman beckoned, squinting at Lucia in what little light survived its journey through the cloud of coal dust that settled over the neighborhood, and through the soot-smudged window.

"Thank you. I've been gone from London these last seven years, and returned yesterday to find my home..." She shook her head. "My residence, recently burned to the ground."

Rose stepped away from her, staring, her head cocked, likely coming to some realizations she hadn't expected. Charlotte whispered something into her mother's ear.

"Yes, Charlotte, I know she's the murderess, and — Rose, is it? — well done, lass. I only wish you'd been quicker about it. It's your gentleman companion I'm more curious about. Not a gentleman at all, I don't think. What's your name?"

Rose took another step back, eyes wide, and covered her mouth with both hands. "L-Lucia?"

Lucia nodded, and Mr. Playfair's sister sighed. She shook her head slowly. "You broke Jeremy's heart, and worse, you stole his soul. How could you possibly remedy that?"

"I don't know if I can, but that's for Mr. Playfair to decide."

"I think Mrs. Playfair might have a say." A new voice, from the doorway behind Lucia.

"Elizabeth, this is —"

"Yes, I heard. Thin walls, open doors. These stairwells are a marvel of modern acoustics."

The woman, Mrs. Playfair, seemed tired, world-weary. In one hand, she held a sack from which a loaf of bread extended; in the other, the hand of a small boy. The boy shuffled behind his mother's skirts.

Lucia fought the urge to be sick. It had never occurred to her that Mr. Playfair might be married, that in seven years, his situation might have changed so drastically. Over those years, she had developed quite an elaborate fantasy of her future life. None of that would be possible now.

"Of course," she said. "Of course." She didn't know what to do. Everything seemed blurry.

It was only when Mrs. Playfair muttered, "Oh, for Pete's sake," and attacked her with a handkerchief that Lucia realized her face was wet, and that the reason she couldn't catch her breath was because she was sobbing.

And it was to this that Mr. Playfair returned.

Mr. Playfair's greeting was, impossibly, and painfully, colder than his wife's, at least until Lucia told her story. Rose was quick to back up her description of her masters' inhumanity, and to hear it told, their cruelty had only grown over the years. Rose also told of finding the generator hidden in her room, and being only nine years old at the time, not knowing to keep it hidden.

"Do you remember what we talked about that day, Mr. Playfair?" Lucia could not bring herself to call him Jeremy, not in front of his wife. Possibly not ever. "About the rechargeable battery? Has anyone succeeded yet?"

"No, not that I've heard of, though my b-budget for scholarly journals has been sadly lacking, of late."

Lucia leaned forward. "I've had some success. Have you paper and pencil? I need someone to validate my findings, and formulate them properly for the patent application." As she sketched out the theory, and a diagram of the battery, she could feel Mr. Playfair's hostility change first to curiosity and then to excitement. "There are questions of safety and practicality that must be addressed, due to the caustic nature of the acids, but that shouldn't stop us from filing the initial patent."

"With what money? If I'd had the hundred quid to p-pay the fee, I'd have p-p-patented the generator."

"That's more than most people earn in a year," Rose said, aghast.

"That's no problem." Lucia reached into her pockets and deposited several handfuls of gold and gems on the table.

"Are you proposing to hire me? Or pay me off?"

"Hire? No, sir, I'm looking for a partner, both our names on every patent, and this is capital investment. You trusted me seven years ago, and though I failed you, I am trusting you now. I will need to leave the country soon, possibly forever. We have yet to figure out where we—"

"New York," Rose injected, her face determined.

"We'll be in New York, and I'll write as soon as we have an address."

"New York!" Charlotte exclaimed. "When can we visit?"

Mrs. Playfair laughed, a startling sound. She caught Mr. Playfair's eye, but he shook his head.

"This is all very sudden, Miss.... Lord, I g-gave away my fortune and I never even knew your full name." Mrs. Playfair patted his hand.

Lucia exhaled slowly. "The last time I even thought of myself as having a surname I was twelve years old." She licked her suddenly dry lips. "Vona. My name was Lucia Vona."

"Still is, I warrant," Mrs. Playfair said. She broke the end off the loaf of bread and handed it to her son, who fidgeted at her knees. "Though if what I gather is true, any papers to prove that might be ash now."

"I d-don't know what to do," Mr. Playfair said, miserably.

"I have been unfair," Lucia said, standing suddenly. "I won't ask you for a decision now. Rose and I will travel to America. I will learn your decision then, and whatever that decision is, I will be happy for you. And you will take this," depositing some more gold on the table, "and have your sister's leg cared for. Come, Rose, New York is waiting."

They were out the door and starting down the stairs when she heard Mr. Playfair's voice. "V-Vona, was it? Your name?"

"Yes."

"Wouldn't do to g-g-get it wrong, on the p-patent."

"Thank you, Mr. Playfair."

The future, it seemed, looked vastly different from what she'd imagined at any time in her life. In retrospect, all those dreams were tinged with desperation. What lay before her was something better: possibility.

And the possibilities were endless.

The Porcelain Princess

Based on Snow White and the Seven Dwarves

DAVID LEE SUMMERS

LBERTA, THE ALCHEMIST QUEEN, STRODE THROUGH THE PALACE when she heard music from the courtyard. She followed the sound and sighed. A beautiful, snow-white porcelain automaton danced and whirled to melodies from an internal music box. The automaton had been commissioned by her one-time husband, the late king, as a shrine for his daughter's heart. She possessed the same ebony hair and blood-red lips as the original. Alberta admired the engineering that went into the porcelain princess. The automaton danced with grace, and she could almost believe the Princess Janara had come to life again.

"She watches, you know."

Queen Alberta startled, then snarled. She whirled and faced… herself. "She is just a doll," Alberta said.

The automaton known as Mirror stood, ticking and whirring. It blinked and cocked its head. "Am I just a doll?"

"You're… different." Queen Alberta continued down the corridor, followed by Mirror. "You were built to speak for me in public."

"I was built to be a target for assassins," Mirror said.

"An indestructible target," the queen amended.

"'Difficult to destroy,' might be more accurate."

"You watch and report." The queen's gaze narrowed. "What do you mean when you say the porcelain princess watches?"

"Do not underestimate her," Mirror warned. "Her jacquard brain is a fine machine. It stores patterns. It learns. The porcelain princess watches you. She is learning about your contacts and how you govern. When you send her on errands, she learns about the city. The people love the image of the princess. She grows popular and she knows it."

The alchemist queen frowned as she climbed the stairs and entered her library. As long as a part of Princess Janara lived, as long as the porcelain princess had her human heart, the king had an heir, a king's child who could build a coalition that could overthrow a king's widow.

The queen narrowed her gaze. "Automata cannot act independently. They must be programmed."

"You have programmed me to simulate independent behavior." Mirror folded her hands in a careful study of the queen's habit. "How different is that in a world of courtly etiquette and public perception?"

The queen proceeded through the library and stepped out onto a balcony overlooking the city-state of Marsstadt. Smokestacks around the city revealed factories that supplied machines to the surrounding principalities. An airship made its way to a mooring tower near one of the factories to deliver supplies and pick up trade goods. Whoever controlled Marsstadt, controlled the continent.

The queen looked back into the library. Mirror had remained behind. It would never do for both of them to appear in public view, side-by-side. An accidental glance would ruin the ruse. "Have you ever considered taking my place?"

"No, ma'am." Mirror approached the door but remained in the shadows. "My existence depends on you. I'm not certain the same can be said for the porcelain princess."

Queen Alberta had taken great pains to assure she controlled Marsstadt. It all started when she had come to the palace as an advisor and the king's alchemist. One day, the former queen and her daughter, Princess Janara, planned to tour the country in an airship – a goodwill tour to cement alliances with the surrounding city-states. Using her alchemical knowledge, Alberta planted several incendiary devices around the airship. It went up in a satisfying fireball just outside the city's gates. King Friedrich's first wife died instantly, and Princess Janara had been mortally wounded.

The king brought in his seven finest craftsmen to build the porcelain princess as a shrine for Janara's living heart. All the while, Alberta comforted the king. Eventually the king married Alberta, but not before he'd made a decree. "Janara is my true heir. Only the person who pledges their life to guarding the porcelain princess shall succeed me." Alberta had no choice but to sign the pledge. A few weeks later, the king succumbed to a mysterious illness and Alberta inherited the dancing doll.

"It seems to me the porcelain princess could use something other than palace intrigue to stimulate her jacquard mind. Please summon the royal huntsman. I will be in my laboratory."

Mirror nodded. "Very good, ma'am."

Later that day, the royal huntsman strode into the throne room. Before him sat Queen Alberta. To her side stood the porcelain automaton in the image of Princess Janara. Instead of a dress, the princess wore trousers and a blouse. Although he thought that odd, the huntsman remembered protocol and knelt before the throne. The queen gave him permission to rise.

"I have decided Princess Janara should be tutored in the animals of the woodlands surrounding Marsstadt," Queen Alberta declared. "I believe no one is more suited to this task than you."

A broad grin appeared on the porcelain princess's face. The craftsmanship that allowed the doll to show multiple expressions amazed the huntsman. The queen cleared her throat and the huntsman remembered to speak. "I would be honored to teach the princess what I can, your highness."

"Excellent." The queen stood. "As this is a momentous occasion, I would like to present the princess with a gift." She opened a box and removed a jewel-studded choker. Setting the box aside, the queen put the choker around the princess's neck. "You look splendid."

"Thank you, stepmother," Janara said.

The huntsman's brow furrowed. He thought the choker seemed an odd gift to mark lessons about wildlife. The way it caught the light and sparkled could startle a deer or rabbit. Before he could consider the matter further, the queen stepped down from the dais and took the huntsman's arm. She led him a few paces away. "Should an accident befall Princess Janara, you must bring me her heart at all costs. Do you understand?"

The huntsman's eyebrows shot up. "Just her heart?"

"She is but an automaton. Her heart is the essence of the living princess."

The huntsman nodded. "Yes, your highness." He turned and faced the porcelain princess. "We may leave when you're ready."

"I'm ready now." The princess sang the words and danced down the steps from the throne's dais. "Please lead the way."

"By your leave, your majesty."

The queen opened her hands and nodded, flashing a cruel grin. The huntsman led the porcelain princess to a steam-powered carriage. As he drove through the city, the princess looked around at the tall buildings, eyes wide. She watched the people walking down the streets. Some of them stopped and waved when they realized the princess rode in the carriage.

Soon, the huntsman and the princess left the city. Although it seemed like it should be impossible, the princess's eyes grew wider at the sight of the trees. They drove for half an hour before the huntsman pulled over beside the road. "Now, we must be very quiet," he explained. "Animals startle easily."

The princess smiled and nodded. As they hiked into the forest, the huntsman pointed out birds and squirrels. The princess seemed as delighted by them as she was by the rarer animals. They crossed a clearing and the huntsman found signs of deer. He looked up and worried as he heard a ratcheting noise, just a little louder than the princess's normal whirring and ticking. It seemed to come from her new choker. He wondered why it would make such a sound and again worried the decoration would startle the animals away.

They continued, following the deer tracks. Soon, the huntsman pointed. Ahead of them, in a grassy clearing, a buck with mighty antlers grazed, making the huntsman dearly wish for his bow. As they watched, a sharp crack sounded. The deer bolted. The huntsman looked over at the princess. She grasped at the choker—which had cracked the porcelain of her neck—then fell over sideways. She no longer made the faint ticking and whirring sounds he'd grown used to. He broke out in a cold sweat. He touched her shoulder, but she failed to move.

He remembered the queen's instructions. If something happened to the princess, he should bring her heart back to the castle. He considered opening her blouse to see if there was some access port to get to her heart, but the thought made his cheeks warm, even though the princess was just a porcelain doll and likely dead.

The huntsman realized he could take the princess back to the castle as is. He tried to lift her and found her heavier than a full-grown buck. Of course, she was filled with metal clockworks. He looked around and noticed foothills nearby. The engineers who'd built the princess worked at mines in the hills. He ran back to the steam carriage, stoked the boiler, and drove to the mining camp.

The engineers were dwarves who had arrived in Marsstadt many years before to ply their trade. They'd soon come to King Friedrich's attention, and he'd given them positions in the palace. After the king's death, Queen Alberta had relegated them to the mines to maintain the machinery.

The huntsman reached the camp and located the shack the engineers used as a workshop and living quarters. He knocked and the engineer known as Julius answered, sneering at the intrusion. After listening to the explanation, Julius summoned the other engineers. "We need to hurry as fast as we can, too much time may have passed already."

They shooed the huntsman back to his steam carriage and had him lead the way to the porcelain princess. The seven engineers mounted mechanized velocipedes and followed on his tail. They soon reached the princess.

Milton examined the choker at her neck. "Insidious," he growled. "This choker was designed to contract in sunlight. It's cut off the fluid links to her jacquard brain."

Leonard knelt down and opened his toolkit. He grabbed a cutter and removed the choker with a flourish, holding it up with a grin. A moment later the princess's eyes sprang open, and she sat up. The only sign of trouble was a series of cracks around her neck.

"Thank goodness." The huntsman wiped the sweat from his brow. "I was afraid I'd have to find a way to remove Janara's heart and take it to the queen."

Arthur gasped, then looked away, as though afraid to meet the huntsman's gaze. "The queen wanted you to bring Janara's heart?"

"If she died, yes," the huntsman affirmed.

Wilhelm looked to his brother Jakob and the two nodded as though sharing unspoken thoughts. "We had better take the princess back to our workshop," Wilhelm said.

Jakob pointed to the cracks in the princess's neck. "You can't return her to the queen in this condition."

Herbert yawned. "I daresay the queen will be disappointed if you bring the princess home at all."

The huntsman considered that. She had made a special point of pulling him aside. It had been the queen who had given the princess the choker. He suspected the engineers were right. As he considered this, the dwarves helped the princess to her feet.

"Bring the princess back to our camp and we'll help you out," Leonard called cheerfully.

The huntsman nodded. He walked in silence with the princess back to his steam carriage. He thought he should say something to her. "I'm sorry."

"About what?" The princess spoke in a melodious voice.

"That you died. That I couldn't prevent it."

She trilled a light laugh. "I didn't die. My brain just lost power for a time. My heart was just fine."

The huntsman frowned as he stoked the carriage's boiler, opened the valves, and followed the engineers back to the mining camp. Once they arrived, he helped the princess from the carriage and into the workshop, where five of the engineers waited. "Will you be able to fix her neck?"

"That'll be easy." Julius sneered. "We're skilled at this. She'll soon be good as new."

Just as he spoke, Milton and Leonard entered with a wooden box. "Take this to the queen," Milton said. "It should satisfy her."

The huntsman peered into the box, then slammed it shut on the still, glistening heart within. "Where did you get this?"

"Mining is a dangerous business and miners die all the time. It came from one of them," Milton declared. "I hate to do it, but if you return with anything besides the princess or a heart, the queen will kill you."

Bile rose in the back of the huntsman's throat, but he nodded and took the box. He knew the engineers were right and this had all been a plot to kill the princess. He couldn't take her back to a woman who had tried to destroy her.

As he returned to the palace, he took deep breaths to calm his own hammering heart.

When he arrived, the queen granted him an audience right away. "I'm sorry to say that I could not protect Princess Janara. She fainted dead away and there were no signs of life." The huntsman's voice hitched on the last words.

The queen nodded in sympathy but did not look particularly distraught. "Did you do as I asked?"

The huntsman nodded. He handed the queen the box. She opened it and smiled. "You have done well. You will find something a little extra in your pay next week." With that, she dismissed the huntsman.

Herbert and Julius lifted the body of the dead miner into a coffin. They would give him a proper burial soon. Milton hated taking his heart, but the princess was key to the engineers' plans to overthrow the alchemist queen. The queen had little interest in Marsstadt or the surrounding principalities other than the riches and power they provided her. Milton and his associates had seen how Alberta had taken control of the kingdom. Now the time had come to take the kingdom back, but it would require careful coordination with their allies.

Arthur sprinkled gold dust into lacquer and used the mixture to repair the damage to Janara's neck. Once the mixture set up, she looked around at the seven engineers. "Will you take me back to the palace?"

Leonard flashed a sad smile. "I'm sorry, Princess. If we do that now, your life will once again be in danger. We won't take you back until we're sure you're ready to be queen."

"You built me to be queen, did you not?" The princess's eyebrows came together. Even though Milton helped to design her face, he still marveled at how realistic it looked.

"We did indeed," Wilhelm affirmed.

"But you still have much to learn," Jakob continued.

"We'll endeavor to teach you what we can." Julius appeared with a stack of books. "However, we're engineers and we have work to do. When we're gone, attend to your studies and let no one in the workshop." He pointed at her. "Do you understand?"

The princess's clockworks whirred and clicked. At last, she nodded.

"Very good." Herbert yawned and stretched. "We've made up a room in our living quarters. We'll begin your instructions and your upgrades tomorrow."

Mirror frowned as she looked in the box. "That heart is much too big to have belonged to Janara and it's been dead at least two days."

"I know." Alberta shrugged. "It means Janara is not really dead and the huntsman deceived us, but it's good enough to convince the city council that she's gone and her death was an accident. It will be a while before she's a threat and that gives me time to dispose of her for good."

Mirror narrowed her gaze. "Do you know where the princess is, then?"

"I know who has the technical skill to repair the princess. Those same meddlers also have an interest in seeing their own puppet take the throne. It's a good bet we'll find Janara at the mining camp."

"What will you do?"

"I'll just have to find a way to dispose of Janara that the miners cannot undo." With that, the alchemist queen went to her lab.

She grabbed a jar of fine, lightweight metal filings, perfect for fouling clockworks. She tried to think of how to deliver it in a way that wouldn't be detected. The porcelain doll's jacquard brain might be observant, but it still delighted in nice things. She spotted an atomizer and some vials containing sweet scents.

She devised a spray that would waft the metal filings into the princess's joints. Once there, it would cause the automaton to seize up. There was no way the engineers could clean the porcelain princess and get her to work again. It wouldn't matter whether the heart still beat. It would be trapped inside a useless body. Over the next week, she tested the spray on various mechanisms and made refinements until it worked just as she hoped.

Once satisfied, the alchemist queen went back to her room and summoned Mirror, who helped her assemble a disguise. When finished, Mirror put her hands on her hips. "Very good, my queen, even I don't recognize you."

Alberta held up a finger. "Don't get any ideas while I'm away. I'm still in charge here."

Mirror sighed. "As I've already said, I don't want to be in charge. However, there is a city council meeting today. I will go in your place, listen, and learn."

"Excellent." Alberta returned to her lab and retrieved the atomizer, then left the palace through the servants' entrance.

Two hours later, she found herself outside the mining camp. She checked her watch. The engineers should be working in the mines, but someone moved within the mining engineers' workshop. She suspected that someone would be Janara. She bent low, hobbled to the door, and listened. Someone definitely shuffled around. Alberta knocked. All sound from within stopped. Alberta knocked again. Still no answer.

The alchemist queen went to the window and smiled, spying Janara inside. Grudgingly, she admired the golden repair work the engineers had done on her neck. "I see you, young lady. There's no sense pretending you're not there."

Janara seemed to release a sigh. She came to the window and opened it. "I'm sorry to deceive you. I was instructed not to let anyone in."

"That's fine, young lady," Alberta said. "I don't need to come in. I'm just a peddler and I'd like to give you a sample of my wares."

"I have no money," the princess protested.

"Such a shame." Alberta sniffed the air. "I smell machine oil... Oh dear... I believe it's you."

The princess looked down at herself. Alberta thought she could hear the protocol gears whirling. "It would never do to smell… unpleasant."

"No doubt the tang comes from those engineers who are said to be about." Alberta revealed the atomizer. "The scent in this bottle is quite enticing. Come to the door and I'll give you a sample. I promise I'll stay outside so as not to upset your masters."

The princess's jacquard brain whirred and clicked for a few seconds more. At last, she nodded. Soon the door opened, and the queen sprayed the atomizer at the princess's arms, legs, and torso. Janara had no olfactory senses, but she was programmed to be polite and knew ladies often liked nice scents. "It seems very nice, but I still have no money."

"That's just fine, dear. I'll check back another day."

The princess closed the door. The queen waited for several minutes. At last, a loud thud sounded from within. The queen smiled to herself and returned to the castle.

The engineers returned home from the mines and found the princess on the floor, immobile. Milton checked her heart and breathed a relieved sigh. "It's only her joints that have seized up."

Julius checked her wrist, then her elbow. "It's like some kind of fine grit has worked its way into her inner clockworks." He snarled. "It's going to take hours to clean this out."

Leonard stood back and sniffed the air. "There's a funny smell, like some kind of perfume. That must have been the delivery method."

Arthur wrung his hands. "How did the queen get that to her? We told Janara not to let anyone in."

"The queen's a tricky one." Herbert stifled a yawn. "With a perfume atomizer, she wouldn't have needed to touch the princess."

Wilhelm held up his hands. "At this point, that doesn't matter. We have two jobs…"

"Revive the princess…" Jakob chimed in.

"…and make sure this doesn't happen again," Wilhelm finished.

Milton sat back on his haunches. "Given how tricky the queen is, how do we accomplish that?"

Wilhelm rubbed his chin. "Princess Janara's jacquard brains are good."

"But she's not experienced," Jakob noted.

"A political alliance." Milton snapped his fingers. "I think the time has come to contact Prince Karl and introduce him to the princess."

Leonard pointed to Wilhelm and Jakob. "You two ride over and contact him." He looked down at the princess and rubbed his hands together. "And we'll set to work cleaning her joints."

A week later, Queen Alberta worked at her desk. She frowned over some figures from the local helium production facility when Mirror entered the office. Alberta looked up. For just a moment, she admired the automaton's beautiful face and envied the fact it would never age without deliberate tinkering. "How was the meeting with the engineers' guild?"

Mirror stepped up and handed a sheaf of papers to the queen. "The meeting went fine, but I suspect you'll be more interested in some of the murmurings I overheard as the guild masters gathered."

Alberta narrowed her gaze. "Tell me."

Mirror folded her hands. "As you know, Julius of the mines was there. Two of the other engineers complimented him on how nice and organized their workshop had become. Julius noted they had taken on an apprentice who paid them back with housekeeping chores."

Alberta frowned. "It sounds as though those dwarven meddlers found a way to revive the porcelain princess."

Mirror held up her hand. "There's more. I have received a report from agents patrolling the woods. A few days ago, they spotted Wilhelm and Jakob riding velocipedes toward Stromstadt."

Alberta considered that. The engineers might have legitimate business in the neighboring city, but Prince Karl had been a thorn in her side. King Friedrich and Karl's father had discussed a marriage to better cement the alliance between the two city-states. "Marsstadt mourns its lost princess. As far as people know, she's dead. The porcelain princess is too well built and she's in the hands of her builders. If I destroy the machine, the engineers will just rebuild her. What I must destroy is the heart."

The queen stood from her desk and swept past Mirror. She had toxins that would stop a heart. The challenge was that the porcelain princess ate only a little to provide nutrients to her heart and those nutrients were heavily filtered. It would need to be a most potent toxin.

Three days later, once she'd assembled what she needed, she disguised herself as an old woman and summoned a driver to take her to a point near the mining camp. She hobbled the rest of the way on foot while the driver waited.

As before, she heard shuffling from within until she knocked. The shuffling stopped immediately. The queen peered in the window. Janara was not in sight. The princess had learned from her earlier mistake. Alberta tried the door – locked as she expected. She applied lock picks and entered. "Ah, what a lovely young lady you are." She held up a basket of fruit with a gloved hand. "Surely you would like a pear or an apple from my basket."

"How did you get in? I am but a cleaning automaton. I am not authorized to purchase anything from you." The porcelain princess narrowed her gaze, and for just a moment, the queen feared the lifelike doll saw through her disguise.

Without waiting for the princess's jacquard brain to process more data, the queen retrieved an apple from the basket. "This apple is a gift. You should taste it to see how lovely they are this season. It would be the polite thing to do."

The princess's eyes snapped wide and the queen grinned. She'd triggered the princess's protocol clockworks. Without having any choice in the matter, the princess reached forward and took the apple. She took a bite. "It is very good," she said after she swallowed.

A moment later, something gurgled deep within the princess. Her eyes rolled back in her head and she dropped to the floor in a heap. The queen rushed forward, unbuttoned the princess's blouse, and opened the hatch in her chest. The heart beat erratically for a moment, then stopped.

With a satisfied grin, the queen left the cottage.

Prince Karl flew his ornithopter over the treetops. Below him, the brothers Wilhelm and Jakob rode their velocipedes toward the mining camp. As the camp came into view, the prince descended, landing in a clearing nearby just as the dwarves pulled up to the workshop door. The door hung open and the two brothers rushed inside. Karl followed them.

On the floor lay a porcelain doll made in the spitting image of Princess Janara before the tragic accident that had destroyed most of her body. A hatch lay open on her chest and her heart lay still within.

Wilhelm groaned and Jakob patted him on the back. "If the heart's tissues aren't dead, we may save her yet."

Karl ripped his flying helmet from his head, peeled off his gloves, and knelt by the princess. With care, he began pushing on her heart so it would pump the life-sustaining fluids like a human heart pumped blood.

Wilhelm pointed to a streak of liquid by the princess's mouth.

"Don't touch it," Jakob warned. "Somehow the queen delivered a toxin strong enough to reach Janara's heart. I'm guessing even a trace would kill you right away. We need to flush her system." He looked at the prince. "Can you keep that going? One of us can trade out if you need."

Wilhelm rushed to a panel and flipped several levers, summoning the other engineers to return from the mine. Once done, he and Jakob lifted the princess onto a table, then began to gather what they would need to flush the princess's system. Soon, the other engineers arrived. They worked throughout the afternoon.

Once convinced they had cleared the toxin from the princess's system, Milton approached the heart with a pair of electrodes. He smiled at Karl who was taking another turn pumping the heart. "You've done a great job, but now we need to see if we can get the heart to beat on its own."

Reluctantly, Karl stood back. Milton applied the electrodes to the princess's heart, then lowered a pair of dark goggles over his eyes. He gave a thumbs up to Leonard, who threw a switch. There was a *zap* and a *pop*. The heart lay still. "Again," called Milton. More electricity crackled through the electrodes.

This time, Princess Janara's heart began beating on its own. A moment later, her eyes fluttered open. The princess's eyes roved the room and stopped on the prince, who suddenly became conscious of his mussed hair and rolled-up sleeves. She smiled at him. "Prince Karl, what are you doing here?"

"I came to discuss Marsstadt and possibly forming an alliance with Stromstadt." The prince gazed into her beautiful, expressive glass eyes as Wilhelm and Jakob discretely closed the princess's chest and rearranged her blouse. The brothers helped her sit up.

Arthur looked from Karl to Janara. "The prince helped to keep your heart alive. We might not have succeeded if not for his tireless efforts."

"I am grateful, your highness," Janara said.

"I am glad our doctors taught me their techniques of heart resuscitation."

Milton held out his hands. "I think we should all clean up and we'll make dinner while you and the prince make plans."

Over a month had passed since Queen Alberta stopped Princess Janara's heart. In that time, there had been no news of the princess. At last, she thought she was rid of the bothersome doll. Alberta strolled through the garden, delighted by the silence, when Mirror approached. The automaton held out an envelope. "There is to be a wedding in Stromstadt. You're invited."

The queen waved her hand. "You will go in my place."

The automaton shook her head. "They won't allow me to attend alone. They want you, in person."

Alberta took the envelope and ripped it open. The invitation announced the wedding of Janara and Karl. "How can a human prince marry an automaton? This is outrageous!"

"It is said he won her heart."

Alberta snorted. "Just because she's marrying a prince doesn't mean I've lost this kingdom." She stormed off to her study.

Mirror followed close behind. "They wish you to dance at their wedding."

"That'll be the day," Alberta growled.

She threw open the door. Inside stood a mechanical armature, like an exoskeleton in the shape of a human. Alberta's eyebrows came together. "What is this?"

"A gift from the dwarves, who have been talking with me. They have a better role for me in the new regime than being a target."

Alberta whirled around. As she did, Mirror socked her in the jaw and the queen crumpled to the ground.

When she awoke, Alberta found herself lying on a table in her lab, strapped into the armature. Struggle as she might, she couldn't break free. Mirror soon appeared, dressed in Alberta's finest gown, prepared for a wedding. "Stand," Mirror ordered.

Alberta vowed to remain still. Despite her wishes, the armature moved. She threw first one leg to the ground, then the other. She stood, facing Mirror.

"Come along, you must dance at a wedding feast. After that, we must attend negotiations allying Marsstadt and Stromstadt." Mirror led the way out of the room.

The queen continued to struggle, even as she was forced to follow Mirror to the airship.

The Pipes Are Calling

Based on The Pied Piper of Hamlin

Patrick Thomas

THE SHIRTLESS, BALD MAN STRUGGLED NOT TO SPUTTER. WHILE THIS struggle might not be described as epic, it was hardly easy. As a matter of courtesy, anyone bound and then hung upside down to dangle unconscious until someone threw a bucket of water at their face might be granted some slack if it took a moment to orient themselves.

Jackson Grimstone wasn't just anybody. He would prefer to die rather than give someone torturing him the least bit of satisfaction.

Grimstone blinked his eyes and forced a smile.

"My thanks for the water. I must've been sleeping with my mouth open because my throat was a tad parched. Perhaps you could fetch another bucket but have the decency to make sure this one is cold."

The water had been taken from a deep well to ensure it was frigid.

"So sorry it was not to your liking," said an overweight middle-aged man sitting on a throne. Apparently, he fancied himself a king but was merely a baron, and that only through an accident of birth. No one mentioned this in his presence, of course, especially if they wanted to continue breathing.

His killing of others was done on the sly, as the actual monarch of Albion, Queen Theodora, frowned on the aristocracy killing her subjects.

Baron Karl Rogan grinned. "Perhaps I should boil the next bucketful instead."

The Spellpunk smiled back. "Be sure to do the decent thing and add some tea first."

"Of course. I would hate to be considered uncivilized. You must be surprised to wake and find yourself once again my prisoner."

Despite the awkwardness of doing so while dangling upside down, the Spellpunk shrugged. "With all the money you've been throwing at capturing or killing me, it was bound to happen sooner or later. Of course, you're assuming that being captured wasn't intentional on my part."

Baron Rogan believed he was known for his calm demeanor, but there was something about Jackson Grimstone that filled the rational portion of his mind with doubt and fury as the Spellpunk had continuously made the baron look the fool, and Rogan was concerned that he might do it again.

Rogan's blood pressure rose as the room around him swayed. No, not the room. Grimstone swung back and forth in his inverted position with all the care of a school child on a swing.

The baron resisted the urge to grab hold of the Spellpunk by his nethers to halt his imitation of a pendulum.

"Nonsense. What benefit could you derive from being my prisoner?"

Jackson Grimstone chuckled. The assassin had managed to capture him—the Spellpunk knew the baron had offered triple the bounty if someone delivered Grimstone alive. The adventurer had no master plan, but that was hardly a reason not to manipulate the mind of a man who regularly hired assassins to end his existence. The record was three in a weekend.

The baron saw the eyes of those in his throne room dart back and forth among themselves, looking for the answer in one another's faces.

Rogan stood from his throne and stepped next to the swinging man.

"Why would you do this?" the baron whispered, not wanting the others to hear. Rogan was not the type of man to hide his torturing ways, preferring to make a show of it. He enjoyed the discomfort and pain he caused others. Even more than that, he relished the way it crushed the spirits of those who watched. The baron knew they each thought of what it would be like if they were the one on the receiving end of his less-than-tender mercies and that those thoughts would resurface if they ever considered rebelling against him.

"You fancy yourself intelligent, brag about how you went to the best school. If any of that is the least bit true, you will be able to tell me," Grimstone bluffed, hoping the aristocrat would supply an answer he could use to agitate Rogan even further. He would have to get him angry enough not to think straight to have any hope of escaping.

Baron Rogan fell silent for a moment. "You're bluffing. Now it's time to get to the fun."

It was apparent from the expressions of those in attendance that the fun would be exclusively the baron's.

"I suppose I should warn you that despite how you've stuck me up here, I'm not a piñata filled with candy."

"What are you babbling about, Grimstone?"

The Spellpunk sighed. Although he was from Earth, those born and raised on the Steamworld had no idea they were all just players in a world designed for the entertainment of aliens. Which meant it was all too common for his comments to fly far over people's heads.

Those born on the playworld accepted the occasional presence of gawkers, floating metal spheres that were cameras broadcasting to the alien Aloff. Having one follow you was considered prestigious. Since most of the Spellpunk's adventures involved what he considered a spherical stalker, it only added to his perceived prestige. Rogan mistakenly assumed that the one present in his throne room was there to watch him, mentally ignoring that it hadn't arrived until the Spellpunk had.

Grimstone turned to stare at the floating sphere. "Sadly, you scum are the only ones who understood that."

"Babbling already. Sad, but I trust you will understand this." Baron Rogan pulled on a pair of rubber gloves that went up above his elbows, then picked up two metal rods attached by wires to a metal box with a crank. The ends of the rods were each covered with a sea sponge. The aristocrat dipped the sponges into a bucket of water. When he pulled them out, they dripped.

The baron nodded to a servant next to the box. With both hands, the man took hold of the crank and spun it rapidly for almost two minutes.

The baron stepped toward the inverted and swaying Spellpunk. "No attempts at wit?"

Grimstone gave another inverted shrug. "I can't say I'm thrilled, but this is hardly shocking behavior."

"That may pass for hilarity among the lower classes, but I have a more sophisticated palate when it comes to entertainment."

The baron prodded the sides of Grimstone's bare chest and pressed a switch with his foot. The current that rushed through the wires to the rods made sparks as Grimstone convulsed, fighting not to bite his tongue and to keep his grunts of pain as minimal as possible.

"You have an impressive constitution, but having been a thorn in my side this long, I would expect nothing less."

The baron again nodded to the servant working the crank, who this time turned it for an exhausting four minutes.

"They say enough current will stop the human heart from beating. I've always been curious as to exactly how much that would take. Thanks to you, I will find out shortly."

The baron stepped in again, metal rods in front of him, but as he lunged toward Grimstone's chest, the Spellpunk suddenly contracted his ripped abdominal muscles and folded himself so that his head came up and smashed the bridge of Rogan's nose.

The pain made the baron drop the rods and stumble back as blood flowed from his nostrils.

"You'll pay for that," Rogan promised.

Grimstone flexed and extended his trunk, so his body swung faster and higher. "Put it on my tab."

With both hands holding his face, Baron Rogan brought back his boot, readying himself to kick Grimstone in the head mid-swing when one of his guards marched into the throne room and stopped in front of him at full attention.

"My Lord, a visitor demands to be seen."

"No one makes demands of me."

"But, my Lord," the guardsman whispered. "It's Lady Vera."

The baron's eyebrows suddenly rose toward the heavens at the mention of the woman's name. "Take her to my quarters and tell her I will join her as soon as I finish here."

"Yes, my Lord." The guardsman marched out with every bit of pomp that he had marched in with.

While his relaying of the baron's message could not be heard, the woman's imperious response was apparent to all those nearby with working ears.

"He will see me *now*."

Half a pair of huge entry doors swung open, and an unnaturally beautiful woman with long dark hair strode in.

The guardsman rushed to get in front of her and block her way.

Unimpressed, Vera brought her knee hard and fast into the guardsman's groin without breaking stride. With a high-pitched moan, the guardsman crumbled to the marble floor.

"Vera, you know not to interrupt when I am attending to matters of state," the baron said in the most deferential tone the Spellpunk had ever heard him use as he wiped the blood off his face with his sleeve.

"Have your men yet figured out where the kidnapper has taken the children?" the beautiful woman demanded.

Beautiful was too mild a word to describe Lady Vera, something noticed by all the men and several women in the room.

"These matters are quite complex. Rest assured, I am doing everything I can to get the missing children of Barony Rogan back."

"Then you better do more," Vera said furiously.

That a woman, even this exquisite one, should dare to raise her voice to him made the baron's fury and fist rise. "Insolent wench…"

Vera leaned back on one leg, crossed her arms over her chest, and glared. "Excuse me?"

The fury in her eyes shone hotter than that in his, which gave the aristocrat pause. He did not wish to anger her, as the consequences for him could be lonely and unfortunate.

"Vera, I allow you some familiarity, but you have overstepped. If you do not leave…"

"The child stealer has taken Cecil."

"What?!" the baron bellowed. "When?"

"Some time while we slept," Vera responded.

"Rest assured, I will bring my…" The baron quickly corrected his words. "Your son home. Grimstone, it looks like you have been granted a small reprieve."

As the aristocrat turned back to the chains, he realized they no longer held the Spellpunk.

"Grimstone! Where is Grimstone!"

"What does it matter?" Vera said. "How will you get Cecil and the other children back?"

"Yes, Rogy, how will you get the children back?" Jackson Grimstone said, now sitting atop the baron's throne. Although his posture was hardly respectful or proper as he sat sideways, still bare-chested, with one leg up on an armrest.

Rogan charged his own throne but was brought up short when, with a flick of his wrist, Grimstone pointed the tip of a sword at the baron's throat. "I've always thought it was foolhardy for you aristocrats to hang crossed swords on your walls. Very convenient, nevertheless."

Fear replaced fury as the baron said, "At least make it quick."

"You have the two of us confused. You're the one who kills unarmed men in cold blood."

"Fine. Then allow me to take down the other sword from the wall so we can finish this like gentlemen," Baron Rogan said.

"Nothing gentlemanly about two people stabbing and slicing at each other. And since I have the upper hand here, giving you a weapon that you will use to attempt to kill me is the second stupidest idea I've heard today."

"Then what will..."

Before the baron finished his sentence, Grimstone had turned to follow where the aristocrat's pupils had darted and saw a guardsman sneaking up behind him, pistol in one hand and sword in the other. The throne stood between them, or the guard likely would have shot.

Before the guard could blink twice, the Spellpunk's arm flashed out, stinging the insides of his would-be attacker's wrists. The gun and the blade clattered to the floor.

Grimstone's follow-up was a slice through the waistband of the guard's pants, causing them to drop to the floor.

Between the wounds and wardrobe malfunction, the guard couldn't react fast enough as the Spellpunk scooped up his pistol.

"Naughty boy. Go over there and stand in the corner," Grimstone ordered. The guardsman looked to his baron for guidance.

Grimstone made the tip of his blade dance through the air between them.

"Don't look to Rogy for guidance. I have told you what to do. Now march to your corner."

The guardsman bent over, pulled up his trousers, and slinked to his appointed corner.

"Well, Rogy, I guess I was wrong about you being disarmed." Grimstone pointed the pistol between the baron's eyes. "I can end you now and make this a better world."

The aristocrat frowned and raised his hands as if they might ward off a bullet. "Whatever do you mean? I don't have a weapon either in my hands or on my person."

"But you have a gaggle of guardsmen with guns and swords everywhere the eye can see." His pistol aimed unmoving at Rogan's face, Grimstone motioned with his blade toward the baron's guardsmen, who now had their guns trained on the Spellpunk. Worry they might hit the baron or trigger Grimstone into firing stopped them from shooting. "Since you can kill me with a word, I'm more than justified to shoot first."

Spellpunk pulled back the hammer, and the Barron went pale.

"All of you, put down your weapons," the baron ordered.

"Even better, pull a tapestry off the wall, wrap all the guns and swords in it, and slide it over here," Grimstone said.

The aristocrat's growl was enough to inform anyone unaware that he was a murderous psychopath. "Do as he says."

Moments later, Grimstone had both tapestry and weapons. He reached in and tucked several single-shot pistols into his waistband.

"If you are not going to kill me or allow me to duel you, what exactly is your plan?" Baron Rogan demanded.

"Besides finding a very deep and dark hole to drop you in? How about you start by explaining to me exactly what happened to these missing children."

"It's far too complex for someone of your lesser intellect to comprehend."

"So says the moron," Grimstone said. "Lady Vera, what happened to the children?"

"Rats overwhelmed the town. We couldn't get rid of them. A brightly dressed man arrived and offered to rid the town of our rodent problem. His method was using an amazing mechanical set of bagpipes. He played, and the rats followed him out of town, but…"

Grimstone grinned. "Let me guess. This Pied Bagpiper didn't get his money upfront, and Rogy stiffed him."

"He had nothing in writing…" the baron said, but Lady Vera nodded.

"The Bagpiper has been luring children away with his music. No one can find them. Someone with more investigation experience is needed. My Lord, have you reconsidered calling in the Steam Table Knights?" Vera asked.

The baron scowled. "I will never allow those self-righteous officers of the law into my domain."

Grimstone chuckled. "Too worried that they'll discover all the nasty things you do and show more interest in you?"

"You need to speak to your betters with respect," Baron Rogan said.

"If I ever meet one, I'll consider it. Since you don't want to involve the Steam Table and your minions are not up to the task, I offer my services."

"What makes you think I have any desire for you to operate within my borders again."

"Maybe for a chance at saving…" Grimstone turned to Vera. "How many children are missing?"

"Twenty-nine," she replied. "And three young women."

"To get twenty-nine innocent children and three frightened women home safely to their families."

"I would sooner swallow excrement than ask for your help, Grimstone."

"Jackson Grimstone, is what they write about you in the *Thames Times* and the other papers true and accurate?" Vera asked.

The Spellpunk nodded. "Not all of it, but largely they get it right."

Vera turned to the baron. "Hire the Spellpunk to bring the children home."

The baron's face darkened, his eyes narrowed. "Who are you, woman, to give me orders?"

Vera stepped forward and repeatedly poked her finger into the baron's chest. "If Cecil dies, I will never forgive you. I cannot think of a worse torture than parents being separated from their child."

"I have to agree with you there." It was well-known that Jackson Grimstone constantly searched for his missing daughter. What was not as well-known was that the two of them had been kidnapped from Earth by the Aloff and then separated. Grimstone hadn't stopped searching for his daughter since.

"If by this time next week, the children have not been returned to their parents safe and sound, I will leave Rogansburg to live in Thames and not return," Vera said. "You will never see me again."

"But what if the children are already dead?" the baron said.

"Was I unclear?" Vera said.

The baron parted his lips to speak again, but Vera covered them with her index finger. "If the next words you speak are not to hire the Spellpunk to bring the children home safe and sound, I will begin packing immediately."

With a posture and expression suggesting that brown waste was indeed about to slide down his throat, Baron Rogan said, "Grimstone, I demand that you go and bring the children back immediately."

The cheek on the right side of the Spellpunk's face scrunched toward his eye as he shook his head. "I don't do so well with demands, Rogy. You're going to have to do better than that."

Through gritted teeth, the baron sucked in a deep breath. "Grimstone, bring the children home!"

The Spellpunk ran his fingers along his scalp as if they were moving through hair he had long ago shaved. "That was an improvement, but you can do better."

"I knew it. He wants to humiliate me to make him do the decent thing. Now all will see what kind of a man the Spellpunk truly is. What horrid acts are you demanding of me?"

Grimstone wiggled his brows. "Try asking again, only this time use the word *please*."

The baron's cheek developed a tick, and he tilted his head to the side like a sheepdog that had just heard a high-pitched squeal that dwelt in the realms beyond human hearing.

"Grimstone, bring the children home… *Please*."

The Spellpunk leapt to his feet, swung his arms to the side, and inclined his head slightly. "I would be happy to."

Shocked that the man who'd been a thorn in his side for far too long had forsaken a chance to humiliate him, yet angry that he still made him look the fool, the aristocrat said, "Good. When will you start?"

"Once we agree on the small matter of my fee."

"I am shocked and dismayed at your callous disregard for the lives of children that you would sully these dealings by asking for money."

"Why? You paid your bounty hunters and killers to capture and bring me here. You promised to pay this Bagpiper for doing what he does. Why should my services be any different?"

"Because you help the poor and destitute for free," Baron Rogan said.

"I do if I like them. I don't like you. Besides, you are neither poor nor destitute. The last time I questioned one of your hired killers, he said you were paying him two thousand pounds to take my life. By my reckoning, you have sent no less than forty-seven assassins to kill me, which means you've paid them 94,000 pounds. Let's double that and round it up for pain and suffering endured on my part and just for you being a general pain in my posterior and call it two hundred thousand pounds."

"That is an outrage. That amount is ridiculous!"

"Come now, Rogy, we both know that your exploitation — both of your people here and those with whom you do business — puts your fortune at least a couple million. That amount is nothing to you."

"Two hundred thousand pounds is hardly nothing. I won't pay it. Instead, I will let the papers know you are too much a coward to save those children."

"I'll tell them you were too cheap and that my feelings were hurt after you tried to kill me." The Spellpunk turned toward the beautiful woman. "Lady Vera, I will be returning to Thames posthaste. Can I offer you a ride?"

The beauty looked from the Spellpunk to the baron, then back to the adventurer. "That would be very kind of you."

Grimstone extended his arm, Vera took it, and they moved toward the huge double doors.

They got within a few steps of exiting when the baron yelled, "Wait!"

"Excellent. I shall require a down payment of half that amount."

"I am insulted by the implications. I give you my word that you shall be paid," the aristocrat said.

"Forgive my distrust, but that vow is worth less than the excrement of the ravens in the Queen's Tower. In addition to the cash, I shall also require the use of your airship."

"Do you realize the cost of putting that ship in the air?" Baron Rogan said.

"Is that pittance worth the life of a single missing child? Particularly that of Cecil?" Grimstone said.

To his credit, the aristocrat's eyes only briefly darted to Vera's face before he answered. "It will take five to six hours to get her sky-worthy."

"Very well. In the meantime, I will need my things returned, the loan of a swift horse, and directions to where the children were taken. I'll leave as soon as I receive the down payment."

When Grimstone returned to the baron's manor, his horse was tired, and he was no longer carrying the large traveling case of cash he'd left with. The baron had, of course, sent men to follow him, but they weren't up to the task and quickly lost track of him.

Vera and the baron met the Spellpunk as he dismounted, carrying a huge canvas sack. The baron scowled at the gawker that had both left and returned with Grimstone, making the baron seem less important to those who watched it go.

"What is in the bag?" Rogan demanded.

"Nunofya."

"What is nunofya?" the baron said.

"None of ya business," Grimstone replied.

"What did you find?" Vera asked.

"Only that it seems as though the children left under their own power via the main road out of town," Grimstone said.

"In other words, no more than my guardsmen," Rogan said.

"Only that I found tracks from men's sneakers," Grimstone said.

"What are sneakers?" Rogan asked.

"Footwear originating far from Albion."

"The dark continent, then? Is one of those miserable orange savages taking vengeance upon my barony?"

"Not that you don't deserve that, but in all likelihood, no. These came from a bit further away than that."

"What difference does having that information make?" the baron demanded.

"Knowing where he's from will help me get inside the Bagpiper's head. Is the airship set?"

"All is ready."

Grimstone approached the mooring tower to see a contingent of ten fully armed guardsmen already onboard.

"No need to send your pretend soldiers. I just need a pilot, although I can do without him, too, unless I need to disembark in a hurry," Grimstone said.

"You are taking my airship, the most valuable thing I own. If you think I am going to allow you to take it without assurances that I will get it back, you are sorely mistaken," Baron Rogan said.

"Oddly, not an unreasonable request on your part. Fine. They might come in handy."

Vera stepped forward. "Sir Jackson..." The Spellpunk had been knighted by Queen Theodora and thus legitimately held the title. "I would like to come with you. May I?"

The baron's eyes widened, and spittle danced from his lips when he spoke. "Absolutely not! Airships are not for ladies, especially one as exquisitely delicate as you."

Vera glared. "I am quite capable."

"On the ground, but up there? Wind currents could crash her, or the air bladder might burst..."

"Lady Vera, I find myself in what would normally be a despicable position of agreeing with Rogy, albeit for different reasons. The wooden gondola will not capsize, nor will the balloon above it burst. And while I am fully confident that you could normally handle the rigors of both the journey and the mission, your emotional attachment to your son will make you act from love instead of logic. In such situations, these actions typically lead to injury or death. What would be the point of saving Cecil only for him to lose you? I ask that you trust me to find the children. Can you do that for me?"

Vera inhaled once, causing a backward journey of mucus from tears restrained too long. "I do not like it, but I understand." She held up a photograph of the boy. "Please bring Cecil and the rest back safely."

Grimstone bowed with a flourish of his right hand. "I shall do my best."

The airship was moored fifteen feet off the ground. The guardsmen had pulled up the gangplank, and not even a ladder dangled from the side.

The baron smirked, knowing the Spellpunk would have to ask for his help to board.

Grimstone ignored the aristocrat. Placing the strap of the large bag diagonally over his shoulder and chest and his goggles over his eyes, Grimstone pointed the tip of his cane up and wrapped its leather strap around his right wrist, holding his canvas bag with his left hand. With a twist of the gold dragon's head handle, a button appeared. With a firm press, there was the hiss of compressed air, and the end of the cane flew up and sprung into a three-pronged grappling hook with a thin wire trailing behind. The hook attached itself to a mast, and Grimstone appeared to fly through the air like a fish being reeled in from the deep.

The metal gawker flew after him.

Once above the wooden deck, Grimstone dropped down. A flick of the wrist later, the line retracted into the cane as the grappling hook collapsed and slid to restore the tip of the cane.

He waved to Vera, enjoying the baron's glower. The guardsmen tried hard not to be impressed.

The Spellpunk turned to the pilot. "Take us up."

Once in the sky, Grimstone said, "You all know the region better than I do. Keep a watch out for anything that seems unusual. An open area now covered, smoke from a spot where nobody should be. Anything like that."

Most of the guardsmen ignored his instructions, but one who seemed barely old enough to shave stepped to the rail to scan the land below. Grimstone moved next to him.

"Who is it?" he said.

"What?" said the young man, his eyebrows raised. He slid his head to avoid the gawker moving in for a closeup.

"Rogy undoubtedly told you to keep an eye on me instead of help, but you are searching intently. I surmise someone you care about numbers among the missing."

"My sister." The young man turned to look the Spellpunk in the eyes. "Do you really think you can find the children? We've looked."

"I've got a better shot than most."

"Well, regardless of what the baron ordered, if you need help rescuing or punishing the bastard who took them, count on me."

Grimstone nodded. "What's your name, son?"

"Dennis."

"Nice to have you onboard. So, did the baron tell you lot to kill me as soon as we find the kids or to just throw me off once we were over some inhospitable territory on our return flight?"

Dennis swallowed hard. "I'm not..." Something over the starboard side caught his eye. "Over there near the river. Those branches look stacked. Trees don't grow in that pattern."

Grimstone adjusted well-camouflaged controls on his goggles, a souvenir from his visit to a higher-tech playworld. In infrared mode, they showed a nearly hidden heat signature of what could be a large group of people. "Good eye, Dennis. If we get too close, they will hear us coming." Grimstone scanned the terrain. "There is a clearing a ways down the river. Land there." His goggles adjusted to telescopic mode. "Company is coming." Dennis had to squint to make out the distant ship coming traveling the London River. "Keep an eye on that boat."

"Why?" Dennis asked.

"Assuming the children are still alive, our bagpiper has a use for them. Unfortunately, there's a large market for human trafficking." Under his breath, he added, "The damn Aloff built Steamworld from scratch. They could have eliminated some ills, but they had to make it entertaining, and few things entertain like human misery."

"How will we get down there?"

"You won't." The Spellpunk opened the bag he brought onboard and snapped poles together. Finding the parts he needed to assemble the simple canvas glider had taken him a while. Who knew that the knowledge of a high school physics teacher from Earth would come in handy so many times? "I will."

Grimstone slipped a harness around his chest, then leapt over the side and took to the air.

Drifting in ever-shrinking circles, Grimstone got close enough to a tree to fasten an anchor rope, then unhooked himself from the glider and swung around the tree until he stopped while the glider crashed into some nearby branches.

The rope he packed was long enough to rappel to about seven feet off the ground. He dropped the rest of the way. Crouching, he scanned the vicinity to assure he was alone and unspotted.

As he moved behind a tree, he debated whether or not to use his secret weapon.

Taking a page from Odysseus and the sirens, Grimstone had fashioned earplugs from paraffin and cloth to block the hypnotic music, which rendered him functionally deaf. If he put them in now, anyone could sneak up behind him unnoticed. If he waited, he might fall victim to the music if the Pied Bagpiper spotted him first.

In the end, he compromised, putting one in and hanging the other off his ear, hoping to insert it before the music took over his mind.

A city boy both on Earth and Steamworld, he crept with extra care through the woods so as not to step on a twig or pile of leaves that would give away his location.

The Pied Bagpiper sat on a tree stump with branches placed behind it to make a woodland throne of sorts. The children were in a wooden cage, a practical decision since the hypnotic state wore off not long after the music stopped. The trio of missing women rubbed his shoulders, left hand, and right foot. A worn white sneaker lay on the ground nearby, and another gawker floated above it all. Everyone except the Pied Bagpiper looked terrified.

The musical kidnapper had the bagpipes attached to a leather strap wrapped around his chest diagonally so it could not easily be snatched away.

"What will you do with us?" demanded one child. Grimstone recognized Cecil from his mother's photograph.

"Not much. I have some friends coming who will take you up the London River."

"Why?" Cecil demanded.

"They offered me a great deal of money."

"I'm sure Baron Rogan would give you more," Cecil said.

"No, he wouldn't. I already offered him the chance to have you all returned just by paying what he owed me. Your idiot baron refused."

The news angered the Spellpunk, but didn't surprise him.

"Our parents would pay you," a girl said.

"I'm sure they would, but these friends have more money than your poor families."

"That's not right," Cecil said.

"And neither was Rogan not paying what he owed. In this or any other world, it's up to you to get what's yours. Worrying or caring about anyone else is a loser's game."

Grimstone slid the one loose earplug into place and crept forward. His plan was simple. Knock out the Bagpiper before he knew what hit him. Like all the best-laid plans of mice, men, and kidnapped Earthlings, it went astray. No sooner had he stepped out from the woods that the underbrush behind the Bagpiper began gushing dozens of rats. Several ran up Grimstone's legs.

Though startled, the Spellpunk did not let out a sound, but the same could not be said of the rats. The rodents' squealing and chattering caused the Bagpiper to spin around. With a grin, he clapped his hands twice, and the rats leapt off Grimstone's legs and went back into the underbrush.

Grimstone crouched to attack the Bagpiper when he was laid low by a blow to the back of his bald head.

Crouching had saved him from being knocked unconscious rather than just having his senses scrambled. A pair of large arms scooped the Spellpunk off the ground as if he weighed no more than a toddler, then dropped him at the feet of the Pied Bagpiper.

Grimstone turned his head, ignoring the pain that shot through his neck, to see a large man standing over him with his feet apart and arms crossed over his chest. Turning his head, he looked up into the face of the child stealer.

"What do we have here?" The mind-controlling musician looked the bald man over from head to toe, pulling the plugs from his ears. "Why, I do declare if it isn't the famous Spellpunk. I've enjoyed reading about your exploits in the *Thames Times*. It's nice to see another Earth expatriate doing so well."

"Since you know who I am, you know it's best for you to surrender now." It would have been more intimidating if Grimstone hadn't slurred half his words.

The Pied Bagpiper smiled as he stuck his foot into his sneaker. "I suppose that might work on these local yokels." The Bagpiper pointed his thumb toward the gawker with him, then the one that had come into sight once Grimstone was captured. "But I know the score. We're from the same place. Your little tricks might be impressive to the people brought up on this pathetic steampunk world, but I have the same advantages you do. More, I'd say, since our benevolent alien overlords saw fit to gift me this." He lifted up his bagpipes, complete with all sorts of extra metal boxes and gears that hardly seemed necessary for playing music but undoubtedly were crucial for using frequencies that control minds.

"Overlords, I'll give you. Benevolent, not on their best day."

"Agree to disagree. Although I'm surprised that you are doing Baron Rogan's dirty work for him. If the stories are true, the scumbag has tried to kill you numerous times."

"They are, but I'm not here so much for Rogy as I am to get the children back. Since you claim to be from back home, you must know that human trafficking and slavery are wrong."

The Pied Bagpiper shrugged. "Back in Jersey, I never would have done anything like this, but I was a loser with a dead-end job. Most of my paycheck went for alimony and child support. I never had opportunities like I do here. Besides, these people are so primitive. It's not like they matter the same way we do. One thing I learned in Jersey from watching the guys who ran things was don't let somebody get away with screwing you."

"Rogan's the one who stiffed you. These kids have nothing to do with it."

"True, but this makes him look weak and ineffectual. Might even inspire people to rise up and kill the schmuck. Plus, this way, I get paid. A lot."

"This is your last chance to surrender," Grimstone said.

"Mark Hamill said it better." The kidnapping musician blew into the mouthpiece and squeezed the bag on his pipes as his fingers danced along the holes.

The Spellpunk made a deep, booming humming sound and put his hands over his ears while doing his best to focus on anything but the sounds of the pipes. Once he saw the others falling under the hypnotic sway of the pipes, he bellowed, "Children, keep shouting *beat up the Bagpiper!*"

As it was the first command they heard while under the sonic spell, the children obeyed.

Realizing what was happening, the Bagpiper stopped playing, but as soon as he tried to speak, the Spellpunk threw a handful of dirt into his mouth, causing him to choke and sputter.

The bellows-like chanting was the only thing being said, which meant the adults had no choice but to obey. The big man and the three women charged the bagpiper to rain blows and kicks upon him.

Despite the assault, the Bagpiper managed to spit out most of the dirt and started speaking, but it was too late. The Spellpunk was on his feet, and his fist connected with the evil musician's jaw, breaking it and knocking the man to the ground.

The Spellpunk plucked the bagpipes from his hands and wrestled the leather strap free as the still-attacking adults pummeled the child stealer.

The Spellpunk looked at the bagpipes in his hands and smiled.

Grimstone emerged into the clearing where the airship had moored, with all the freed victims following in his wake. The Pied Bagpiper and the big man had their arms bound behind their backs, and the Bagpiper had a gag tied tightly around his mouth and broken jaw.

Dennis came running out to scoop his sister up in a hug.

Still holding the child, the young guardsman walked to the Spellpunk. "Thank you, Sir Jackson, for getting the children back."

"It was my pleasure."

Dennis put his sister down and told her to join the other children. "You remember that question you asked me earlier?"

Grimstone's eyebrows shot up in surprise. "I do."

"Our orders are to take the children below deck and not allow you back on the airship. We were told to kill you here."

"Thank you for telling me, Dennis, but doesn't that kind of ruin the plan?"

"I certainly hope so. The others may still try, but I wanted you to know that my gun and my blade are at your service. I will not allow the savior of Rogansburg's children to be harmed while I yet draw breath."

"You're a fool and a traitor, Dennis," said the leader of the guardsmen who had his pistol and blade drawn. "Come over here and help stow the children like you're supposed to instead of dying for scum like the Spellpunk."

Dennis drew his gun and sword and then stepped beside Jackson Grimstone.

Rather than reaching for a traditional weapon, the Spellpunk played the bagpipes. Seconds later, all the guardsmen and the airship pilot stiffened.

Dennis stated the obvious. "You used the bagpipes to take over their minds. Why aren't I and the people you freed entranced as well?"

"The moron who had the pipes never bothered to try all the different things they could do. The sonics can be focused in one direction at a small group or even one person. Collect their weapons, please."

"Are you going back to the Baron's Manor now? He won't be happy," Dennis said.

The Spellpunk grinned. "I'm counting on it, but first, we will visit some folks on a ship who think it's a good idea to traffic children and introduce them to some music-loving rats."

It was almost dusk when the airship flew over Rogan Manor. The baron rushed out, eager to hear about the Spellpunk's demise. He was considerably put out to see Grimstone lowering the gangplank.

With an order from Grimstone, the guardsmen and pilot disembarked, stopping mere feet from Rogan only when the Spellpunk yelled, "Halt!"

"Grimstone, you cowardly, thieving dog! I see that you failed. You best return my money!"

"I wouldn't if I could, as I've already arranged for it to be distributed back to the people from whom you extorted it via excess taxes. I would hardly call rescuing all the children and a trio of women a failure."

"You again prove what a magnificent liar you are. I see no children."

"I am indeed magnificent, but the children have all been returned to the town. I stopped there before coming here."

Vera's head snapped up. "All the children?"

"All but one." The Spellpunk stepped to the side, revealing Cecil, who ran down the gangplank into his mother's waiting arms, both weeping tears of joy.

Vera whispered, "Thank you, Sir Jackson."

"Happy to be of service. Now, Rogy, give me the second half of my fee, and I'll be on my way."

"You are a greater fool than I took you for Grimstone if you think I'm going to give you another shilling. Who are all those men bound on the deck with all the red marks?"

"Slavers the Bagpiper was going to sell the children to."

"And my men captured them? Excellent. I'll make sure they receive severe punishment."

"Your men were of no use, with one exception. And these river slavers will be turned over to the Steam Table Knights for trial, as will the Pied Bagpiper and his lackey."

"Nonsense. What did I pay you for? I will take custody of the prisoners."

"No, you will not. And you just stated you're not paying me. At least not in full."

"Grimstone, you forget who holds power here. Guardsmen, take Jackson Grimstone into custody. If he resists, kill him. Repeatedly."

Pointing the bagpipe's controllers at the guardsmen who'd remained at the manor, Grimstone played a song that vaguely resembled *Danny Boy*, stopping them in their tracks.

The baron's pupils went wide, realizing what was to come.

Later, after a twist of the aiming controls, another refrain, and some commands from the Spellpunk, the baron signed another document granting Grimstone the ownership of the Barony treasury, anything he could carry, and the airship itself.

Moments later, the baron and his guardsmen were loading up the airship with every last shilling the baron owned—over two million pounds—along with several other valuable odds and ends.

Vera watched in amazement as the baron finished emptying out his home.

"Won't he come after you for this?"

"His assassins didn't do him any good. Rogy won't have much left to hire more with. He doesn't have much stashed in banks as he doesn't trust them not to tell Queen Theodora how much money he actually has, which is why he keeps almost all of his cash here. As for the legalities of me getting all this and possession of his airship, this document will need a witness's signature to help me get away with it." He held up the paper and a fountain pen. "Would you do the honors?"

"Did you really give away the hundred thousand you took with you?"

"I did."

"Are you going to give away all this too?"

"All? No, but quite a bit of it."

Vera sighed. "I cannot. He is my son's father even if he will not acknowledge him."

"The Bagpiper had been in communication with Rogy and made him an offer to secure the children's return. Rogy refused to pay."

The color drained from Vera's face as her visage became one that would give even a Valkyrie of legend pause. "Are you certain?"

"I am."

Vera turned and rushed toward the baron, her long nails out like a harpy, obviously intending to strip the flesh from his face, but the Spellpunk caught the furious mother with an arm around her waist.

"Rogy deserves far worse, but not when he's unable to enjoy the misery or defend himself. May I offer you another option? Now that I own an airship, I will need a crew. Dennis has already signed on. He stayed behind to guard the slaver's ship, which I am claiming as my spoils under the Queen's maritime law."

"But you are not in her navy."

"Teddy likes me." Vera's brows rose at Grimstone's causal addressing of the Queen. "Since he did help me, I'm going to make sure Dennis shares the credit for capturing the slavers. You mentioned earlier that you felt you could do well onboard an airship. I would be happy to offer you a job as a pilot."

"But I have no idea how to fly an airship."

Grimstone dismissed the concern with a wave of his hand. "I can arrange for the training and license. The position includes quarters onboard for you and your son. That is if you want to get away from Rogy."

"I do, but if he petitioned the courts for custody of Cecil…"

"Then he would have to acknowledge the boy as his son, which would cause him to lose face among the aristocracy for having his only heir out of wedlock. He cares too much about his reputation to do that. And if he tries to come after you, he'd have to go through me first."

Vera genuflected and motioned for her son to come closer as the gawker dropped down for a better shot.

"Cecil, what did you think of the airship?"

"It's amazing."

"What would you say if I told you we could live on board?"

"We could? Yes, please, Mother. I would like that very much."

Vera stood. "Grimstone, I accept your job offer."

"I'm glad to hear it. Gather your things, and let's go turn this scum over to the Steam Table Knights."

The Binding Clause

Based on Rumpelstiltskin

Cynthia Radthorne

THE ROAR OF THE SUSPENDED TRAM WHOOSHING OVERHEAD RATTLED the bottles and glasses on the shelves of the tavern. Yet no one inside paid the slightest heed. If you habited the Leaky Grommet, it was all just part of the ambience.

The work week was over and the place alive with its own noise as workers raised their glasses, spending their wages on their one good meal in a seven-day. None gave a thought to those well-heeled riders sailing past in the carriages above on their way to their rich estates. Tonight was their own night, time to ease their exhaustion before yet another back-breaking week of mindless toil.

Emily sat alone at her usual table. While the Leaky Grommet was the gathering place for most of the city's engineers, she was still the anomaly. A woman engineer, looked upon with equal measures of disdain and distrust: what could a woman possibly understand of steam tables and friction coefficients?

Thus, she ate by herself, surrounded by tables of laughing, increasingly inebriated men. She didn't even know why she bothered coming to the Grommet; it just made her even more depressed than her job. Spending her day fixing broken hydraulic fittings was not why she had endured four years of hazing at Cambridge for an engineering degree.

A rough clanking of gears heralded the arrival of Hazel, the serving automaton. Her treads crunched over the detritus thrown on the floor by patrons as she rolled up to Emily's table. Little pistons *whooshed* softly as Hazel extended an arm, a pitcher of ale grasped in her metallic fingers. "More, Miss Cleverton?" rasped the tinny artificial voice.

"No, thank you, Hazel. You're sounding a bit creaky today; may I tighten you up a bit?"

The automaton's head swiveled around to check for the publican, but he was busy at the bar. Swinging back so that her glowing arc-lamp eyes settled on Emily, the voice said quietly, "Thank you, miss."

Smiling, Emily opened a panel on Hazel's side. Deftly, she tightened several of the wing nuts that she knew always worked loose, and untangled some of the control cables that had a tendency to get wrapped around other internals. Closing the small door, she patted Hazel's arm. "There you go, not quite good as new but maybe hold you until next time."

Hazel's little head bobbed up and down. "Thank you, miss." She trundled off, much more smoothly and quietly now. Glancing at the bar, Emily saw the publican frowning at her. He never liked Emily messing with his 'property.' Finishing off her ale quickly, she waited until his back was turned, then dropped her payment on the bar before slipping out the front door.

A few moments after she left, a man rose from his booth in the tavern and went to the bar. His hooded cloak left most of his face in shadow, though a few locks of longish grey hair curled out from around the edges. The cut of his shoes showed he was no working engineer, though; footwear that fancy rarely graced the likes of the Grommet.

He motioned to the publican, who asked him, "What can I do ya, Gov'ner?"

The tram thundered overhead, shaking the rafters, the smell of the lubricating oil seeping down into the tavern as it passed. The cloaked man slipped a £100 note under his hand across the bar top toward the publican. "You will tell me everything you know about that girl."

Several days later Emily's world suddenly turned completely upside down.

She was just tightening up one of the countless leaking flanges among the maze of pipes that crisscrossed high up along the ceiling of the Nugatory Industrial plant, a poorly conceived rat's nest of tubing and a maintenance nightmare. Boring and demeaning work, but at least it was a paycheck.

Her real passion was her research on automatons. Every evening she tinkered with whatever parts she could afford, experimenting with new and better ways to make them work. She had, in fact, already had several research papers published on the topic. Not that anyone at Nugatory ever read them or even knew such papers existed…

As she climbed down to the catwalk from the pipe fix, hanging her pneumatic spanner back onto her belt, her supervisor walked up. He had to shout over the hiss of steam and noise of machinery from the factory floor below. "Boss wants you." He gestured firmly downward with his finger. "Now."

Packing up her tool kit, Emily hurried down the many ladders leading to the floor. *This cannot be good,* she mused. *What in the world does he want with me?*

Once she entered the office block, the cacophony of the factory suddenly stilled as the hydraulic door closed behind her. Approaching Mr. Meddleson's open office door, she peered in nervously.

He paced in front of his desk, his expression behind his bushy walrus moustache clearly agitated. From a waistcoat far too tight, a little watch chain barely peeked out from its pocket. Emily's gaze moved from Mr. Meddleson to the other occupant of the room, if such it could be called. Next to her boss stood the most human-like automaton she had ever seen. It wore clothing, a uniform of some sort, covering its body and limbs, with a hat perched atop its head. If she didn't know better, she would have said it looked like a —

"This chauffeur isn't going to wait all day, Cleverton!" Meddleson snapped. Impatiently, he waved her into the room.

"Yes sir, I am sorry… sorry," she managed to squeak out.

"This," continued Meddelson, waving at the automaton, "belongs to Lord Sniffian. It will be taking you to his office." Emily opened her mouth to speak but Meddleson held up his hand. "He's not a man to be kept waiting. Just go." She looked back at the automaton, which, without a word, nor even a hint of mechanical noise, gestured toward the door and stepped through. Equally silent, she followed.

The chauffeur guided Emily to an elaborate self-propelled carriage, folding down the small steps for her to enter. Before doing so, she took a moment to appreciate the exquisite engineering of the carriage. Dual chains led from the drive gear at the rear boiler to both the front and rear axles, a feature she had read about but never seen in person. The oil reservoir was mounted above the boiler, with the control piping for it tidily strapped along the roofline leading to the front, where the chauffeur would sit perched atop the driving box. It was all smartly done and must have been vastly expensive.

The automaton was still silently waiting for her so she hurriedly climbed inside, whereupon he retracted the steps and shut the door. The interior was magnificently appointed, all red velvet cushions and gilded metalwork. As the vehicle trundled down the street, Emily felt more than a little uncomfortable. Here she was, still in her dirty overalls, in a conveyance fit for royalty! She hung well back from the carriage windows to avoid being seen. The long ride gave her more than enough time to worry anew about what this Lord Sniffian might want with her.

A puff of excess boiler steam as the chauffer routed energy to the brakes finally heralded their arrival. They rolled to a stop before the imposing façade of a rather grand townhouse. An automaton doorman, looking much like the chauffeur, opened the carriage door and unfolded the steps.

Emily took a deep breath. This was not the sort of day she had been expecting. Not at all.

"Sit down, Emily." Lord Sniffian smiled affably as he held out the chair for her.

The walk from the intricately carved front doors of the townhouse through the ornately decorated hallways was all a bit of a blur. Not until reaching the office, richly paneled in fine wood, did she feel able to get her bearings. The room contained a single massive desk, a magisterial-looking executive chair, a lone bookcase on one wall, a rather grand window overlooking the city below, and little else aside from its occupant and the visitor's chair she was being directed to.

A thin, rather reedy man with overly long grey hair in an unkempt mish-mash atop his head, Sniffian cut an unprepossessing appearance, though he wore a finely tailored suit and shoes shined to a mirror per-fection. All of which Emily took in at a glance as she perched hesitantly on the edge of the chair.

"Let me get right to the point, Miss Cleverton." Sniffian took his seat behind the desk, which was covered with all manner of small engineer-ing tools: calipers and loupes and gauges. A large magnifying glass on an articulated armature hovering above a rather smart looking miniature steam pump. Impressive—and not at all what she had expected a member of the nobility to have scattered about his desk.

"I have read all your research papers. Yes, don't look so surprised; your work is really rather phenomenal. All of this," as he waved a hand to encompass everything beyond his office door, "is a result of having nothing but the finest engineering minds on payroll. That is what has made the Automata Works the industry leader that it is today."

Automata! Now it made more sense: the immaculate chauffeur, the impressive steam carriage. Sniffian owned the largest automaton factory in England, probably the world. Why would this man have the slightest interest in her research? He could hire the best engineers the world over to work for him.

He steepled his long fingers, gazing at her over them with eyes that felt slightly unnerving. "I mention the caliber of my staff to explain my interest. You see, to rise above the competition one must offer what others do not have, envision what others cannot see." He leaned forward, placing his hands flat on the desk, his eyes never leaving hers, as if they wanted to ensnare her. "You have that vision, Emily. Your talents have been wasted. I can see the incredible potential in you. And it belongs here, with me. With Automata."

Emily sat absolutely stunned. Aside from Nugatory, not a single factory had been willing to employ her, let alone any of the first-rate engineering firms. Now the owner of the best of the best professed he wanted her to work for him!

Recalling Nugatory, however, sent a pang of guilt through her. "But... but I am under contract already to Mr. Meddleson..."

Sniffian chortled. "Oh, my dear, I *own* Nugatory. Well, not openly, of course; through a variety of—shall we say—partnerships. I can assure you, Meddleson will not be an impediment." The bony fingers of one hand rapped lightly across the surface of the desk. And still those eyes of his would not release hers. "Do you wish to accept my offer?"

Trying to keep her excitement in check, Emily nodded vigorously. "Yes, I would! I would very much so!"

A smile crept slowly across Sniffian's countenance. "That's my girl." One of the dancing fingers reached out to flip a small lever on the desktop. The door behind her opened and three men carrying briefcases entered, as if they had been waiting for their cue. "Now we just have some formalities to conclude to make things official."

In unison, the three expressionless men opened their briefcases. Each contained a document written in dense hand-lettered calligraphy. Sniffian produced a cylinder from his waist coat pocket and pressed a button on its side. It unfolded into a magnificent golden pen, complete with steel nib and a feather on the opposite end that slowly unfurled. "Sign each of these, please." And he handed her the pen.

She took it a little shakily. "What am I signing?"

"Our employment agreement." The corners of his smile edged almost into a smirk. "Value given for value received. It is always how I do business."

The first man leaned forward with his open briefcase. She tried to read the document but the lettering was so ornate, and the language so full of legalese, that she could not fathom what it said. "Can you... can you tell me what it all says? I mean, what is it exactly that you want me to *do*?"

The fingers returned to their drumming cadence, a bit more impatiently now, it seemed. "It is very simple. I am offering you a position with Automata as a Vice President of Engineering, with your own office and staff. Much better than spending all your working life fixing leaking flanges or cavorting in seedy taverns, wouldn't you agree?" The fingers suddenly stopped drumming. "Your work, of course, becomes the property of Automata. Standard industry practice. Just sign all the documents and we'll get you set right up so you can meet your new staff."

Little alarm bells clanged all over the back of her mind. How did he know so much about her? Even the Leaky Grommet! Plus, it made no sense whatsoever for her to be offered such a position. And yet... A vision of hot grease dripping on her face, narrowly missing her eyes, as had happened just last week, popped into her head. All her working life, doing that... or maybe, just maybe, having the proper tools and resources to make a difference....

She put pen to parchment and began signing.

The little alarm bells did not fall silent when she was summarily hustled out of Lord Sniffian's office the moment she had signed the last document. "Take care of her!" he had called out as the nameless men in suits led her away, their briefcase duties now concluded. They ushered her back downstairs to the marble entrance foyer of the townhouse, then turned on their heels in unison and abandoned her where she stood. At a loss as to what she was supposed to do now, she reached for the handle of the front door when a voice came seemingly out of nowhere.

"Allow me, Miss Cleverton."

A sudden movement beside her made her jump but it was another of the almost-perfect automatons springing to life, extending a silent mechanized arm to grasp the doorknob.

"Th-thank you," she stammered. "I'm not sure wha—"

"My name is Ichabod. I have been detailed as your primary assistant. If you would be so kind as to accompany me, I shall escort you to the clothiers. The Master has requested that you be suitably attired for your new duties." The automaton stepped through the doorway and toward another waiting carriage, one rather less sumptuous than the last.

Completely uncertain of what she had now gotten herself into, Emily dutifully followed.

Over the succeeding weeks her worries slowly vanished. True to his word, Sniffian had provided her with an office in a prime location in the city, fully staffed with a dozen engineers, all of whom reported to her. The fellows all had existing Automata projects they were working on and so her time initially was spent reading reports of their progress. Through it all Ichabod was loyally present, assisting her with any issues and making sure everything ran smoothly.

At the beginning of her fourth week, she plopped the last of the progress reports down atop the pile on her desk. "Finally! Ichabod, I think I can now say with confidence that I am caught up."

From his perch near the door, where he continually watched through the glass windows of the office partition toward the engineers working in the room beyond, the automaton silently swiveled his head around to look at her. "Indeed, Miss Cleverton. You have absorbed an astonishing amount of material."

Emily sat back and stretched. "Well thank goodness it's done. Now I can get started on some real research."

"That won't be necessary, Miss Cleverton."

She laughed. "Well, I may be the woman in charge, Ichabod, but I still want to keep my hand in things! I can't let these fellows out there do all the hard work!"

"There is no need, Miss Cleverton, for any additional research on your part. The Master already has all the data he needs."

A feeling that she had not had for some while made a little warning ding in her head. "Ichabod, I have not yet *done* any new research to give to Lord Sniffian."

The automaton's head swung away from her, back to watching the engineers outside. "New research is not expected, nor indeed desired, miss. The existing research is sufficient for his purposes."

In an instant, the little bell in her head became a piercing claxon. If Sniffian did not want her to actually do anything, then… what existing research did Ichabod mean?

And then it came to her. All those papers she had signed, the "value given for value received," his immediate dispatch of her out of his office after the signing…

He did not want her as an engineer. He wanted the research she had done on her own, her treatises on automaton design. But those belonged to *her*. She had created those long before Sniffian had sought her out, they were not a part of her employment with the company. They were *her* ideas, not something she would have bartered away just for the opportunity to sit in a glass box and do nothing all day except read other people's reports.

She stood up and retrieved her long coat, scarf, and hat from the brass hat rack. "Come along, Ichabod. Take me to Lord Sniffian's townhouse, please."

The automaton had tried to dissuade her from the journey, indicating that "The Master" was very busy. But she insisted, and thus now they both stood, waiting, in the marble foyer. And waiting. And waiting.

After an hour had passed, Ichabod's voice box activated. Emily knew that sound very well by now, a little click and a tiny whir from his mechanism before the voice kicked in. Before he could utter a word, she held a finger to her lips. "Shush!"

The automaton stayed silent.

Three hours passed, and finally the house automaton, a silent model, came to escort them to the office. This time Sniffian did not hold a chair out for her.

"What exactly is it you want?" he said without preamble, never rising from behind his still-cluttered desk. "I am a busy man and I don't like dealing with petty complaints." Emily's keen eye noted that none of the implements on that desk had moved an inch since her last visit here. It was all for show.

She slowly settled herself in the chair opposite the desk, refusing to be ruffled now. In the carriage ride over, and throughout the clearly intentional wait downstairs, she had had time to reflect on what Sniffian had tried to do, what he *had* done. Which was now her task to undo.

"Thank you, Lord Sniffian, for consenting to see me and Ichabod. Hopefully this will not take up too much of your time." From her satchel, which she had retrieved from her flat on a detour from the office, she pulled out a small pile of periodicals. "These are the journals that published my research on automatons. As you can see from their publication dates, they all pre-date my employment with Automata."

Sniffian had retrieved the folding pen from his waist coat pocket, slowly twirling it in his fingers. As before, his gaze never left hers. It was unnerving, the way he didn't look away, but she forced herself to stare back and not flinch. His voice was flat. "Your point?"

She shuffled the journals into a tidy stack. "The point being that this research is my property, not Automata's. *I* created it, on my own, using my own brain and resources. No Automata resources were involved in its creation."

The pen never stopped twirling in its little circle. "Anything else?"

She waited for some sign of resignation, or perhaps even acknowledgment that he had overstepped in his conduct. But there was nothing, no emotion at all. "That—that's about the size of it, yes."

He slammed the pen down upon the surface of the desk with a mighty crack. Startled, Emily nearly leapt up off her chair.

Sniffian leaned forward, forearms on the desk, the long fingers curling into fists and then flexing outward again. Still never taking his gaze from hers, he spoke quietly but intently: "Ichabod, be so good as to read back to Miss Cleverton the text of what she signed."

The automaton read off some convoluted legal phrases and try as she might she could not make heads nor tails of it. Abruptly, Sniffian raised a hand. "Stop! There. Read that again, please."

Ichabod's soulless voice intoned, "All research from Employee (defined in Paragraph 1.a.12 as being Miss Emily Cleverton of 42 West Surrey St.) is henceforth the intellectual property of Employer (defined in Paragraph 1.a.13 as being Automata Works, Ltd. of 111 Financial Way), there being no defined initiation or termination date covering said research."

The automaton fell silent. The only sound in the room came from the soft dripping of a hydraulic water clock on the bookcase shelf.

Emily tried to keep her hands from shaking. "I—I do not recall reading that, nor agreeing to it."

"Girl, you didn't read any of it, so eager were you for a little title and the trappings of respectability. And you *did* sign your acceptance of the terms, believe me." He spun his chair to gaze out the window, rocking slowly, each movement making a grating little squeak from the springs. His tone changed to one of utter boredom. "You've had your say, now get out, flange fixer."

She fought the urge to cry; *That is not going to help anything,* she told herself. *Think! You have maybe five seconds to turn this around before getting demoted back to the Nugatory pipes, if even that.*

What had he said, back on that first day? "…one must offer what others do not have, envision what others cannot see." That's it, I don't need the full solution right now—I just need to keep one step ahead of him until I *can* find the solution.

Carefully, slowly, she slid the journals back into her satchel. "That's really rather a shame, you know. The articles in the journals were just the preliminary concepts. I was about to publish the final piece, the one that shows how to achieve independent thought in the automaton."

The chair springs stopped squeaking. Yet Sniffian did not turn back to her. "You are bluffing. All you had was in those already published reports."

Gotcha! Slowly she stood up and tied the belt of her coat around herself. "Well now you'll never know for sure, will you."

He spun back, his face a snarl. "I own *everything* you produce, gutter rat. And no journal will dare publish any findings of an employee of mine without my consent; they know their legal obligations."

"Who said anything about publishing it at all? It just won't go anywhere. Not to the journals and," as she sauntered over toward the door, "not to you."

Her fingers were already on the doorknob, and she thought she had overplayed her hand, when with considerably less affability than their first meeting he commanded, "Sit down, Emily."

Having resumed her place in the chair, she saw now she had his full attention once more. His fingers gripped the pen as if to snap it in half. His voice was strained now. "Give me one shred of evidence that you have anything at all to back up your boast before I have you thrown out of here and blacklisted from every business in this city."

Her mind had been racing furiously ever since she had committed to this course. Stall, delay, get more time; that was the objective in this moment. She had to keep him guessing until she could work out a way to get her rights back.

On a sudden inspiration, she turned to the automaton. "Ichabod, are you alive?"

Immediately, he answered in his smooth mechanical voice. "No, Miss Cleverton. I am an automaton."

Now she had to take a chance. Ichabod had been Sniffian's spy all along, and would clearly obey every wish of his 'master.' But she had been able to observe him closely at first hand for some time, his reactions to events and questions, so this was a calculated gamble but worth trying. "Understood. Ichabod, do you *want* to be alive?"

There was silence. Inwardly, she breathed a sigh of relief.

Sniffian laughed out loud. "*That* is your proof? A stupid question to a piece of machinery?"

It was Emily's turn now to hold Sniffian's gaze. "Yet you notice he did not answer, Lord Sniffian. Is it because his coding cannot conceive of the question, and thus *had* no answer? If so, automatons will always be limited to simple tasks and never achieve the potential to assist us with truly difficult tasks. Then again, perhaps Ichabod *does* have an answer to that question. But he will not say, either out of loyalty, or because he lacks the capacity to express it clearly. Either way, *I* know how to bring those concepts to life within the automaton. And from the research I've done, you know I am capable of it." A bold bluff but she had to go out on a limb to make this work.

Sniffian's lanky fingers splayed out across the desktop. His eyes narrowed, as he looked at Ichabod. The automaton did not move.

After a long awkward pause, Sniffian picked up his folding pen (how did the casing survive in that man's hands, she wondered) and began twirling it again. His tone had changed and she knew before he finished his sentence that she had won this round. "Even if what you say is true, for this research to be of value to me, then clearly you must provide it. Which means you want something in return. State your terms and I will decide if I think it is worth it."

All the while she had been pondering how far to go with this. In the end, she decided that nothing short of total victory would keep her safe from the likes of Sniffian. Clearly his contacts would allow him to ruin her life unless she had the means to protect herself. And there was only one way to do that.

"I want a wager. If I lose, I give you all the automaton sentience research without reservation or compensation, no strings attached."

His eyes looked keen at that prospect. "And in the event you win this bet?"

"I become the majority shareholder of Automata Works."

This time his laughter boomed. "You are insane, girl! Why would I ever agree to such terms?"

"Because I will let you dictate the wager to be made."

The twirling pen stopped and the smirking smile returned. "Done." His finger pressed the little lever again, and once more a troop of suited men came through the door. "Here is the wager, then, flange fixer. You must provide my true family name. By tomorrow at sunset. If you can't, you are bound to me and must give to me all your work on automaton sentience. In the impossible circumstance that you can, then you will be made majority shareholder of Automata." He pressed the small button on the pen and it unfolded once more. With a sneer he handed it to her.

Emily felt utterly exhausted. It had been a full twenty-four hours since she and Ichabod had left Sniffian's office, contract in hand for the wager. What she had thought should be a relatively easy task, finding his family name, had instead turned into a series of frustrating dead ends. She ought to have realized he would not have given her a task that could be easily accomplished.

She had set out with the automaton crisscrossing the city, hunting in libraries and archives for the history of Lord Sniffian and Automata. But everywhere she turned it was the same story: the man seemed to have sprung out of whole cloth. Aside from some vague allusions to having come originally from Germany, there was nothing. She suspected that his fortune had gone some way to suppressing any information about his past.

Now here she sat in her office, only a couple of hours left before Sniffian's deadline, and she still hadn't the faintest clue of the man's family.

"Can I provide any refreshments for you, Miss Cleverton?" Ichabod's voice, while never changing timbre, nevertheless managed to sound sympathetic.

Head in her hands, Emily muttered, "No, thank you, Ichabod." But that exchange sparked an idea. She looked up at him to where he stood in his usual spot by the door. "Ichabod... may I examine your mechanism?"

She could almost sense his hesitancy. "If you wish, Miss Cleverton." He stepped over to the desk and turned away, so that his access panel faced her. She slipped the little catches aside and opened it, marveling at what she saw inside.

Her engineer's heart found the design exquisite, all very clean and tidy. Cabling neatly tied, the rods and gearing perfectly machined and amazingly intricate. So vastly different from Hazel at the Leaky Grommet. And yet both were automatons, both worked essentially the same way. Each had a regulator board that provided the parameters for what they could and could not do. That was in fact what she was searching for, as she had a thought, a very far-fetched one, but a last grasping at straws.

She found the board, partly buried behind a bundle of flexible hydraulic tubes going to his lower extremities. "This should not hurt, Ichabod, but I want to try something. Please pardon my fingers." With some difficulty she unseated the regulator board and disconnected it. To her surprise it was exactly the same as Hazel's. A common board, used everywhere.

A whirring noise came from above her, the prelude to Ichabod speaking. His head swiveled 180 degrees and tilted down to look at her. "Yes, I would."

Emily looked up. "Sorry? You would what, Ichabod?"

"Like to be alive."

She sat dumbfounded. Jaw agape, she stared down at the regulator board in her hand. "That—that really *was* all it needed? To remove the regulator to give you... thought?"

"No," replied the automaton. "Not just that." He spun his body around to face her and laid his mechanical hand on her shoulder. "It is much more than that. It is... being treated with respect. I have watched you closely for some time now. And you have given me the same respect you give to humans. That allows me to... understand... some of what you are. What I would... like to be."

She set the regulator board on the desk. "Then," she whispered, "this is not going back inside you. I'll be going back to tightening flanges but at least you will have found some purpose." She got up and began collecting her things from around the office. "I'll save you the trip back here, once Sniffian kicks me out."

"That won't be necessary, Miss Cleverton."

"It's fine, I don't want to cause you any trouble with him."

"You misunderstand me…. Emily." His use of her name made her stop and stare at him. "Before Lord Sniffian assigned me to you, I was his personal valet for many years. My listening receptors record everything I hear. That data has never been deleted. Including Lord Sniffian's private communications with his attorneys and others." He picked up the regulator board from the desk, held it over the waste bin, and dropped it in. Then he looked at her.

"His family name is Rumpelstiltskin."

The Six Clockwork Swans

Based on The Six Swans

CHRISTINE NORRIS

KADIE'S FOOTSTEPS WERE ALL BUT SILENCED BY THE THICK PERSIAN carpet as she crept across the library. The tall windows that lined the one wall showed a clear night sky full of stars and a full moon that made turning on the gas lamps unnecessary. Thick shadows lay in corners where the moonlight didn't reach. The last of the church bells' midnight chimes still hung in the air, its resounding *gongs* giving Kadie the perfect cover for her journey down the stairs, across the marble hall, and through the library door.

The household had been in bed for hours, except for the night maids, who were in the kitchen gossiping over their tea. As mistress of the house, it was her right to be in the library whenever she pleased, so sneaking shouldn't be necessary, but she knew she was being watched. And being so close to breaking the curse, she couldn't take a single chance.

The library seemed to hold its breath as she passed the shelves of books. The framed portraits of generations of her husband's family stared down from above, their dour expressions silently judging her. She had been told all of their names but didn't recall a single one at this moment. There were only six names that mattered to her.

Her foot caught on something, and suddenly she was falling. She flung her arms forward to stop herself and slammed her palms into the edge of her husband's enormous heavy desk, her knee into the side. Tears pooled in the corners of her eyes, and she gritted her teeth to hold back her cry of pain and shock. After a few seemingly eternal moments, the pain passed, and Kadie was able to gather herself enough to stand. She looked down and saw the architect of her stumble — a wrinkle in the rug. She silently cursed it and resumed her trip to the farthest corner of the library.

She tossed a nervous glance over her shoulder to make sure she was still alone. No one had heard her unfortunate crash into the desk, it seemed. She stood on tiptoe and reached as high as she could, the tips of her fingers grasping the edge of one of the books on the top shelf. With a *snick* softer than a whisper, the bookcase swung open. Kadie grabbed the oil lamp she kept on a shelf just inside the door and lit it with the matches she kept in the pocket of her skirt. A few yards down the stone-lined passage, she pushed on one, worn smooth, and the hidden door swung silently shut. The little oil lamp only put out a small circle of light, but she walked with quick and sure steps, her footfalls echoing along the narrow passage. She could have had no light at all, and she would know the way, so often had she traveled this corridor.

She had discovered the secret passage completely by accident, just a year after Daniel found her in the tiny cottage in the woods and brought her to his home. His was a magnificent manor house at the center of the city over which he reigned as Duke. A far different place than her home in so many ways.

The library had been her refuge from almost the moment she had arrived, and one rainy afternoon while she was looking for something to read and hiding from her mother-in-law, she reached for the book that opened the door. The passage had been dark and full of cobwebs, obviously unused for many years. But with a little sweeping and the hidden lamp, it had become almost welcoming.

The other end of the passage opened into a comfortably sized room with windows near the ceiling that allowed the moonlight to pour inside like silver. Kadie had never been able to figure out where this room was within the house, either from the inside or looking at the house from the outside. It was as if it existed just for her.

She inhaled deeply, letting the scent of machine oil and dust fill her nose before she placed the lamp on a small table beside the door and, in a few minutes, the rest of the lamps were lit, and she was ready to get to work.

The flickering yellow light bounced off the glass doors of the cabinet where she kept the collection of tools she had gathered in the last six years. She never took them from the room; if she were ever caught with even the smallest screwdriver, it could mean her death. In this realm, technology like clockworks and machinery were heresy.

Her workbench stood against the back wall. Beside a small pile of spare gears and cogs, five small music box movements sat in a neat row, gleaming in the light. The first was the largest, and each decreased slightly in size. In front of each sat a small card with a name written in her own elegant script—*Albert, Broderick, Charles, Dorian, Edgar.* The sixth movement lay in pieces on the bench in front of a small stool with a cracked leather seat. Its label waited off to the side. *Flynn.* Kadie gazed at the names, picturing each of her brothers in turn. Their faces had begun to blur in her memory. If all went well, she would see them again today.

Kadie sat and took a deep, cleansing breath before lifting the small screwdriver in her callused fingers and tightening the screw that held the cog in place. *Almost done, and yet still so far to go.* It hadn't been easy to keep her work a secret; these stolen moments in the workshop had been harder to come by, especially with her mother-in-law keeping an ever more watchful eye.

This would have been so much easier if she had been home, or even still at the cottage. Her father's realm was a hive of mechanical things. Clock shops, mechanical vehicles on the streets, airships in the skies above. Her father loved anything mechanical. Her room in the palace had been filled with clockwork toys, many he had made himself and given to her on birthdays and holidays.

That had been before he had married again.

Her stepmother hated her and her siblings. Kadie had no idea why, nor why she had been spared from her curse. When her brothers had disappeared, she had grabbed what she could carry and ran. From the capital city and into the forest, she ran so far she had no idea where she was. She followed the forest road until she discovered an abandoned cottage. Inside, she found a corner and cried herself to sleep.

That was where her brothers had come to her. At sunset, six clockworks swans landed in the yard outside her door. One by one, they transformed into her human brothers. Kadie was overjoyed to see them and hugged and kissed each on the cheek.

"How is this possible?" she had said. "Who did this to you?"

Her brothers said nothing, only looked at her sadly. She brought them inside and, for hours, tried to get them to speak, but none would utter a word, no matter how she pleaded.

"They cannot speak. Their voices have been stolen," said a voice behind her. Kadie turned around to see who had spoken. Just as the little mantle clock she had taken from her room at the palace chimed midnight, a woman appeared in a cloud of aether, wearing a shimmering gown of copper and silver, with a crown of gears and cogs upon her brow. On her back fluttered wings of the most intricately scrolled metal, the gears that drove them working silently.

The Fae Queen of Clockwork.

She approached Kadie, concern and sadness written across her otherworldly features. "They have been cursed to be clockwork swans by day and human only from sunset to sunrise." She nodded to each of them, sympathy in her eyes, then turned back to Kadie.

"You can free your brothers, but it will not be easy. You must construct a music box for each of them to restore their voices and their bodies."

Kadie scoffed-—was that all? She had spent her life around springs and gears. A music box would be simple. She had never built a music box, but she would learn. "I will happily do that."

"Of course. I will do whatever I must to help my brothers."

The queen held up a hand. "It will not be that easy. From the time you begin, you will have six years exactly to finish, or else your brothers will remain in their clockwork bodies forever."

Kadie nodded. It seemed a reasonable timeframe to complete what should be a simple task.

The queen glanced at her brothers, who shook their heads in protest, but she continued. "There is something else. Once you begin, you may not speak a word nor laugh. If you do, your brothers will perish."

Kadie gasped. She gazed at each of her brothers, all looking back at her with the same blue eyes. Eyes that matched her own, that matched her father's.

She lifted her chin defiantly. "That won't be hard. There's no one to talk to out here in the forest anyway."

The queen smiled. "You have courage, child. And I can help you just a little." The queen pulled a rolled sheet of paper from her skirt and handed it to Kadie. She unrolled it—a diagram and instructions to build a music box movement.

Kadie took the diagram and held it tightly. She nodded. "I will break the curse."

"Remember. Six music box movements, six years. Not one word from your lips." The queen leaned over and planted a kiss on her head. "Good luck."

And in another moment, she was gone. Her brothers silently objected, shaking their heads and with gestures telling her she could not do it, that they would be fine spending half their lives as clockwork swans. She waved all their objections away.

"I know you think I'm unable to do this since I am the youngest of you and the only girl."

Broderick smiled gently, his face relaying every worry and fear he could not speak.   Kadie stroked his cheek, already rough with missed days of shaving. "You are my brothers. My heart would break if this were your fate, and I did nothing to change it. And I am the strongest-willed of all of us. You know I am. You cannot change my mind. I will begin tomorrow. But for tonight, I will sing, and we will dance until dawn."

When the sun peeked over the horizon, her brothers waved a sad goodbye as their bodies changed to metal and gears, and they soared off into the sunrise.

A sudden sound jolted Kadie back to the present. She dropped the screwdriver and whirled around, looking for the source of the noise. Something scuttled in the dark to her right, and she narrowed her eyes to try and pierce the shadows. It was probably just a mouse. They were ubiquitous, especially in the less-used areas of the house. Whatever it was moved again, and it sounded larger than a mouse. She crept across the room to where the sound had come from and tapped the side of the cabinet with her foot, then a table beside it.

With an unearthly howl, a long-haired creature of gray stripes and long whiskers shot out from beneath the table and leaped onto her workbench. Kadie jumped back. The beast gazed at her with bright green eyes.

Copernicus, her mother-in-law's wretched cat. He was always underfoot, it seemed, trying to trip her or send her tumbling down the stairs. Kadie pressed her lips together, biting back all the curses she had for the animal. She was not about to let this miserable beast cost her everything. She swatted the cat away, and Copernicus hissed and ran off. Kadie sat heavily on her stool, breathing deeply to allow her shaking hands to steady and her heart to slow from the marching band bass drum beat it was currently keeping.

She picked up one of the completed movements and wound the key. A beautiful melody played one that reminded her of Edgar's laugh. The song soothed her nerves and lifted her spirits. She set the movement back on the bench, proud of how far she had come.

The first two years of her quest had been devoted to her simply learning how to make the movements. It was a simple task to not speak, as there was no one to speak to most of the time. But figuring out how to build a music box, then create a melody for each of her brothers had been her first big challenge. Despite the queen's remarkably specific directions, her earliest attempts at making the movements hadn't worked at all. On her first attempt, the spring would not wind. On the fourth, the music that erupted from the mechanism sounded like the voice of a demon. Definitely not reminiscent of Albert at all.

She had had some help. Once in a while, a tribe of Nomads would stop in the clearing near her cottage for the night, and she would trade with the toy and watchmakers, for parts and knowledge. They had never minded that she didn't speak. Couldn't speak. They somehow understood what she needed and why and were fully willing to help as best they could.

Almost every evening, just as the sun set, her brothers would fly to the cottage and transform. Kadie would feed them a hot meal, and they would sleep. During those years, Kadie and her brothers developed their own language, using their hands and facial expressions to communicate.

Kadie shook her head, clearing away the cobwebs of memory, and returned to her work. She lifted the drum from its box. A cylinder of polished brass flecked with small raised bumps. This was half of what created the box's melody. When the movement was wound, the drum would turn, and the bumps would lift various teeth on a finely tuned metal comb placed beside it. The comb played a note as the tooth was released. She had crafted each drum by hand, using her mind's ear to create a melody representing each of her brothers. It was this that took the most time, and it was imperative it was perfect and the cylinder was placed correctly.

Kadie took a deep breath, letting it out slowly as she maneuvered the cylinder. It clicked into place, and she closed her eyes and let out the rest of her breath. All she needed to do was put the comb in place and give all six boxes a final inspection. She should have plenty of time to gather them all up and get to the forest by sunset. Both she and her brothers were almost free.

She reached across the workbench to retrieve the metal comb. Her fingers wrapped around empty air. She looked up, but there was no sign of it. Panic rising in her chest, she picked up the closest lamp and searched every corner of the bench.

No, no, no! She knew she had left it sitting beside the cylinder. Had she seen it when she came in tonight? Now she doubted her own memory. Frantic, she pulled open drawers and looked in boxes. She patted her skirts in case she had absently slipped it into a pocket. After thoroughly searching the workshop, she had to face the horrible truth. It was gone.

She pressed her lips together, anguish and frustration wanting to cry out. There was almost no time left, and if she couldn't replace the part before the sun rose, her chance would be gone. Once Daniel, his mother, and the rest of the household awoke, too many eyes on her would make it impossible to slip away. She trusted none of the servants. They were all loyal to the Dowager Duchess and likely would report any suspicious movement on her part.

She had no choice. She would have to go now, in the dark, and pray to the Fae Queen of Clockwork she could get what she needed.

Kadie carefully packed up the other five movements, their labels attached, and put them into a large satchel. The last one, she scooped up the unfinished movement and a few tools, then wrapped them and added them to her bundle.

She looked at the clock she kept on the shelf, a replica of the beloved mantle clock she had had to leave behind in the cottage. She had built it herself, just as she had made the pocket watch hidden in her bodice, which she pulled out and checked against the clock. One o'clock in the morning. They would be asleep, of course, like everyone else. But it couldn't be helped. This was an emergency. She tucked her watch away again, making sure it was secure. The workshop was a necessary risk, but keeping a clock on her person was outright dangerous.

She pulled open one of the drawers in the workbench and stared at the contents for a moment. When she had built what lay inside, she never thought she would need to use it. It had been a lark to see if she had the skill to make such a thing. Her hand trembled a little as she touched the handle.

It would be prudent to take a weapon, wouldn't it? She was a woman venturing alone on the street in the middle of the night. It was perfectly reasonable to want needed to protect herself. She slipped her hand into the drawer, withdrew the small sonic pistol, then dropped it into the pocket of her skirt.

Kadie extinguished the lights in the workshop, grabbed her lamp, and hurried down the secret passage and through the library. In the entrance hall, she did not even glance at the grand staircase that led back to her room and her comfortable, warm bed but instead made for the foyer and the huge, richly carved wardrobe. She pulled out her warmest cloak and wrapped it around her shoulders, then sneaked through the dining room and to the servant's stairs. At the top, she stopped and listened—the maids had finally gone to bed, it seemed. Still, she made her steps slow and careful as she descended into the kitchen. Embers from the evening fire glowed in the hearth like the eyes of devils watching her. She shivered at the thought.

Kadie slipped through the back door and out into the chilly night. The moon had begun its descent but still gave enough light to see. The path from the kitchen to the stables was clear enough, but she turned away and headed across the gardens through the park that surrounded the manor. It was half a mile to the hedge that marked the edge of the estate. If she hurried, she could reach the outskirts of the city in an hour. Her destination was The Dredge, as it was known, the poorest part of the city. Deep in the Dredge was an underground network of people called The Makers.

Kadie had sought them out over a year ago when she needed to find more parts for her music boxes. They had been suspicious of her at first, of course, as they were of anyone asking about anything mechanical. She had disguised herself but felt at least some of them had guessed her identity. Eventually, she had earned their trust, even without being able to speak. Most of them could read, so note-writing had been their form of communication. Of course, they had no idea about the curse—who would believe that?

Kadie reached the end of the gardens, the hedge just fifteen yards down a gentle slope. She lifted her skirts and ran. Dew clung to her stockings, soaking them and the hem of her cloak. She reached the wall of greenery and slipped through the space she knew was there. On the other side, she stopped to catch her breath. The cobblestone street glistened in the light of the moon and the street lamps. No one was in sight, and all the windows of the shops and homes were dark. No one to see her pass.

She walked down the street, determined, her direction clear. Three blocks down, she turned left. Shadows lurked in corners, and Kadie started imagining people in every shadow. She reached into her pocket and wrapped her hand around the handle of her pistol. As much as she feared using it, having it gave her some comfort.

Heading for a shortcut down an alley that would take ten minutes off her travel time, Kadie hesitated when she saw how dark it was.

No darker than the forest at night. Kadie pulled her shoulders back and dove into the alley. Shadows enveloped her, pulled at her cloak and hair as she made her way, keeping her eyes on the light at the end of the alley, hand on one wall so she wouldn't stumble.

Kadie broke free of the passage and landed on the sidewalk. She pulled her cloak around her, got her bearings, and started to run. Down another three blocks, then a right turn. The buildings began to look shabbier, and the streets less clean. A man sat on one corner, unconscious, a bottle tipped over beside him. She slowed down when she reached the edge of the Dredge. She had only been here in the daylight. There weren't as many streetlights here, and people had long since doused their lamps and gone to bed. She stopped at the end of the first block, unsure which way she needed to go in the dark.

"Stop!"

The shout reverberated, the sound bouncing off the empty buildings. Kadie froze, the unexpected order pinning her in place. Five uniformed men materialized from the darkened doorways across the street. In seconds they had surrounded her. Kadie pulled off her hood, showing her face to the guards and glaring at them defiantly.

If they knew who she was, they didn't care. One guard, their captain by the look of his uniform, stepped forward.

"In the name of the Dowager Duchess, you, Duchess Kadie, are under arrest."

Kadie didn't think. Her hand moved on its own, pulling out her weapon and firing at the guard. A blast of sound erupted from the end, blowing the guards off their feet and shattering windows along the street.

She turned and ran blindly into the Dredge. Streets became a blur, and she turned so many times she lost count. When she finally stopped in the doorway of what might have been a boarding house, she knew she was lost. She checked her watch. Two o'clock. Not that it mattered now. She couldn't go back to the manor or plead her case to Daniel. Now she needed to find the Makers, get the part, and get out of the city to the forest.

"*Psst.*"

Kadie pulled herself further into the shadows of the doorway and hoped whoever it was would just go away. The pistol was still in her hand, but it needed to charge for fifteen minutes before she could use it again.

"*Psst. Hey, Duchess.*"

Damn. Kadie peeked out and saw a boy no older than twelve. Tall and thin, in a threadbare coat and trousers. He waved her out.

"C'mon. Come with me. I know a great hiding place."

Kadie hesitated. She didn't recognize the boy, but that meant nothing. She decided to trust him. He likely knew where the Makers were and could take her there. She had nothing to give him in return, though, and cursed herself for forgetting her reticule and change purse. She followed the boy deeper into the Dredge, though alleys and streets much narrower and dirtier than those in the rest of the city.

"There she is! I've found her, captain!"

The guards appeared like spectres out of nowhere. Kadie panicked — her pistol wasn't ready yet.

"We have to run, miss. Follow me." The boy took off, leaving Kadie to catch up as they dashed through the Dredge's labyrinth of streets.

They came to what turned out to be a blind alley. Panic squeezed Kadie's chest like a vise. They were trapped.

The boy ran to the wall and pressed on a stone. It popped out from the wall like a knob. With a quick turn, a door appeared in the seemingly solid facade. He waved at Kadie to follow.

She hadn't made it three steps when one of the guards caught her. The boy waited half a second, fear and worry in his eyes. She couldn't call out for him to *GO!* but hoped her expression made her point for her. He gave a sad wave before letting the door shut, sealing the wall once more.

The guard grabbed Kadie's arm roughly, and she winced in pain. He then snatched her satchel and looked inside. Her heart jumped as he pulled the incomplete music box movement from the bag.

"You are under arrest for possession of illicit machines and suspected Technomancy." The captain tossed the music box in the bag and dragged Kadie toward a waiting box wagon. He shoved her inside and slammed the door shut. Two guards jumped on the back, and two clung to the sides. The captain climbed up beside the driver, who whistled to the exhausted old mare that pulled the wagon. The horse flicked its ears and then moved slowly forward, dragging the wagon behind.

Kadie watched between the bars as they moved through the streets. Everything remained still and silent except for the wagon's wheels and the *clip-clop* of horse hooves. Her heart was in her throat as they left the Dredge. Soon she recognized where she was and realized where they were taking her.

The wagon rolled into the empty town square. At the center, a fountain of carved stone gurgled, its sound reverberating off the large and impressive buildings that lined the green. A tea shop, a modiste, a bookstore. The church took up one entire side, the crown jewel with its carved spires and gargoyles. Kadie had spent every Sacred Day since her arrival in this realm inside its sumptuous chapel, listening to sermons about the evils of machinery and technology.

The wagon pulled around the square and stopped in front of the most somber looking of the large and impressive buildings directly across from the church.

The Meeting House.

The captain jumped from the front seat and walked around to the back, his ring of keys jingling. He unlocked the door and pulled Kadie out onto the sidewalk. She would not let herself cry, though tears burned in her eyes. How had she come all this way only to be caught at the last minute? She had been so careful, hiding her work, never uttering a sound.

The guards pushed her toward the stairs. She resisted.

"Don't make us hurt you, Duchess," the captain growled. "We will drag you if we have to."

Kadie was glad her skirts were long; they hid her shaking knees as she climbed the stairs to the Meeting House. She tried to bury her fear and remain brave, but it was a tremendous struggle, with fear seeming to gain the upper hand.

Kadie had driven by the Meeting House many times, of course, but never been inside. She had no reason to ever enter it, and no desire, especially when she heard the things that went on inside, whispers from the staff when they thought she wasn't listening.

At the top of the front steps, the Meeting House's huge double doors stood open, a gaping mouth in the stone facade of the building. Kadie walked through, feeling as if she were being swallowed by a monster. The air in the foyer was stale and still. Someone had come ahead and lit the lamps, which only partially dispelled the gloom that hung over this place like a storm cloud. The hall was a well-appointed cavern, two stories tall and thirty feet wide. The ceiling might have been painted with cherubs and clouds, but it was cast in half-shadow. A huge sweeping staircase took up the center of the room, leading to an upper floor that sat completely in darkness.

"This way, *my lady*." The captain sneered as he shoved her to the left toward a small, unassuming door in the corner. He unlocked it and ushered her into an empty, plain hallway lit by cheap oil lamp sconces. The smell permeated the space, the walls around the lamps and the ceiling stained with soot. There were no windows, making it seem even more narrow than it was. It gave off a sinister air that made Kadie shiver.

Her feet felt like lead as she walked toward the unknown. The captain had no words for her, friendly or otherwise, so she had nothing but her imagination to provide her with answers to her unspoken questions.

At the far end of the hall stood another door of rough, unpainted wood, the domed heads of the nails jutting from it like knuckles. Kadie did *not* want to go through that door. She didn't even want to know what was on the other side.

The captain pulled her to a halt, then fumbled with his keys to find the correct one. It was the largest of the bunch and black as pitch. The sound it made when the captain turned it in the lock made Kadie's blood run cold. As the captain pushed it open, the hinges let out a high-pitched scream, crying for oil.

The smell that emanated from inside brought only one word to Kadie's mind: *horrific.* A combination of stale air, a dirty stable, and something Kadie couldn't identify but might have been the scent of misery. She resisted the captain's first attempt to show her through the door to this nightmare.

"Sorry, Your Grace, it's late, and I've got no time for this. On you get." Which he punctuated with a shove that jolted her over the threshold.

The prison boasted three cells, all slightly larger than her water closet at home. Each had one small, barred window set high in the outer wall, the other three walls made of iron bars. Kadie was led to the last one and assisted through the door. She squeezed her eyes shut to stop her tears from falling, so she only heard the door shut with a terrible *clang.* The guard's steps receded, and the door of the prison closed with a thunderous *boom.*

Kadie stood in the cell, listening to the silence. When she opened her eyes, she could barely see her surroundings. A single lamp had been lit, its weak pool of light not doing much to illuminate the prison. The only thing in the cell was a pile of straw, which smelled moldy. Kadie's nose wrinkled at the scent, but she couldn't just stand here. Who knew how long she would be kept prisoner? The weight of everything that had happened in the last few hours overcame her, and her knees buckled with exhaustion.

She wanted to scream, to beat her fists against the stone floor, and rage at the top of her lungs. Instead, she pulled off her satchel and opened it. She carefully pulled out each music box movement and set them on the floor. With her legs folded in a tailor's seat, she took her small screwdriver and tightened every screw, inspecting every gear and the teeth of each comb. She clung to the barest scrap of hope that she would still be able to break the curse, despite her current predicament.

She lifted the smallest mechanism and held it in her hand. The one she had made for Flynn. Her twin, her best friend. She wondered if he had gotten taller since she had last seen them almost two years ago. Their meetings had grown less frequent since she had been brought to Daniel's duchy in the middle of this strange realm. When she first came here, they had visited often, flying into the gardens at the far end of the estate, where Kadie could meet them.

Then she became Daniel's wife, and sneaking out became not only impossible but dangerous. The Duchess had duties to attend to, and she was constantly surrounded by people. Not to mention, her mother-in-law's spies were everywhere. If anyone had spotted her meeting her brothers, Kadie would have been arrested long before today.

She set Flynn's unfinished box back in the bag and scooped up the others, carefully packing them away. Stretching her arms over-head, she let out a huge yawn. Then she tucked the bag under her arm, arranged her cloak around her, lay on the dirty straw, and fell asleep.

"Time to get up, Your Grace."

The proclamation was followed by a completely unwelcome banging. Kadie forced her eyes open and sat up. An unfamiliar guard stood outside her cell, banging on the bars with his club. Kadie could see him clearly and realized that it was full daylight. She leapt to her feet, clutching her satchel tightly.

The guard smiled and shook his head. "Still nothing to say? Maybe once you're upstairs, you'll loosen your tongue."

He slid the door open and reached toward her, meaning to grab her arm. Kadie shook him off, choosing to walk herself out with as much dignity as she could muster. The long hall didn't seem as frightening today, and sunlight flooded the foyer. The robins-egg blue walls and white trim looked almost friendly during the day, but Kadie would not let herself be fooled.

The front doors flew open, and Daniel stormed in.

"Kadie!" he cried and ran to her side. "What have they done? I only just heard you were here. I'm so sorry, my love." He stroked her hair, tangled in knots from sleep. He turned to the guard. "Release her, now. You have no authority to do this."

The guard's face went white as trim in the room. "I-I-I, Your Grace, I-I-I-"

"Bring her upstairs," someone called from above in a demanding tone that could not be ignored. Kadie thought the voice sounded familiar, but the room's acoustics distorted the sound, so she couldn't be sure. The guard looked toward the source of the voice, then at Daniel, and he gulped.

"I'm sorry, Your Grace, but I have my orders." He turned his back on Daniel, grasped Kadie gently, and steered her upstairs. Daniel followed right behind them, muttering curses and threats toward anyone he thought responsible for Kadie's arrest under his breath.

At the top, she was led down the hall, through a set of open double doors, and into a large room. Dozens of chairs had been lined up in rows with a break between that formed a center aisle. A few people sat in attendance, and Kadie realized they were all servants in Daniel's household. The chairs faced a long, tall bench at the front of the room. Behind the bench, presiding above it all with a grin that re-minded Kadie of a cat who had just caught a juicy mouse, sat her mother-in-law.

"Ah, there you are." the Dowager Duchess' voice dripped with false sweetness. "At last. I have been waiting here for hours. Years, actually. You shouldn't keep me waiting, you know." She drummed her fingers on the bench, then stretched them out and inspected the huge rings on her fingers.

"Mother! You did this? Stop this nonsense this instant." Daniel stood where he had been since he arrived, by Kadie's side. "What is wrong with you?"

The Dowager Duchess gave him a pitying look, then turned to Kadie. "My son is a good man with a kind heart. And a good ruler. But he has always had a blind spot when it comes to you. Never took my concerns seriously. I have tried to tell him repeatedly that something is not quite right about you. A proper lady who doesn't speak? For certain, a true high-born girl knows how and when to speak. But you—" she looked Kadie up and down in distaste, "—don't speak *at all*. Not a single sound in the four years since my son found you in that grubby little cottage and brought you here. Not a single word, even at your own wedding." The Dowager Duchess narrowed her eyes at Kadie.

"It's... unnatural. How you got my son to marry you at all makes me even more suspicious."

Daniel stepped forward. "Mother, I demand you cease this farce immediately. I married her because I love her. She is kind and loving. Her smile lights up a room and my heart. She is every inch a lady and a perfect Duchess. She does not speak but is a wonderful listener. You, on the other hand, listen to no one."

The Dowager Duchess wore a look of pity for her son. Then she glanced down at something beside her and bent over to pick it up.

"With all the other eligible ladies, titled daughters of the realm, that I brought to you, you chose this little nobody with no history or background? No, she had to have done some sort of witchcraft to make you marry her. I have tried for years to figure out what she was up to, and last night I found out. And I have my best and most loyal spy to thank."

She deposited Copernicus on the bench. The cat looked just as smug as his mistress as he walked in a circle, rubbing his head against her hand and purring loudly. Kadie's heart plunged to her stomach.

"He, the good little boy he is, brought me this." She lifted her other hand to show them something small, but Kadie already knew what it was. The light caught the metal of the music box comb, sending a single beam of light across the room.

Daniel looked confused. "What is that? Mother, I'm begging you, give this up now, or I swear — "

The Dowager Duchess looked up at someone entering the courtroom. The captain of the guard strode through the door and marched right to the front.

"My dear captain, please present the evidence."

The captain bowed to the Dowager Duchess, though he looked sideways at Daniel. "Absolutely, Your Grace." He relayed the story of Kadie's capture the previous evening. When he mentioned the sonic pistol, there was an audible gasp from the audience.

"Three of my men still can't hear properly today, Your Grace. She assaulted us."

"I see," the Dowager Duchess responded as if she were hearing it for the first time. "And what did you find in her possession when you arrested her?"

The captain reached over and pulled the satchel away from Kadie. She struggled to keep a hold of it, but he ripped it from her grasp.

"These, mum." He opened the bag and pulled out each of the music boxes. Kadie kept her eyes glued to the precious pieces, which at this moment were both her lifeline and her damnation.

The Dowager Duchess curled her lip in disgust. "Are those — machines?"

The captain nodded. "We also found tools on her person as well, Your Grace. It would seem she built these abominations herself. "

Her mother-in-law looked closely at the music box movements, a look of fearful fascination on her flabby face.

"This must be how she put my son under her spell, bewitched him with the tune of a music box. Technomancy! Witchcraft! I knew you were an unnatural creature. Who knows what nefarious purpose she had for these." She waved her hand, and the captain took the movements away, sweeping them into her satchel in a heap.

"This realm, unlike our heathen neighbors, has strict laws against owning or building such things as these. Anyone who uses tools must have a license and be a member of a guild. Stonemasons, carpenters, jewelers, sculptors, and the like are permitted to use their skills to support and build our community. *Machinery*, such as clockworks, tinkers, or... music boxes, are forbidden. They are the tools of witches."

Kadie wondered what the old hag would think about her workshop.

The Dowager Duchess stopped and took a deep breath before continuing. "The evidence is clear. You are a witch and must be punished." She failed quite spectacularly if she was trying to hold back a smile.

"The punishment for Technomancy is clear. You will be put to death. Today."

Kadie stepped back in shock, her fist in her mouth to stop her scream. The servants in the gallery gasped, then muttered to each other gossip that would reach every corner of town within the hour.

Daniel said nothing, only stared at Kadie, confusion and hurt in his eyes. At that moment, she wanted nothing more than to tell him everything, to comfort him and tell him that she loved him too. She reached out a hand to him, hoping for comfort.

He stepped away, a small motion that felt like he had slapped her across the face.

The guard and captain grabbed Kadie and dragged her from the room, down the stairs, and back to her cell.

"I'll see you later this afternoon, *Your Grace*," the captain said with absolutely no respect. He reached into her bag and pulled out the tools, then tossed it in behind her. "Keep your dirty clockworks. You can hold on to them as you hang." He waved the tools at her. "But you'll do no more Technomancy in this lifetime."

He closed the cell door and walked out. Kadie let her tears flow; she had no energy to stop them. She cried, sitting in the middle of her filthy cell until she had no tears left.

How could she have been so careless? Everything was undone by a stupid cat! Her anger and frustration boiled, and she had to stop herself from pulling every music box out of the bag and throwing them against the wall. They were useless now anyway. She would never get to see her brothers again. She would die, and they would stay as clockwork swans forever. At least they would live.

She looked into the satchel at the boxes, then closed the bag and put it down beside her. Even now, when it seemed beyond hope, she couldn't bring herself to do it.

"Hello."

Kadie looked up. Daniel stood there on the other side of the bars. His look of betrayal broke her heart.

"Nothing to say, even now? My lo... why? I will listen to any explanation you can give me. Please just... say something."

Kadie's eyes pleaded with him. He had never learned the hand signs she and her brothers had used to communicate. Even if she could tell him, it would only make things worse—to tell him she broke the law in order to break a curse? They would hang her twice if they could.

She pressed her lips together and backed away from the door.

Daniel looked at his feet. "I'm sorry. If you had something to say, some kind of explanation, there might have been a way for me to save you. But not if you don't speak for yourself."

Kadie pressed her lips together tight. She could save herself right here, but at what cost? The minute sound left her lips, her brothers would die. Her choice was clear. Kadie remained silent.

"Then there's nothing I can do." Daniel turned and walked away, his eyes glinting with tears. At the prison door, he stopped. "Goodbye."

Kadie watched him go, then flung herself to the floor in despair, her fate sealed. She fell asleep and dreamed of her brothers, made whole again, all laughing in her father's clockwork gardens, with both real and mechanical birds singing from the trees.

Then she dreamed of the Clockwork Queen. She appeared just as she had on that night in the cottage, surrounded by ethereal light. She leaned down and kissed Kadie on the forehead.

"You have been so incredibly brave and must continue for a little while longer. "

Kadie jolted awake. She sat up and brushed the dirty straw from her hair. The sun that came in through the little window above her had shifted. She pulled out her watch and checked the time. It was late afternoon—they would be coming for her soon. She stood and wiped her face, then did her best to smooth her hair and dress, so she didn't look quite such a mess for her execution.

The squealing hinges of the prison's door announced the guards. Four of them, including the captain, stood outside her cell, their faces grim. The captain unlocked the door and opened it, waiting.

Kadie held her head high and the satchel with the music boxes close to her chest as she walked out of the cell. The guards fell in beside her as they led her out of the prison and down the hall. In the foyer, they turned her toward the front door of the Meeting House. The doors stood wide open, the low light of approaching sunset painting everything pink and orange. They took Kadie through the doors, out to the town square. Kadie stopped cold and felt the blood drain from her face.

They had erected a gallows right in front of the Meeting House. Not once in all the time she had lived here had she heard of a public execution in the town square. The captain nudged her down the stairs, and when she slipped and almost fell, two guards grabbed her and forced her the rest of the way down, then up the steps to the gallows. She walked across the platform, where the noose hung above a closed trap door.

The Dowager Duchess stood right front and center of the crowd, which struggled to fit within the square. Everyone, it seemed, had been told, and Kadie wondered if the Dowager Duchess had ordered everyone to attend or if they were just curious to watch their own Duchess die. At the back of the crowd, she noted a small group of concerned and horrified faces, some of which she recognized. The Makers had come. The boy who had tried to save her wept openly. A girl whose name Kadie didn't recall had her arm around him. She looked furious.

Daniel stood beside his mother, his face a mask of misery. Kadie put all her feelings for him into her thoughts and hoped he would somehow feel them. She wasn't angry with him; she had betrayed him to save her brothers. She could only imagine how he felt.

The captain placed Kadie under the noose and ripped her satchel from her hands. A second guard pulled a scroll out of his jacket and unrolled it.

"All who are gathered here, you are to bear witness," he said in a voice that carried across the square. "To the execution of this woman, Kadie Appeline, Duchess of the Realm, for the crime of Technomancy. She has been sentenced to hang by the neck until dead."

Kadie barely heard the words, her heart pounded so loudly in her chest. All she could do was stare at the sky. Her last sunset.

The guard rolled up the scroll and returned it to his jacket. The captain placed the noose around her neck, and Kadie's body started to shake uncontrollably.

The Dowager Duchess turned and faced the crowd. "But before we execute her, she, and all of you, will witness the destruction of her fiendish works."

The captain moved to the side of the platform and stood in front of a table that had been placed there. He reached into Kadie's satchel, took each music box movement from the bag, and set it on the table. He added her sonic pistol to the collection, brought from inside his jacket. Then he bent over for a second and grabbed something under the table. He held up his hand to show the crowd the hammer gripped in his fist.

The word "NO " formed deep in Kadie's chest. She inhaled deeply, using every ounce of her strength to hold it in, even now. The captain raised the hammer, ready to smash Albert's music box.

A sudden sound from above stayed his arm. Every head turned toward the sound in unison.

Six birds, silhouetted against the sunset, flew toward the town square. The first and largest swan dove at the captain, metal wings and feet flapping. The captain threw his arms protectively over his head. A second swan flew in to help, and the captain leapt from the platform. Four more clockwork swans landed on the gallows, each one smaller than the one before.

"More machines?" the Dowager Duchess screeched. "Her familiars have come to save their mistress! Guards, destroy them!"

Guards climbed back onto the stage, clubs ready to strike. The swans fluttered to the table, landing in a line, each behind a music box. As the sun set, they bent their heads down and swallowed each swallowed a mechanism.

For a moment, no one breathed, and no breeze blew. The guards froze in their tracks.

Each swan grew, their metal feathers falling to the ground in a cacophony. Wings turned to arms, and bird feet grew long and separated into toes. In less than a minute, the clockwork birds had vanished, replaced by six young men wrapped in feathered cloaks, each with eyes that matched Kadie's. They raced to Kadie's side, surrounding her.

"What is going on here?" Albert's voice sounded strong and clear. Broderick and Charles stood to their full heights, their posture and expressions promising pain upon anyone who dared challenge them. Dorian reached over Kadie's head and removed the noose from her neck.

"We are executing a Technomancer!" The Dowager Duchess' face turned red as she shouted. "She is a witch, and you must be demons come to save your mistress."

Charles stepped to the edge of the platform so that he stood above the Dowager Duchess. "What a completely idiotic thing to say. Who is the authority in this place?"

The Dowager Duchess opened her mouth, but Daniel stepped forward before she could say another word. "I am the Duke, and she... is my wife."

"Then you should know all that has happened." Edgar turned toward Kadie. "You can tell him. The curse is broken."

Kadie could hardly believe it. They were here, all her brothers together and whole. And speaking! Then Flynn grasped her hand. He opened his mouth, but no sound came out.

Kadie's joy slipped. Could her twin not speak? His music box had been incomplete; enough to break the curse but not enough to restore his voice. She stroked his head, his hair thick and curly.

"I... am... sorry." Those were the first words she had uttered in six years, and she could only manage a whisper. Flynn shook his head and, using his hands and their special language, told her he understood. He walked with her to the front of the platform. She opened her mouth, wondering where to begin. But before she could say a word, the world began to spin, and she fainted.

She woke in her own bed, the sun coming through the tall windows of her bedroom. She pushed herself to sitting, and the first thing she saw was a mechanical songbird on her bedside table.

"There she is! Awake at last?" Dorian sat in a chair next to the door. He stood and came to her side. "You gave us quite a fright, Princess." He squeezed her hand and then went to the door.

"She's awake! Everyone, she's awake!"

In an instant, the room filled with people. All six of her brothers crowded around her bed, happy to see her awake.

Daniel came in last, walking slowly, stopping a few feet away from the group. "Hello, Kadie."

"Hello, Daniel."

He was unable to hide his surprise at the sound of her voice. "I... I don't know what to say. 'I'm sorry' doesn't seem to be enough. But I am. So very sorry." He looked around the group. "Your brothers were kind enough to explain everything. Who you are, and about the curse. When I heard what you had done, what you had given up, I knew this wasn't something evil. It was love."

Kadie wasn't sure how to respond. "I am sorry, too. I couldn't tell you, as many times as I wanted to."

Daniel waved away her words. "You owe me nothing. And if you want to leave, return to your kingdom and your father, I won't stop you."

Kadie didn't know what to say. Her entire life for six years had been consumed with breaking the curse. She hadn't even thought about what would happen next.

"That is discussion for another day, I think." She loved Daniel deeply but would need to think about what she wanted the rest of her life to be. The one thing she was sure of was that she wanted to spend time with her brothers.

Flynn waved the rest of them out of the room so she could rest. They filed out, single file, but Daniel stopped and turned back.

"I believe this is yours." He pulled her screwdriver from his pocket and set it beside the mechanical bird. "If it makes any difference, my mother will no longer be living here. I've sent her away to spend time at court. A *long* time. I made it clear that it would be far too soon for my liking if she never returned to the Duchy."

Kadie laughed out loud, and it was a glorious sound.

Dress for the Occasion

Based on the Emperor's New Clothes

GORDON LINZNER

HER SCREECHES ECHOED THROUGH THE HALLS OF THE TERNION SHIRTWAIST Factory. They could be heard over wheezing boilers providing power to the lights, chattering young seamsters and seamstresses, even whirring steam-powered fans as the latter struggled against the August heat wave. Across the road, travelers waiting at Paterson Township's railroad station stared along the tracks, thinking the distant sound might be an approaching locomotive.

Bradley Reynold, private secretary to company head Truman Connor, cautiously opened the door to his employer's private office. He found Connor bent over his desk, hands clasped before his thin frame, knuckles white, eyes shut.

"It appears Miss Minuchi is calling on you again, sir," young Bradley advised.

Connor looked up wearily at his employee.

Maxine Minuchi, recent heir to a small fortune from her late father, had purchased a majority share in Ternion only a few months earlier. Her major — and, judging from her attitude, only — reason for doing so was to use the company's state-of-the-art technology to create for herself the finest clothes ever seen. And maybe some designs almost as good, for Ternion's customers.

Connor's life had grown increasingly hellish since her acquisition.

"You couldn't have told her I was out of the office today, Bradley?"

"I've yet to see her in person myself, sir. Only heard her shouts."

"As has everyone else in the building, I'm sure, and within a two-block radius as well. I was making a joke."

"Yes, Mister Connor."

"Admittedly, not a very good one."

"No, Mister Connor."

Connor sighed again. "You'd best prepare to show her in."

"Not necessary!" boomed Maxine Minuchi as she barged into Connor's office. For this meeting, the stocky woman wore the most intimidating of her score of business suits, one blacker than black, its lapels so narrow they could barely be seen. Connor could hardly miss the thick bundle of blue and white fabric tucked under her left arm. Her austere outfit, lack of an aide, and the fact that she carried the burden herself, rather than having a menial do so, did not bode well.

Minuchi glared at Bradley for a long, uncomfortable moment, then turned to his employer. "Shouldn't this child be on duty at his desk, Connor? We are, after all, on business hours."

"Bradley just stepped in to inform me of your... presence." Truman looked past Minuchi's thick shoulder pad to dismiss his secretary.

The young man had already slipped out of the office.

"Never mind!" Minuchi tossed the bunched-up cloth onto Connor's desk, scattering paperwork. "The real problem here is this dress your people made for me two days ago! It was — is — a disaster!"

"I had it designed to your exact specifications, Miss Minuchi," Truman Connor countered. "I even verified them personally."

The wealthy matron crossed her arms, lips curling in a well-practiced sneer. Her voice lowered half a decibel.

"What I gave to you, to your people, was only a rough draft. One I expected a so-called expert in the fashion industry, like yourself, would properly embellish. Instead, at last night's ball, this — outfit — was overshadowed by nearly identical ones worn by two other women. One of whom I identified as a mere clerk."

Connor raised his hands in protest. "I assure you, Miss Minuchi, my best workers were assigned this task. I know you have a busy schedule, but if you had made time for a fitting, perhaps...?"

As if his words of praise had somehow summoned them from the depths of the factory, the women who'd worked on the garment in question suddenly entered Truman Connor's office.

The room began to feel cramped.

"This is her?" asked Blanche, the taller of the pair.

"It has to be," observed her buxom companion, Rosa.

"Ladies," Connor began, "I don't think this is the right time..."

Minuchi silenced him with an angry glare.

"You're the ones who made this dress?" she snapped, pointing to the fabric she had heaped on Connor's desk.

"Yes," they answered in unison, moving closer.

"At least three other women at last night's event wore nearly identical dresses. One of them didn't even work there!"

Connor held his tongue rather than point out the change in numbers. By the time Minuchi left, she might claim up to a dozen similarly clad attendees. Or a score.

Blanche met the woman's eyes. "Were they more impressive than this one you wore? Or only equally so?"

Minuchi shrugged. Her voice dropped another half decibel. "The latter, I suppose."

Rosa tilted her head. "Was yours not even a little lovelier than theirs?"

"A tiny bit," Minuchi admitted, after a moment. "That's still not good enough!"

"However, it does demonstrate, Miss Minuchi," Blanche replied, "that my partner and I did our best work."

"Within the limitations of what we had to work with," apologized Rosa.

Truman offered his employees one more wary side-glance but continued to hold his tongue. Whether it was their attitude, their tone, or their phrasing, the workers were having a calming effect on the owner, at the same time piquing her interest.

"What limitations?" Minuchi asked.

"We only had access to the same materials as every other local manufacturer," replied Blanche. "With a larger budget, we could have used the most gorgeous of silks..."

"The finest gold threads..." added Rosa.

"And the necessary time to assemble it perfectly," Blanche concluded.

Minuchi blinked, then turned to Connor. "This was your fault! Not providing adequate materials!"

"Ternion Shirtwaist does well enough," the man protested. "Better than most competitors. But we haven't the resources for such high-grade materials. No one has."

"I do," Minuchi promised. She snatched a notepad from Truman's desk and began scribbling on it. "Order whatever you need. Spare no expense. Charge it to me." She held out the scrap of paper. Before Connor could grasp it, she added, "Should you disappoint me, there will be consequences."

"The only people to be disappointed," Blanche interrupted, taking the slip herself, "are those unfortunates who have poor taste, or are too simple-minded to appreciate quality work. Such people will see nothing."

That seems unlikely, Minuchi thought, though she found the idea tempting.

Rosa leaned forward. "We can make you a dozen dresses, if you like, each one more engaging than the other. It will, of course, take us a bit of time to create such garments worthy of a woman of your stature."

Nothing succeeds like excess, Maxine decided. "Very well. Next week, I am formally unveiling a statue of my late father, Arnold Minuchi, in front of the railroad station across from here. You will finish my dress in time for that event." She phrased the words as a statement, not a question.

Blanche and Rosa exchanged a glance, then nodded in unison.

Minuchi extended a hand to seal the deal. Both women stepped back, slipping their hands behind them.

The rich woman's lips twitched.

"Our apologies, Miss Minuchi," Blanche offered hurriedly. "My partner and I had been unloading a horse cart earlier. We have not had time to properly wash up."

Rosa nodded. "Not every supplier can afford a fleet of steam-powered vehicles."

"These days, too," Blanche pointed out, "there is always a danger of plague."

"However slight," her partner added.

Truman Connor did not entirely buy the women's excuse, but he again remained silent. The last thing he wished to do was interfere with the rapport his employees had built.

"Your concern is appreciated." Minuchi lowered her hand, then looked at the longcase clock standing behind Truman's desk. "Now, I must be off to an appointment with my homeopath." With those words, Maxine Minuchi spun about to march out of Connor's office.

Truman Connor turned to his employees. "I knew you two were persuasive when you convinced me to hire you last year without so much as a recommendation. Yet what you just accomplished, turning Maxine Minuchi's mood from anger to anticipation in minutes, is beyond amazing."

"It's a gift," Blanche admitted.

"Sometimes a curse," responded Rosa.

"Though not on us."

"Not usually."

Connor clasped his hands together. "Whatever the source of your charm, please, tell me what you need for this job."

"A private room, where we may work long hours without disturbance, will suffice," Rosa said.

"You should also spread the word around Paterson," suggested Blanche. "Let everyone know that Ternion Shirtwaist is creating the most beautiful dress in the world — in history — for our benefactor, Maxine Minuchi."

"A dress so lovely," her partner added, "that it will, as mentioned, be beyond the vision of simpler folk, those with poor taste, low intelligence, or otherwise unfit for their jobs."

That would truly be an achievement, Connor mused. Were such a thing possible, he might use it to identify which of his employees were truly competent.

Although a garment with that kind of power might also prove beyond the vision of a man of Truman Connor's own humble beginnings.

Finding silk of a quality capable of outshining any produced in Paterson, a town famous for such material in the late 1800s, would be impossible for anyone lacking Maxine Minuchi's resources. Even her staff found the task difficult.

Yet they got it done.

Every scrap of imported Japanese silk available in nearby New York City was delivered to the Ternion Shirtwaist Factory by train just before noon the next day. Spools of golden thread also arrived from upstate factories by late afternoon.

Blanche and Rosa set to work immediately, seated behind their steam-powered sewing machines. At their request, and with Miss Minuchi's urging, these had been moved into a small workroom separate from the main factory. To compensate for flickering overhead gaslights, a kerosene lamp not only provided additional light but also heated a steam boiler to drive their machines' motors, well into the early morning hours.

Such uncommon activity could hardly go unnoticed by the local citizenry. Word quickly spread through the streets of Paterson. In little more than twenty-four hours, nearly every man, woman, and child in town knew that their wealthiest resident had ordered Ternion Shirtwaist to create the most beautiful dress in the county, the state, perhaps in all of history. Added to this knowledge were rumors that the garment would be so stunning that simple, ignorant people could never comprehend its beauty, and would therefore be unable to see, let alone appreciate, the final result.

The desire to admire the garment when it finally appeared in public, accompanied by a fear that being unable to do so might reveal one's lack of taste and intellect, only added to the excitement.

Maxine Minuchi herself began to feel uneasy, an unusual sensation for her. She was, after all, the wealthiest woman in New Jersey, possibly the wealthiest on the eastern seaboard. True, her fortune had been inherited, not earned, and she was no longer quite as rich as she was the day her father died, but that status nonetheless counted.

Suppose, however, she was not as astute as she believed herself to be? What if her life was a lie?

A ridiculous notion.

Yet...

She much desired to know how the work progressed. The simplest way to do so would be visiting the two women directly herself. But... there was that 'simple' word again.

To be safe, she ordered her Chief Executive Officer, Hiram Butterworth, to check on Blanche and Rosa's progress in her stead.

"What do you think, Mister Butterworth?" asked Blanche excitedly. "Have you ever seen such a vibrant mix of colors?"

"And the pattern!" added Rosa. "So intricate, yet so subtle! I doubt that either of us shall ever be able to surpass our present work!"

Butterworth stared at the wall to which the two partners pointed. He saw only bare brickwork.

He squinted. Still, nothing.

Yet his employer, indeed the entire town of Paterson, was primed to expect something fashionably spectacular.

It occurred to Butterworth, after all his years working for the Minuchi family empire, that perhaps he was not worthy of his job after all, that he lacked the necessary taste and complexity.

His career, his livelihood, would be destroyed, should this flaw be uncovered by Maxine Minuchi herself.

"Never have I seen such stunning work!" Butterworth exclaimed, a statement that was technically true. "I doubt I can do a description justice. Please, ladies, talk me through every single detail, so that I may impart them in full to Miss Minuchi."

"With pleasure!" the women replied in unison.

"You should also advise her," Blanche added, "we need a few more yards of quality silk."

"And many more spools of golden thread," Rosa put in, "to raise this project to the level of perfection Miss Minuchi deserves."

"I shall be certain to include your request in my report," Butterworth agreed as the seamstresses drew him nearer the seemingly empty wall.

Two days later, Maxine's Chief Financial Officer, Wayne Walston, also appeared at the Ternion Shirtwaist Factory on behalf of his employer. He, too, could not see the dress, even as Rosa and Blanche hunched over their sewing machines, furiously fidgeting away, occasionally brushing aside the steam that whistled out the sides. Fortunately, his friend and colleague, Hiram Butterworth, had described the dress in detail. He knew exactly how he should react.

And how to report back in a way that would satisfy his employer.

Maxine Minuchi made her decision. If those two executives had no problem seeing this allegedly wondrous creation, she certainly shouldn't! The more she heard about the dress, the more she needed to see it for herself, now, before the garment was completed, so that she might get the full flavor.

On entering the workroom the day before the dress needed to be finished, Minuchi—alas!—found her concern justified.

Blanche led the woman towards the display wall, then held out her right hand, palm up. "Feel how light this fabric is!" she gushed. "How comfortable!"

"You'll hardly know you're wearing it," Rosa chimed in.

Minuchi wriggled her fingers above the taller partner's open palm. If she concentrated hard enough, she might indeed feel... something.

"I should take it home now," she announced in her most privileged voice. "My father's statue is to be unveiled at noon tomorrow."

"But we have just a few more last-minute details, to make it perfect," Blanche replied. "Surely you noticed."

"Of course, I did," the wealthy matron lied.

"Then others would notice, as well," Rosa chimed in. "None of us want that to happen, do we?"

"Of course not." These ladies were indeed persuasive, and, so far, Maxine Minuchi had not found them to be wrong.

"Come by here early tomorrow morning," Blanche suggested. "We can do a final fitting, and you can lead your procession from here to the railroad station plaza."

"We've added this lovely train to the dress, if you'll pardon the pun," said Rosa, holding her hands waist high.

Blanche raised an eyebrow. "Perhaps the gentlemen who visited us earlier on your behalf could accompany you, hold the train up so it doesn't drag in the streets."

"They did seem quite impressed." Rosa grinned. "I'd think they would be proud to assist you."

As if they have a choice, Minuchi thought. She'd avoided the fitting nonsense last time. Still, it would prove useful to be accompanied by two other people who actually saw the dress and could quietly fill her in on the details.

"How does the waist feel?" asked Blanche, putting down her measuring tape. "Is it too tight?"

"Not at all." Minuchi gave the expected answer as she made a half-turn in front of the full-length mirror she'd had hauled into the workroom. "I barely feel it."

Rosa smiled. "As it should be."

Maxine Minuchi made another half-turn in the opposite direction. How impressive this must appear to others!

"Could you look this way now, Miss Minuchi?" asked the photographer from the Paterson Daily Press.

"It's a pity your little Kodak can't capture all those vibrant colors," opined Hiram Butterworth. His fingers twitched, holding up one corner of the train. At least, he hoped he held it up. The cloth was light as a feather.

"Indeed," agreed Wayne Walston, beside him. The Chief Financial Officer struggled to maintain his own uncertain grip on the delicate cloth.

Truman Connor abruptly poked his head through the open doorway to Blanche and Rosa's workroom. "It's quarter to noon. Almost time for the ceremony."

"Perfect timing," said the seamstresses, clapping their hands in unison. Walking on either side of the wealthy woman, followed by her two executives with their own arms outstretched, they led Minuchi to the exit closest to the railroad station.

A slight breeze sprang up that morning but did little to relieve the August heat. Minuchi bowed, waved, and smiled at the citizens lining the street that led to the station. Twice she almost curtsied but stopped in time. The act would have seemed condescending, in her mind.

Halfway to the statue, she heard a child's voice suddenly call out "Bloomers!"

Minuchi halted, turned, glared into the crowd. A boy of four or five pointed at her, laughing.

"Do my undergarments show?" she whispered harshly to her executives. "Are either of you, by chance, pulling too hard on my train?"

Both men shook their heads.

"The train is only an attachment, separate from the skirt," explained Walston.

"And there's barely a breeze to ruffle that delicate material," Butterworth confirmed.

Minuchi frowned, glancing down. She saw nothing amiss with bra or bloomers. If her employees claimed her new dress looked fine, who was she to deny it?

"Bloomers!" the child repeated, letting loose another sharp laugh.

Minuchi sneered in his direction. "You don't know what you're talking about, boy. For your parents' sake, stop it. Now."

Instead, the boy repeated himself again, this time joined by other nearby children.

"Bloomers! Bloomers!"

A few adults joined in the chanting.

A child may be naïve, but at his age the boy's sight should still be pure enough for him to see the dress. Paterson's citizenry slowly realized not one among them was capable of seeing the fabulous outfit they'd been told to expect.

Because there was none.

Minuchi turned to her executives. The way they grasped the alleged train did not, on close inspection, look right. She abruptly slapped Butterworth's hands away. He fumbled to regain their position.

"You don't feel any cloth at all, do you?" she hissed. "Either of you."

Both smiled sheepishly.

"Where are those two seamstresses?"

The men shrugged.

"No matter. I'll deal with them later. Continue as you are. I have no other choice but to go through with this." She raised her voice.

"Somebody, send those photographers away! They've taken more than enough pictures. And their newspapers could never duplicate these brilliant colors!"

The ceremony continued as planned, apart from that slight delay and the increasing snickers among the crowd. Minuchi laid a wreath against the statue's pedestal, followed by a greatly truncated speech about her father's many accomplishments, including the establishment of this very railroad. Duty done, she insisted Butterworth—or Walston, she didn't care which—hire a coach to transport her back to the factory, rather than continue this charade any further.

Before she could board, however, she was blocked by the county sheriff and three other men. One of the latter was a Pinkerton agent with whom she'd had business in the past.

His expression told her the usual bribe wasn't an option this time.

"My apologies, Miss Minuchi," the sheriff offered. "I've been asked to bring you in for an interrogation regarding several possibly shady business deals you may have been involved in over the past year. Most recently, involving some very expensive, unpaid-for Japanese silk."

Minuchi snorted. "This is insane."

"I have my orders."

"Very well. Give me time to change. I can't go to your office looking like this."

"You may want to rephrase that," said the Pinkerton agent, shifting his gaze to stare at the cobblestones under his feet. "You sound like you admit to being in violation of indecent exposure laws, as ruled by the New Jersey Supreme Court in Van Houten v. State, back in..."

"Hold on," the sheriff interrupted. "I was told, for this event, that you are wearing the finest dress in the state, Miss Minuchi."

"Well, um, of course," she muttered.

"Surely you'd wish to impress your inquisitors with your fashion taste."

One deputy struggled to restrain a laugh.

Minuchi glanced at the Pinkerton agent, who continued looking away. Apparently, even the most corrupt of that group could not excuse her.

Angrily, she pointed toward Truman Connor, watching from a discrete distance. "Tell those women they've not seen the last of me!" she screeched.

The sheriff and his companions then bundled Maxine Minuchi into the horse-drawn carriage by which she'd meant to make her exit, now headed for a very different destination.

Returning to Ternion Shirtwaist, Truman Connor slowly made his way to Blanche and Rosa's workshop. The ladies were celebrating inside with a warm kiss. Several, in fact, until they noticed his presence, and likely more than that had he not intruded.

Connor could not hide his scowl. "You two seem awfully happy, considering you've just given Maxine Minuchi more than sufficient cause to destroy this factory. Even if she goes to prison, unlikely given her status and wealth, she will still have plenty of influence."

"Which is why," Blanche offered, "we are leaving your employment immediately."

"You're quitting?"

"No," explained Rosa. "You are firing us."

"For our egregious behavior."

"Announce it publicly, so all of Paterson knows."

"Explain how you were taken in by our con."

"After all, we can be, as you said, very persuasive."

Truman's eyes widened in surprise. "Why? I mean, nobody really likes Maxine Minuchi, but the pair of you took this scam much too far."

Blanche grew somber. "Recently, a good friend of ours, Eloise, got on bad terms with Miss Minuchi. Despite following up with frequent apologies, some of them sincere, she continued to be harassed by that woman. Once Eloise lost both home and husband, she gave up, wandering in front a train just north of that very station."

"We only found out how depressed she'd been afterward," Rosa added. "Otherwise..."

"My god," Truman whispered. "I remember that incident. I was on a business trip in New York at the time."

Blanche nodded. "Our research showed this was hardly the first time that woman ruined other people's lives."

Rosa bowed in agreement. "The humiliation we put her through today, along with our providing the state with records of her numerous shady deals and outright crimes, hardly makes up for that."

Blanche clasped Rosa's hand. "Still, we settle for what we can get."

Connor's jaw slackened. "I had no idea. You never mentioned this to me."

"You didn't need to know."

"You're right," Connor replied. "I don't. It's not safe for you to remain in Paterson, or even in New Jersey. Let me offer you a severance package to help your escape."

Blanche shook her head. "I fear that would not help you get back into that woman's good graces."

"I'm not sure I want to be," he admitted.

"Think of your workers, then," said Rosa.

"And," Blanche added, "we did put aside a bit of savings."

"In the brief time you two have worked for me?" Connor then noticed, for the first time, two thick luggage bags perched in one corner, with a pair of shoulder bags leaning alongside. The former seemed a perfect size for conveying bundles of high-quality silk; the latter, for carrying dozens of spools of golden thread.

What Connor did not see was the dress in which Maxine Minuchi had arrived that morning.

"As my partner told you," Rosa continued, "we managed to squirrel away more than sufficient assets for moving on. There's a new world opening up out west."

Blanche wrapped an arm about her partner's waist. "Did you know, Wyoming was the first territory to allow women the vote, retaining that law even after it became a state?"

Connor turned at the sound of horse's hooves clattering against cobblestones outside.

"That must be our hired carriage," Rosa observed. "It has been a pleasure to work for you, Mister Connor. We trust Ternion Shirtwaist survives this little hiccup, and truly apologize for any inconvenience we may have caused."

"That horse-drawn transport seems a bit old-fashioned," Connor observed.

"Steam-powered cars are too heavy and slow," Blanche replied. "And for us to be seen waiting at that station, with so much luggage, might seem a bit suspicious." Each woman hefted a large suitcase and a shoulder bag. "We'll catch a westbound train in..."

Connor cut her off. "Don't tell me. The less I know, the less likely I might let something slip."

"True, man," Rosa said, winking, as the women took their leave for-ever from the Garden State.

Ala al-Din and the Cave of Wonders

Based on Aladdin and the Lamp

DANIELLE ACKLEY-MCPHAIL

Come, Best Beloved, and sit you by my feet. I shall tell you a tale such as sister Scheherazade could have scarce imagined… a tale oft told but little known. A tale of a foolish young man born seemingly of humble means but destined for glory and betrayal and, yes, Child of Adam, great love, though that is a tale for another day.

The night is for the telling of tales of which the morning may bear Truth. In the oldest of days and ages and times, there was, and there was not, a great evil that reached across the desert and beyond…

ON THIS DAY, AS WITH ANY OTHER, ALA AL-DIN LOUNGED AGAINST the low stone wall which edged Kashgar's famed bazaar, chin lifted and eyes half-closed, doing his best to appear to have no care in the world. In truth, he peered beneath his lids at a group of foreigners from the west gathered at the gate, bustling like industrious seed beetles as they set up intriguing paraphernalia to take photographs of the famed market, or so he had been told. Deep inside, a part of him yearned to move closer even as it ached that such things were lost to him. Worth it, to return home and tell his mother all he had seen, only these were British soldiers, part of an expedition led by a man called Sir Douglas Forsyth. Such important men as that would not welcome his presence.

Frowning, he scratched gently at a bit of dry skin on the stump of his right wrist and adjusted his skull cap, turning his gaze away from temptation, as he should have done at age eleven when he'd tried unsuccessfully to steal extra food so his mother would eat.

Ala al-Din resettled himself against the wall, angling his head away as he basked in the warm sun and the cool breeze, glad he had chosen a place upwind from those selling livestock. If only he could so easily avoid the chatter of the young boys around him. Most waited eager and hopeful to earn some coin for delivering messages or purchased goods for those desiring to shop unburdened. Ala al-Din wished only to be left in peace, or so he told himself. Let them run from one end of the oasis town to the other and back again all the hours of the day.

Not he. Why, when no one would trust either messages or goods to his care?

Of course, this is not to say he didn't come to his feet with all the others when opportunity neared. It would not do to be seen as idle, even if he held little hope for his effort. He straightened as purposeful footsteps approached, but did not push forward, as the others did, yammering and bouncing as if to display the wealth of energy they possessed, surely making them best suited for the task on offer.

Ala al-Din tensed, slouching to seem smaller and younger, just in case, as a tall man with skin like dark sandstone strode toward them. A finely knit white kufi covered his head, and a rich blue djellaba flowed around his body. If Ala al-Din had to guess, he would say this man hailed from Africa… likely Maghreb, given his manner of dress. Such foreigners were no odd sight along the Silk Road, any more than the British were. Kashgar was a hub of trade, and merchants the world over journeyed there, traveling by caravan or airship, and once, a most magnificent contrivance he'd learned was a Selden auto-mobile prototype. And Ala al-Din had little to do but watch them.

His attention must have lingered too intently. The westerner locked eyes with him, or so it seemed. Ala al-Din shrank back even further, disturbed by the stranger's intent gaze. Let one of the others collect the coin they were so eager for. Ala al-Din would wait and comb the ground on his way home for any cash dropped in the day's commerce, as was his practice so that his mother would not question how he filled his hours. He could hardly confess to her that no one would entrust him with their goods, once they had seen his stump, assuming—not incorrectly—that he had been punished for thievery. Why would that day be any different?

Except the westerner pushed past all the others, coming to stand firmly and with determination before Ala al-Din.

"You, boy. What is your name?"

Warily, Ala al-Din tucked his arms behind him, hiding the fact that one sleeve of his coarse cotton khalat had been pinned over an empty wrist. He looked up into those powerful eyes and found himself locked in the man's gaze as if compelled.

"Your name…"

"Ala," he muttered. "Ala al-Din."

"And your father?"

A scowl twisted Ala al-Din's expression as he fought the impulse to answer and lost. "Mustafa, the artificer."

Satisfaction flared in the stranger's gaze. "Allah be praised!"

Ala al-Din flinched as the man threw his arms around him, lifting him up as the other runners scattered like startled swan geese, some sulking, others already looking for the next to offer coin.

The stranger set Ala al-Din down but kept a grip on his shoulders.

"My boy! I am Kaddour, your uncle."

"Your..." Ala al-Din's words stumbled as his thoughts swirled in confusion. His mother had told him his father had had a brother, but that he had died. "He's dead. My father."

Kaddour frowned and peered intently into Ala al-Din's eye before nodding with a semblance of sorrow. "As he believed I was, but as you see, I am not. Let us go to your mother and share with her these good tidings."

Ala al-Din shrugged just enough that Kaddour's hands fell away, then he nodded, though unease threaded his belly. Together they left the bazaar, and Ala al-Din led the way to the street nearby where craftsmen set up their workshops, his steps growing more reluctant the closer they drew. At one time, his father had a shop right on the street, with a proud metalwork sign proclaiming 'Mustafa the Artificer' hung above the door. Now... Well, now, his mother's finances allowed her a tiny room on an alley off the street, and a cloth banner embroidered with 'Tahmina the Tinker' tacked beside the door. Ala al-Din and his mother slept in a tiny alcove at the back, able to afford nothing more.

When Kaddour saw the banner bearing not Al al-Din's name, but his mother's, and the threadbare tapestry draping the entrance, his brow furrowed, and his head cocked ever so slightly to the side. "Surely my brother provided better for his family. Did he not at least pass on his craft?" While the words were solicitous, Ala al-Din would swear that the tone held barely veiled pity.

He frowned and tugged at his handless arm.

Before he could comment, the curtain rings jingled as Kaddour swept the cloth aside.

"Welcome..." his mother called out, only to trail off at the sight of him and the stranger with him. "Can... can I help you?"

The man looked around as if tallying the value of all he saw, and finding it wanting, his nose wrinkling at the faint scent of dust and dank that permeated the space, no matter how they aired it. Ala al-Din's muscles tensed, and a phantom tingle danced about the end of his stump as if his missing hand fisted. Supposed family, or not, Kaddour had no call to cast even silent aspersions on his mother's efforts. She kept a neat shop, with well-crafted offerings, within the best of her meager means. At that thought, Ala al-Din's belly soured with guilt. Had he not been a foolish and lazy boy, he might be hale and whole this day, and he and his mother would not be reduced to sorting trash piles in the alleys of Kashgar for usable parts when their coffers ran dry.

"Apa..." — mother — Ala al-Din began only to have his words trampled.

"Allah willing, I can help you, my sister," Kaddour answered with a brief bow, stepping into the shop and leaving Ala al-Din to follow behind.

His mother's confusion deepened into a frown, and she turned her gaze on Ala al-Din.

"Kaddour-aka came upon me in the market, he says he is my father's brother."

Her eyes widened briefly before narrowing. "And how would he know this?"

The man stepped forward, his arm gesturing as if to draw her eye, rather than direct it.

"Please, Tahmina, does your son not look the image of my brother, Mustafa, in his younger days?" Kaddour pointed toward two pictures above Tahmina's workbench — a photograph of Ala al-Din's parents on their wedding day, next to a daguerreotype of his grandparents on theirs. "Even as I am a reflection of what my brother would have been had he grown older?" The westerner held no tension in his body as if his words were given and irrefutable. And perhaps they were as Ala al-Din watched a shadow of doubt waft across his mother's gaze. Her eye narrowed and she worried the barest edge of her lip as if torn between belief and disbelief.

"Mustafa did travel from afar before settling in this place. And you do bear some passing resemblance," she murmured, her tone conflicted, as caution and hope fought for control. "What is it that you wish?"

"Merely to assist my brother's family in their time of need, now that I have found them. To restore them to the honorable station they would have held had he not been taken from us too soon."

While Ala al-Din could take no exception at the man's specific words, faint warnings echoed in his thoughts at the skillful manner in which his supposed uncle emphasized them with subtle precision, fanning the flame of his mother's hope until it flared with more strength than her caution. Of course, she toiled all day in this alleyway hovel, while Ala al-Din spent his days observing all manner of speech and careful maneuvering among those frequenting the market. He exercised his suspicion more often than she, while his hope had been trampled and smothered until a mere shadow of her own.

And still. He wanted to believe, and so he remained silent as his mother smiled and offered to fetch tea from their precious and limited store.

And thus, in a mere matter of days, Kaddour — with his own hands — helped them sort through their meager belongings. Ala al-Din and his mother were swept from their alley and into a storefront on the very street where the famed Mustafa had once plied his trade, with proper household quarters above the shop. By what means it had been procured Ala al-Din could not say and did not want to know. He was hesitant to question their good fortune, for his mother's sake.

He smiled and watched on as his mother fluttered through the shop like a jeweled songbird in her new khalat and richly colored rumol. She darted from the workbench where Mustafa's journal sat in place of honor — filled with designs he'd made and those he'd only imagined — to the various shelves, laughing as she ran her fingers through baskets of gears and over spanners and calipers and all manner of delicate tools and materials meant for fine workings of the sort that would see them well-appointed for years to come. They suddenly had the materials for nearly any job, be it clockworks or automata or similar intricate-but-frivolous contraptions the wealthy commissioned to lord them over others, rather than the work-a-day pumps and locks and cruder workings that had been all they could manage with scavenged parts.

Ala al-Din tugged at the sleeve of *his* new khalat, made of colorfully patterned cashmere, with embroidery at the cuffs, and reached up to brush his fine, white skull cap. Though of higher quality, he could not call the new clothing more comfortable than the old, as self-conscious as it made him feel, as if he pretended to higher than his station, though his uncle scoffed at such concerns when Ala al-Din voiced them.

"What use can you be to me if you wander Kashgar looking like a beggar?"

If not for the joyful and carefree way Tahmina explored the shop, every so often exclaiming with glee, Ala al-Din would have walked away from Kaddour without hesitation. To see her so happy, with the weight of worry lifted from her brow… There was much a son would bear to preserve a mother's well-being, no matter the doubts that might niggle his mind.

"Come, come, Ala," his uncle said, tugging him from the shop before Ala al-Din could protest. "Let us visit the neighboring shops and introduce you around."

Ala al-Din frowned. Not only were these the people who had known him all his life… or at least for the beginning of it… but why should *he* matter? Any hope of his building delicate machinery had died six years ago when his hand had been taken, and the memories of what his father had taught him had faded to near uselessness. He hung back until his half-empty sleeve stretched between them, and Kaddour finally realized he no longer followed like an obedient child. Once the man stopped and turned, Ala al-Din pulled his arm from Kaddour's grip.

With a nod, he said, "I bid you a good day, but I am needed here." He then pivoted around to return to the shop and help his mother. As soon as he turned, the newly hung sign above the door caught his eye, proclaiming to all Kashgar that this was the establishment of Ala al-Din the Artificer.

"What? What is this? That cannot be. It is not true."

"What do you know, boy?"

"I have not been a boy for a very long time," Ala al-Din muttered, glaring over his shoulder at Kaddour, his brow furrowed.

"What would happen, do you imagine," the westerner growled, leaning in close to Ala al-Din's face, "were we to advertise Tahmina the Tinker above that shop?"

Mulishly, Ala al-Din set his heels and his jaw likewise, not backing away.

"Answer me!"

"My mother would get the recognition she deserves for her work."

"Wrong! She would be treated as if she still did business in that hovel in the alley. Her wares would be overlooked because the custom would have already made up their minds."

Ala al-Din wanted to argue, but unfair is not untrue.

"And why my name and not your own?"

Something flared in Kaddour's gaze, heat and smoke and smoldering embers. His tone, however, remained calm, almost dismissive. "My talents lay elsewhere than the mechanical, boy, and none know me here. Better to build on their familiarity with your family."

Rather than fan the flame, Ala al-Din remained silent, nodding in acknowledgment and nothing more. His recalcitrance was not lost on Kaddour.

"I will do my best for you and your mother, Ala, but you must trust me."

Every instinct screamed at him not to do so, but at his back, Ala al-Din could still hear his mother's hums as she reordered the shop to her liking, every so often punctuated by a delighted giggle. How could he take that from her? And for what cause? Other than the deceit of the sign, Kaddour had done nothing out of order. And still, Ala al-Din held misgivings.

"Who will believe I can craft with one hand?"

Kaddour frowned briefly, before giving a slow nod and reaching out to guide Ala al-Din back toward the shop. "There is truth in this. We shall deal with that first."

Overly conscious of the mechanical hand strapped to his stump—a simple hand-shaped clamp crafted by his mother, from designs found in his father's journal—Ala al-Din followed his uncle through the city streets and into the market. They strolled seemingly without purpose, Kaddour stopping to examine copper fittings at one stall, and *tsk*ing over ill-cut gears at another, but always taking a moment to introduce Ala al-Din to the merchants and ask about their wares, while throwing in a random question or two about the countryside, or the Silk Road, or the bands of nomads traveling the sands. At first, Ala al-Din dismissed it as idle chatter, until he noticed a pattern in the questions, slight variations, but always fundamentally the same, as if Kaddour sought something but didn't quite know where. Ala al-Din's mind puzzled over it until he could remain silent no longer.

"What is it you search for?" he asked, as Kaddour sorted through a bin of spare cogs and gears and twisted coils of copper wire as if treasure might lay beneath, but all the while asking his peculiar questions.

If Ala al-Din were not so close, he would have missed the hiss his uncle swallowed as he snapped his head around to fix Ala al-Din with a hard stare. "Nothing, boy, I merely seek to familiarize myself with the region where I will be making my home."

Straightening, Kaddour turned away from the merchant's wares as if they hadn't moments before held him seemingly riveted. Without another word, he strode off with purpose, leaving Ala al-Din to hurry after.

He would have scarce caught up if his uncle hadn't stopped abruptly. Ala al-Din stopped a short distance away to observe as Kaddour settled on a short stone wall near one of the storytellers that regaled the crowd for whatever coin they would toss her. Though he pretended to adjust his sandal, Ala al-Din noticed the cant to his uncle's head, the ear angled to hear the tale being told, and the way his hands stilled in the middle of their task, as if to ensure it was not too quickly done. It had been some time since Ala al-Din had paid any attention to the tales told in the market, so he could not say what story the woman told, but as he moved closer, her words wove a picture of a hidden cavern far beneath the desert where trees bore jewels in lieu of fruit and a Shah's treasure waited to be returned to his rightful heirs. She described great metal beasts and dangers untold, the sulfurous stench of demons, and an ageless beauty bound by invisible chains, guardian of the ages. *"Are you Ins or are you Djinn?"* he heard her murmur in the telling of her tale, her voice exotic, though her features were no different from those born to call this place home. Whether by nature or artifice, she held her audience enthralled.

Ala al-Din wanted to laugh at such fanciful descriptions, only Kaddour had given up all pretense and hung on the woman's words.

With an uneasy feeling, Ala al-Din slowly withdrew, making his way back to the shop that bore his name, but not to his credit.

In the dark hours before dawn, Ala al-Din woke to a violent shaking of his shoulder. He reared up and drew away, a cry on his lips and his empty sleeve flinging out as if it still bore a fist, only to have his shout muffled by a rough hand and his blow batted away.

"Stop it," Kaddour hissed. "Get up and come with me."

When Ala al-Din tried to speak, the westerner pressed his hand firmer. "Do you wish to wake your mother? To give her more worry than you already have in life?"

With a glower, Ala al-Din slowly shook his head.

"If you come with me, it will ensure her continued good fortune." Though his tone bore no threat, the implication hung heavy in the air.

Ala al-Din rose from his pallet and dressed in silence. Though he could not say why, he strapped on his likeness of a hand before following his uncle downstairs and through the silent city streets. They left with few to note their passing, venturing out beyond the oasis and into the desert proper.

As they traveled the sands, he had call to be grateful for the brand-new khalat holding the warmth to his body. This close to the cold season, the night had grown chilled with the setting of the sun.

"Uncle," Ala al-Din called out, "where do we go?"

"Shh!"

"It is cold, and I am tired, if there is no purpose to this journey I would as soon return to my slumber."

Kaddour turned and stalked back to where Ala al-Din had stopped, his expression the epitome of solicitous.

"I need your help retrieving something I have lost. Something taken from me. Once I have it, none of us need work again unless we chose to do so. Can you not imagine how that would be? No more loitering in the market to be shunned by those seeking runners, no more make-work for Tahmina, who may choose what to build at her pleasure. Would not your father, Mustafa, desire this?"

"What is this thing we seek?"

"An intricate beast of the air, a mechanical falcon crafted in the finest of handwork, with delicately formed gears the size of a pea and thin plates sheathing its clockworks in the seeming of banded feathers. And for the eyes, two rare black diamonds swirling with the steam inside."

Ala al-Din considered Kaddour's words. While the working sounded exquisite, he could not fathom how such a thing would accomplish all that his uncle promised. "The market is full of such machinations. What makes this one of such note?"

In the dark, it was difficult to see the truth of Kaddour's expression. Did his features shift and harden, or was it an illusion of moonlight and shadow? He remained silent overlong, but finally… "To me, its value is beyond measure. Made long ago by your own father's hand, a present for me, snatched away before it could be given."

Ala al-Din frowned. His father had been gifted, and his talent had done well for them, but never could he remember such workings as

Kaddour claimed. Not even written down in his father's journal, where he had tracked all his designs to aid with future innovations. But then, who was he to dispute Kaddour's claims? By the time Ala al-Din was born, his father's workings had turned toward practical designs.

"How will this thing accomplish what you claim?"

"Why, my boy..." The pause was not long, but Ala al-Din noted it... as if Kaddour searched the recesses of his mind for an answer without question. "Can you not imagine the acclaim the shop will garner with a machination of this magnificence on display? The custom would come in droves such that you... your mother could choose among them to her heart's desire and be paid so handsomely that it would matter not who was turned away."

Oh, to have such coin. Ala al-Din thought longingly of the photography equipment used by the British expedition. With their finances restored, he might secure the like for himself. From what he had seen, photography was a skill he could learn with but one hand, particularly with his new prosthetic. And with Kaddour here to look after mother, perhaps Ala al-Din might venture out into the world—where his one well-meant indiscretion would no longer plague him—and capture its wonders on film.

"Come!" Kaddour barked. "We haven't much time."

They wandered a while longer, their path seemingly guided by the details garnered in the market, though mostly by the storyteller's tale. Finally, Kaddour stopped when the promise of the sun barely kissed the sky and made it blush. Before them lay a crumbled column, ancient stones weathered and worn smooth, once balanced high as if an archway to the desert, positioned on the edge of an oasis much smaller than the one Kashgar had grown around. Ala al-Din just stood there, awkward and uncomfortable, as his uncle searched the ground, for what only he knew. Finally, Kaddour straightened with a triumphant cry. Spinning back around, the westerner came close, fervor burning in his gaze as he gripped Ala al-Din by the shoulders in an echo of their first meeting.

"Listen, boy. Listen close. I am about to open the way we seek. You must remain silent and move swiftly, for only you can venture forth to find the treasure we are after."

Ala al-Din shook his head. "I do not understand. Why me?"

"Why, you are slighter than I and thus will fit through the passage."

Against such blatant fact, Ala al-Din could not argue. He nodded, and Kaddour turned back, arms raised until the drape of his robe obscured any view Ala al-Din may have had. The man muttered and shook and stamped on the ground… and nothing happened. Kaddour tried again, his voice louder, his tone more commanding. Still nothing.

Ala al-Din was puzzled at his behavior, and softly repeated the syllables he'd heard quite clearly the second time, rolling them around in his mouth before they whispered past his lips.

Suddenly, the earth rumbled and jumped beneath their feet.

"Ay!" Kaddour called out, stumbling back against the toppled stones and falling on his rear as the sand slid away to reveal a maul in the earth, rimmed with blunt stone, like teeth. "Go! Go, boy. Touch nothing but the falcon, or surely you will never return if you do. The guardian of the cavern is quite fierce."

With a nod, Ala al-Din stepped forward to the edge of the maul, staring down into the darkness. Before he could turn to ask how he should descend, a hard shove met with his back, and he tumbled down the hole.

When consciousness—if not sense—returned Ala al-Din rolled his aching body over to stare up at the circle of sky above him. Wheezing out a breath, he scrambled to his feet, the opening taunting him, just barely three feet out of reach. If his limbs were all sound, he might have jumped up to catch the rim and pull himself free. Not today. A single beam of light sliced through the darkness. Where the light hit, it revealed Ala al-Din looking rumpled and dusty but, for the most part, unharmed, and beneath his feet, a floor mosaic of precious gems. He was about to call out to his… uncle when a frantic thought pierced the fog shrouding his mind.

You must remain silent…

As he moved off down the passage, the darkness receded. Not completely, but enough that, with squinting, Ala al-Din could just make out his way. He took care not to shuffle or scuff, taking only slow, sure steps lest he wake whatever guardian lurked. The barest scratch of dirt on tile taunted his ear, and unseen motes of dust tickled his nose, but Ala al-Din made no sound as he moved forward with deliberation, straining to hear any noise to betray another's presence.

He heard nothing but his own strained breath.

The further he traveled down the passage the more the darkness receded, giving way to the promise of twilight as a faint but increasing splatter of glow adorned the walls. Ala al-Din reached out and delicately brushed the points of light, encountering a layer of soft tufts that darkened where he touched. He pulled his hand away, rubbing his fingertips together, marveling at the faint shimmer left behind with the barest hint of moisture. Lichen. He had heard tales, though he could not say if they were true, of long-ago miners chipping the surface layer of lichen-covered rocks to make crude lanterns where they dare not carry flame.

The deeper he traveled into the cavern the brighter the passage seemed until he could make out the arch of an opening expanding into a larger space that seemed to glow even brighter yet, with a subtle lavender hue. With caution, he crept forward, staying close to the stone wall, peering past the opening to a sight of true wonder.

A soft gasp escaped his lips.

The light flared brighter, and of a sudden, Ala al-Din felt pinned beneath the weight of a thousand stares. He dare not move, but his gaze darted about the chamber taking in the massive dome of the chamber braced by a latticework of brass-fitted glass tubes from which the light emanated. Beneath that stunning dome lay a treasure beyond Ala al-Din's imagine. Beyond his comprehension. Beyond his very dreams. Casks of gold and jewels and vessels with wax stoppers that might hold anything from rare spices to exotic scents. At the center of the trove stood a bejeweled throne—a broad platform beneath a canopy ornamented with two peacocks that bespoke a Persian influence. And surprisingly, along the edge of the trove, piled haphazardly, without regard, lay common goods as one would find in any market. He saw no sign of a falcon, clockwork or otherwise, though along the curved wall he could make out a string of what appeared to be mechanical camelids.

Scarcely the same thing.

On the far side of the chamber, however, past the treasure, Ala al-Din spied something most perplexing.

A workshop. As alike his father's as to be unmistakable.

Ala al-Din stepped forward into the light.

A sound began to build, like the hissing of the desert's fury as the sands themselves rose up to express their displeasure. From nowhere, a gust of hot air—the breath of a demon?—brushed wherever his skin lay bare, tugging his khalat and snatching away his skull cap. Swallowing his cry, he hurried to grab the covering back, stumbling among the treasure in his haste, disturbing it.

"Thief!" a voice called out, both harsh and melodious at once. It reverberated through the chamber, pinging off the glass and jangling the fine metalwork among the trove.

Memories of that long-ago day… the fear… the thrill… the panic as the guards seized him… worse, as the blade bit his flesh, then bone, despite his pleas and cries…

He reared away, fighting a grip that was not there. Something sharp caught his wrist, tugging, slicing. All flooded back, tearing a scream from the depths of Ala al-Din's heart.

A biting, metallic scent like rusted iron fanned his terror until then and now melded into one desperate nightmare as a hot trickle of blood dripped off his fingers.

A gasp sounded throughout the chamber, as soft and gentle as the first cry had been harsh. It held notes of wonder and not quite disbelief, but most of all, it held hope.

"Son of Persia… Blood of the Nadar Shah… Be still. Be welcome. Be at peace. Be healed."

A warmth suffused the cut on Ala al-Din's wrist as the lavender glow dimmed and swirled in soothing patterns, and a plume of violet vapor drifted in the glass cylinder above his head. Eyes formed as the plume took the shape of a beautiful woman made of smoke.

Ala al-Din's frantic breath slowed, then stilled, and his eyes widened. "Are you Ins or are you Djinn?" he murmured without thinking, though the answer was clear.

The vapor woman danced and laughed as if he'd been clever, her color brightening with her delight.

"We have waited long for the rightful heir."

Ala al-Din's eyes went wider still until pupil and iris were but concentric dots in a pool of white. His breath panted from his chest as he took in her words and made a frightening sense of them. Carefully, he climbed to his feet and stood clear of the legendary mounds. He may no longer listen to the tales in the market, but that did not mean he had not heard them. Who *hadn't* heard of the famed lost treasure of Nadar Shah, and his equally lost bloodline? Even as far east as Kashgar.

By sheer force of will, he stilled his heartbeat and slowed his breathing.

"No," he stated, not with force or fervor, but with solid, unwavering conviction. Such wealth, such obligation, such *risk* a treasure of that magnitude represented would build chains to shackle his dreams and desires.

He had already lost one life and would not sacrifice another. "No," he repeated.

"I do not understand..."

"Such, I do not wish for myself. It is not a life, it is a procession, where the needs of all others dictate your steps"—here he held up his right arm—"I have not done so well with such choices."

"But..."

"I am certain I am not the only one, the shahs were said to sow nearly as much seed as farmers. Your kind is ageless, another will come along."

Ala al-Din turned and walked back down the passage, not stopping until he stood beneath the maul, squinting up at the bright blue sky.

Kaddour's head moved into view, occluding the light, his gaze maniacally eager. Unease gathered in Ala al-Din's belly. His own arguments echoed in his thoughts as he stared up at the embodiment of his fears.

"Where is it, boy? Hand me the Djinn!"

Ah, so that was what drove his uncle, dreams of limitless power enslaved to his every desire.

Ala al-Din squared his shoulders and held his head high.

"There is no mechanical falcon."

"Liar!" Kaddour growled, all semblance of benevolence leached from his expression.

"Come see for yourself, *uncle*."

"Stay there until you find it, *boy*," he hissed back before uttering a guttural string of words wholly unfamiliar to Ala al-Din, despite a lifetime living in a hub of global commerce.

"No! No!" he yelled over the strange syllables, leaping, his hands reached out to grab the lip of the maul, but unable to grip. "Damn you, Kaddour! May the fires of Jahannam burn you black for all eternity!"

His words had no effect save to punctuate his helplessness. As the final syllable fell from Kaddour's lips, a whirlwind swept in, burying the maul—and Ala al-Din—beneath the sands.

Ala al-Din seethed in the darkness for a very long time. Long enough his belly grumbled, long enough his bladder complained. Long enough, he began to notice the faintest of lavender glow.

"Djinni," he murmured. "Is it you he sought?"

"I do not know," she murmured back, strengthening her glow until Ala al-Din saw the single glass pipe leading back toward the cavern. "Perhaps."

"But no. He sent me to retrieve a clockwork falcon."

The glow flared until the antechamber lit up like a fever dream. "*What?*"

"A falcon. I was to take the falcon and nothing else."

"Shahin," the djinn uttered with a breath. "My brother, of sorts. He is no longer here. Please… you must warn him."

Ala al-Din narrowed his gaze, his suspicion newly rekindled. "I told you…"

"No! I do not seek to sway you… trap you. I cannot leave this place of my own accord, and if this sorcerer knows to target the falcon, he knows Shahin is bound to it. Please… it is a terrible thing for the djinn to be coerced."

He knew the feeling. And in that moment, Ala al-Din filled with an overwhelming sense of dread akin to the djinni's. How could he have forgotten? His mother. Alone and at Kaddour's mercy.

"I cannot," he said softly, true regret giving weight to his words. "I cannot leave my mother unprotected from my uncle…"

The lavender glow deepened to the purple of a bruise, cutting him off. "That one is no kin to you! He is a sorcerer from a far-off land, only eager to add to his power that of a djinn."

Ala al-Din frowned, torn as to what to do.

"I cannot be as you wish."

"My only wish now is that you warn my brother. Anything else is a concern for another day."

"But my mother…"

"And can you help her from here?"

A snarl twisted Ala al-Din's lips. At every turn, his hand forced… and he with but one of them.

"Can you free me?"

"Yes."

"Can you restore this?" He held up his handless arm.

A sense of unease filled the chamber as if a creature made of light and smoke could squirm.

"Can you?"

A soft huff faded into the stone walls.

"After a sort."

"Explain."

"I am a djinn, not a god. I cannot create flesh. I can take what has been crafted and refine it, give it grace and function and form, but not flesh and blood."

Ala al-Din latched on to the only word that mattered. "Function."

"After a sort," she repeated, reluctance drawing out her words. Her response stirred remembrance. Echoes of past dealings observed in the marketplace. Classic avoidance masked as cooperation. Canting his head slightly, he watched her as he asked his next question.

"Will you fix this?"

"I may or I may not."

Straightening, Ala al-Din stared direct at the djinn and uttered two words: "Fix it."

A moment of silence before she answered, "As you wish."

Light, a pale lilac, nearly white, descended in tendrils that wove around his prosthetic, caressing it, tracing the lines and joins, feeding through the gaps to illuminate the inside, light pushing out again through the seams until Ala al-Din fairly felt it pulse. Gradually, the glow faded. "Is it done?" he asked, his words taut with anticipation.

"See for yourself," she murmured, her glow dimmed, though he could not say from overuse or displeasure.

Nigh on holding his breath, Ala al-Din bent his will to flex the fingers, to flare them out flat as the clamp configuration would never allow. And as he wished it, so it was.

"Thank you," he breathed, his fingers still dancing before him as he studied them with awe.

Looking up to where she floated in the pipe—a mere spark of her former glory—he vowed, "I shall warn Shahin."

A faint pulse, and no more.

Worn, then, he answered for himself. And he settled down to nap until she was restored.

Ala al-Din woke next to a wooden bowl filled with gemstones nearly indistinguishable from plucked fruit: amber apricots and amethyst grapes, sapphires like perfect round blueberries plump with juice. He took up a ruby like a bright red cherry and marveled at the lapidary skill it would take to craft such a thing. Looking up to where the djinni had perched last night—day? he had lost track—he met her gaze, itself like onyx or black diamond.

"Thank you, but neither my teeth nor my belly is up to such fruit."

She nodded her concession. "These are to sustain you and your household by other means, now that your… *patron*… is disenfranchised."

"I was told to take nothing."

"Such warning does not apply to those of the blood, whether or not they seek to claim it. These are but a small portion of what is rightfully yours."

Rather than consider that temptation too closely, he offered her his own nod, then, remembering his promise, he asked, "My thanks. Have I leave to deliver these to my mother before I set out?"

The djinni frowned faintly upon him. "No need. Shahin will find you soon enough. Once sensed, your blood is like a beacon to those charged to serve… to *protect* the Afsharid dynasty."

A shiver coursed down his limbs as he wondered who else might take interest in his blood.

"Djinni, I wish to go home now."

If not for their new shop and restored good fortunes, Ala al-Din would have thought his encounter in the Cave of Wonders, and all that led to it, a fever dream. He had awoken in his bed with seemingly nothing out of order. The sound of his mother's singing drifted up from the workshop below, and his clothing lay waiting to be donned, but as Ala al-Din rose and began to put them on, each layer he lifted revealed the marvel of the magicked hand beneath. In fact, though the prosthetic had not yet been strapped on, the fingers clenched as if gripping his pants to pull them up. The garment in question fell from his left hand to puddle on the floor.

Ala al-Din reached for the prosthetic and affixed it to his stump with no measure of discomfort, other than a bit of leeriness. It sat comfortably with nary even an itch to annoy him as he went about his day.

"Allah, be praised," he murmured as he finished dressing and went downstairs to help his mother.

And thus, their days went on for several fortnights, with no mention between them of the transformed hand or the bowl of jewels hidden beneath the hearthstone against future need. The custom came, out of curiosity, if nothing else. Kaddour did not, more curious still. Ala al-Din held himself ready for the day the sorcerer surfaced, under no illusion he would just walk away. In the meantime, he applied himself to the study of Mustafa's journal, desiring to aid his mother as he had failed to do in the past. He had not her passion but did possess a measure of skill. They worked contently side by side. It felt good to have an honest claim to the sign above their shop, though still, he would have preferred his mother receive the recognition due her.

As memory faded into the background and routine relaxed his guard, there came a night when Ala al-Din ventured out after dark to deliver a newly completed commission bespoke by Yaqub Beg himself, Emir of Kashgaria, and for which, surely, they would receive no pay. He consoled himself with the knowledge that others would covet the prestige of possessing clockworks crafted by the Artificer to the Emir. And if not, they needed not the coin, having no desire for great wealth, beyond their needs.

Lost in his musings, Ala al-Din barely noticed the sound of shuffling in the street ahead of him as he wheeled his handcart toward the Emir's compound. When four figures emerged from the shadows to block his path, he stumbled to a halt, the cart clattering behind him as he dropped the handles to the ground.

Before he could react, or even speak, two others seized him from behind.

Within moments they dragged him away down an alley, leaving the cart abandoned in the street.

"What do you want of me?" he asked, not for the first time, though the thugs repeatedly ignored him, binding his hands behind him and pushing him to his knees. Ala al-Din did not resist. Even unbound, he could not have stood against five assailants, and escape was unlikely with so many to block his way.

"Time to make good on our agreement, boy."

Ala al-Din tensed at the familiar voice, cursing himself for letting down his guard. He remained silent as Kaddour emerged from the shadows to stand before him.

"And where is my falcon?" he asked.

Looking up to meet the westerner's eye, Ala al-Din did not bother to shield his hatred.

"There was no falcon," he answered, relieved his "uncle" had not asked about djinn, only the vessel, and so he could answer honestly.

"How did you escape?"

"I did not." And such was true. Escape implied action on his part.

Snarling, Kaddour chanted too low for the words to reach Ala al-Din's ears. As he did so, he raised his hand, his fingers curled. Ala al-Din gasped as that grip wrapped like a steel band around his throat. The sorcerer lifted him from the ground high enough that his legs dangled, without once touching him. He hung there and did not fight it.

"How did you escape!"

"I did not." Ala al-Din answered, his words strained. "I woke in my own bed."

The grip on his throat tightened, and still, he did not fight, merely holding Kaddour's gaze in defiance. To struggle would be to give the sorcerer satisfaction, and any futile efforts would only weaken Ala al-Din. Instead, he contorted his arms behind his back, his flesh hand twisting to unseat his prosthetic.

As they glared one another down, a strident cry sounded above. The scream of a bird of prey, unnatural in the night. For an instant, Kaddour's focus broke, his startled gaze snapped upward. Ala al-Din's feet hit the ground, as did his mechanical hand, and he pictured it scrabbling across the distance to seize the sorcerer by the throat. Swift and sure, it scurried. Before the man could react, it locked down tight in a crushing hold, cutting off the sorcerer's breath as he tried to resume his chanting. Ala al-Din shook off his now-loose bonds and watched as Kaddour gasped his final breath. The thugs fled, honor-bound to no one, particularly the dead.

Again, the falcon screamed overhead, triumphant.

Ala al-Din retrieved his miraculous hand and seated it back in place, striding with purpose back to the street, leaving the rubbish in the alley.

Someday, Shahin, he thought, *you and I will meet. But not this night.*

Heart of Stone

Based on Stone Soup

MICHELLE D. SONNIER

November 12, 1872, Somewhere in eastern France

THINGS HAD NOT GONE WELL FOR LYSE DE MONTRE IN MARCKOLSHEIM. She hadn't wanted this assignment in the first place but had no choice. Sending a crow back to the French Council of Witches with news of her failure had galled her. However, the pitying look from Peldyn in Epfig, when she'd arrived filthy and exhausted, with her clothes torn to shreds, stuck in her craw worse than informing the Council. Pity was just not something Lyse could abide. But starving, covered in mud, with winter hard on her heels, Lyse had no choice but to let Peldyn cluck over her like a brooding hen. First, feeding her food, then information. She told Lyse to head north and slightly west to Dambach-la-Ville. Her sources said the town might be more receptive to the Council's mission.

Peldyn smiled and chirped optimistically about the chances for success. *It is easy for her,* Lyse thought. Already comfortably embedded with the citizenry of Epfig, with a warm bed every night along with company if she wished it. She'd accomplished the first part of *her* mission. She was ready to whisper the right words into the right ears to fan the flames of resistance. Her plump rosy cheeks evidence that she never had to worry about an empty belly.

The truth was things had not gone well for Lyse in some time. A fraught and tangled road brought her here, to the shadows of the Vosges mountains, headed for yet another place where she would not know a soul. She sat close to the remains of her dying fire, knees pulled up to her chest. She poked at the fading coals with a stick, spreading them out a little to burn out faster. She'd risked as much fire as she dared. Just enough to warm a cup of tea and take some of the cold from her fingers and toes. She pulled the thick dark wool blanket Peldyn provided tighter around her shoulders. But she could not chance a truly useful campfire that might catch the eyes of patrolling soldiers of the German Empire.

Lyse let the gloom of the darkness around her guide her thoughts. She sank into her memories. They folded around her like a familiar, tattered cloak. Maman was dead. It was the last argument she'd had with her father after years and years of arguments. A sunny afternoon, an empty watch shop and Lyse chided her father for giving Monsieur Coumet yet another extension to pay for the watch already back in his pocket. Papa lost his temper and shouted that he would not allow his child to belittle him.

"It's MY shop!" he roared.

"You couldn't run it without me!" Lyse shrieked back.

Then, every clock, every watch, suddenly went mad. Hands twirled around their faces, little bells jangled, wooden cuckoos screeched. Papa fled the shop. As the cacophony slowly died, Lyse locked the door and turned out the lights. She went upstairs and cried herself to sleep. The next morning, both of them tried to pretend that the day before had never happened. But then the witches came.

Lyse was not a wild witch, a woman with magic springing up in a bloodline that had never shown talent before. It seemed that Maman came from a line of earth witches from the southeast of France. The Council had thought her line barren. Maman's great-grandmother was the last in that branch to show any magical talent. They'd lost track of Lyse's grand-mere when she moved to Paris. Grand-mere failed to register Maman's birth with the Council, and all was lost to the dusty archives. Until Lyse let loose a surge of technomancy, and the Council's Guardians tracked her to the watch shop.

Lyse never forgot the look of fear in Papa's eyes.

The fire shrank to embers. Lyse wiped the wetness from her cheeks. She huddled under the blanket against an outcropping of stone. With a whisper of magic, she set light wards around her, just enough to warn her if someone came close while she slept. She closed her eyes and tried to claim sleep's oblivion.

Lyse woke in the morning to find a light coating of frost on her blanket and hair. Breath puffing out in front of her, she scanned the sky. Sharp, crystal blue with no softening clouds. The day promised to be colder than yesterday, and the night colder still. Lyse sighed and contemplated the ashes of the previous night's small fire. The old wounds in her heart began to ache again as the dark shadows of her past paraded past her mind's eye. She shook her head sharply. Not again, not so soon.

She stuffed her emotions down with a firm hand and tied her bedroll to her pack in swift, jerky motions. No need for tea or a little warmth this morning; the last leg of her walk to Dambach-la-Ville would get her blood pumping and warm her up. She shouldered her little backpack with all her necessities for living, then slung a much larger canvas bag across her front. It clanked as she settled it lower on her chest and toward her left hip. It was full of her tools and all the bits and bobs she'd managed to collect during her training. She regretted bringing everything with her, especially the mystery box the dorm mother gave her just before she left. The bag hung so heavily.

Lyse gnawed on the last hard heel of bread and leftover cheese rind, courtesy of Peldyn. The witch of Epfig was generous, practically re-kitting Lyse out. And she wouldn't hear of any promises of satisfying the debt. At first, it made Lyse uncomfortable, then embarrassed, and finally, highly suspicious. Lyse viciously tore off another mouthful as she stomped along the cart track north. *How dare she?* Peldyn knew how the Council ran things in Paris. Lyse swallowed her last hard scrap of cheese rind with a grimace. But done was done. She'd needed the clothes and food desperately. There was nothing she could do about it now.

Lyse hitched up her pack and tried to force her thoughts onto happier trails. Not that there were many in the wilds of her mind. But she had been lucky enough to meet Arabella Helene Leyden just once, while she was training. She knew all about Madame Leyden, the first technomancer in the world. Lyse studied her as part of her training. During a trip to the Continent, Madame Leyden generously took the time to visit with France's newest technomancer, Lyse herself. Of course, the French Council would not allow Madame Leyden to be alone with Lyse, not since the English witch had stolen the girl who might have been France's first technomancer out from under their very noses. It had been nearly twenty years, but the Council had a long memory. France laid claim to quite a few technomancers now, but they remained rare enough. Having the first spirited away still stung.

That sunny afternoon with Madame Leyden for an authentic English High Tea had been marvelous, one of the few happy memories she'd had since Maman died. Naturally, they'd discussed technomancy, and Lyse learned far more that afternoon than she'd learned from her tutors in the previous month. And the food! Endless tea, sandwiches, tarts, pies, both savory and sweet, cookies, and an array of pastries Lyse had no names for… Not a mouthful of it was charged to her account with the French Council, and it left her full enough to skip dinner and avoid another meal charge.

The business of a Council charging a young witch for her training and keep had shocked Madame Leyden. Apparently, in England, all witches were bound to a House, and the House was bound to them. A young girl manifesting power outside the established Houses was soon adopted into an existing House. In France, any witch not born to a House was unaffiliated. If the girl seemed like she might be a strong witch or if she were the child of a wealthy family, she would be adopted into a House readily enough. But those like Lyse, with no family connections, or of small or moderate abilities, had to make their own way. Of course, the French Council would never allow any witch to starve or be so untrained that she could not use her powers.

As soon as Lyse's powers were confirmed, the Council assigned her a mentor to guide her training and a room in one of their dormitories. They also assigned her a little ledger with a red leather cover. For every night spent under a Council roof, every meal eaten out of a Council kitchen, anything the girl might use, the dorm mother made an entry in the girl's ledger. If the girl had family, they might send money to help with the balance. Or if she proved particularly promising in training, a House may choose her and pay off the bill for their new member. Or they could be like Lyse, and, once trained, work for others until the debt was settled. This Council mission to the territory so recently ceded by France to Germany to end the Franco-Prussian war was brutal and dangerous. But it also promised to pay well enough that Lyse's years of debt would be nearly wiped clean.

It didn't take long for Lyse to hit her walking stride. Anything to keep warm in the thin November sunshine… But keeping her mind from roving where she didn't want it to was harder. Like pushing her tongue against a sore spot on her gums, she kept returning to painful memories.

The day she finished training, she was offered a larger room in the boarding house for unaffiliated witches rather than the tiny cell she'd been allotted during her training. She asked the dorm mother if she could think about it, then went for a walk. The larger apartment would be nice. It would actually have windows and be mostly rodent free. But it would also cost more, adding larger debits into her little red ledger. Without thinking about it, she found her way to the 17th Arrondissement.

Glancing up at a street number, she realized she was but a street over from Papa's watch shop and the sunny apartment above it. The revelation bloomed in her mind like sugar on her tongue. She could live with Papa. Surely, he'd made peace with who she was by now. Almost laughing, she scampered down the street, clutching her hat to her head. She almost slipped off the curb and twisted her ankle when she stopped dead, nascent laughter lodged in her throat.

A ladies' millinery now occupied the space where her father's shop had been. The shop painted cornflower blue instead of the stately maroon Maman had chosen. The apartment windows above the shop hung open, and a strange woman watered the cheerful flower boxes. Lyse shook her head back and forth, tears gathering in the corners of her eyes.

She turned on her heel and bolted, believing her father had fled from the shame of his daughter. When she returned to the Council Dormitory, Lyse told the dorm mother she would be staying in her current room and asked for the list of Council missions available to a witch of her level.

On the road to Dambach-la-Ville, Lyse knuckled tears out of her eyes. She needed to think of something more soothing to the mind. She turned her thoughts back to her one and only meeting with Arabella Leyden. They'd shared so much. Lyse had been dumbfounded to find out that English witches were not always pushed to develop additional magical strengths during their training as French witches were required to do. In England, they were allowed to follow their natural inclinations to their heart's content and never develop any of the more basic skills that a witch in France would consider so crucial.

Lyse shook her head, thinking about how much trouble she would have met on this mission if she hadn't known basic self-defense skills, shields, and a bit of fire magic. The idea of having to worry about keeping matches dry, or, Goddess forbid, trying her luck with flint and steel, was completely alien to her. It was no wonder that English witches always traveled together and that high-born witches were usually assigned a Guardian to watch over them.

As much as Lyse hated to think about the rigors of her training and the debt it left her in, she had to admit that it had served her well. Had she been born on the other side of the Channel, she'd have a House and somewhere to go without debt. But she would be soft, not nearly as self-sufficient as she was. Lyse heaved a deep sigh and paused, rubbing the back of her neck. There were values to both systems, but there was no sense in trying to decide which she would choose as the best. She'd been born where she was born, which had decided her fate.

Before she could move on to darkly ruminating, and the possibility of working all her life to still be in debt to the French Witches Council, Lyse spotted Dambach-la-Ville in the distance. The picturesque little town nestled on the eastern slopes of the Vosges. Arrayed around the town were neat little fields mostly put to bed for the winter. Some small plots nearer the old medieval wall surrounding the town still had a last few hardy fall vegetables, carrots and cabbages and potatoes, waiting to be harvested. But the grape vines that produced the wine that made the town famous were neatly trimmed and settled in, ready for a long winter's nap.

As she approached the town, Lyse admired the wall around it. It looked sturdy, still in good repair despite its age. She frowned, however, when she came to the front façade to discover the gate closed. Glancing up at the sky, she noted there was still a good hour of daylight left, even for a short November day. She'd planned to get into the town before sundown to find a room and a hot meal in a local tavern, paid for in the money Peldyn gave her before she left. She'd hoped to ingratiate herself with the residents by fixing their mechanical things, and from there eventually make herself part of the community so she could feed information back to the Council, as was her mission. They needed to know who had the will and ability to help a resistance against the German Empire. But now the closed oak gate confounded all Lyse's plans, for the evening, anyway.

Lyse tilted her head back, shielding her eyes from the sun, searching for any signs of life on top of the wall. Perhaps she could still get them to let her in if she played the weary traveler well enough.

She let her tool bag drop with a clanking thump and the loudest sigh she could manage. Then she stretched and rubbed her lower back and neck. The tired groan was not faked, but she put more volume behind it. Still, no head popped over the old stone battlements. Lyse sighed quietly. Cupping her hands around her mouth, she shouted into the crisp air.

"Hallooo? Anyone home?"

Lyse waited. She strained her ears for the slightest sound. Was that a murmur of voices muffled behind the stone? Or was it her imagination playing games with the breeze that tickled her hair?

"Halloooo?" she called again. "Is there any room for a weary traveler? I have good coin. I can pay for a meal and a bed."

This time Lyse was sure she heard voices on top of the wall. Quarreling voices. Lyse tried to temper the hope growing in her breast. If they were bickering, then there was a good chance at least one of them argued to let her in. She shushed the dark voice in the back of her head that they could just be debating the way to kill her. A quick gunshot to the skull? Perhaps old-fashioned arrows to conserve gunpowder. Or let her in and quietly slit her throat after she let her guard down…

A middle-aged man popped his blond head up over the edge of the wall. Lyse couldn't tell what color his eyes were from this distance, but she could tell he was not pleased to see her.

"What do you want?" he called down.

"A bed and a hot meal, just as I said. I have good French francs to pay. I can show you."

"We've been sold off to the German Empire, or haven't you heard? Francs are not supposed to be legal tender here," he said. Lyse thought his voice sounded marginally less unfriendly than it had the moment before.

"I can work for my keep," Lyse shouted back.

Another head popped up beside the first man. A bald man with heavy gray whiskers on his prodigious jowls said, "Oh, come now, Claude. She's obviously a young lady alone, and she needs us."

Claude rubbed his chin in thought. "A young lady alone…" He paused. Turning to his companion with wide eyes, he exclaimed, "She must be a spy!"

The older man tried to soothe Claude. "Now, now, she may not be a spy…"

"A foul collaborator with the German Empire!" Claude would not be soothed. "Come to use her womanly wiles to report back whether we are toeing the line!"

"Claude, she could just be a witch! Witches often travel alone," Claude's companion reasoned.

Claude narrowed his eyes and leaned over the edge of the wall to hiss at Lyse. "A witch…. Just like that foul creature who tried to root herself here over the summer? The one who reported us to the Empire?!"

"But, Claude…" The bald man plucked at the man's sleeve, trying to pull him back.

Claude yanked his arm away. "Aubrey is *dead* because of what that witch reported about him." He turned back to Lyse. "Go away. We cannot risk you. We will not harbor anyone we are not sure of."

"But, Monsieur, I can assure you…" Lyse began.

"No. We don't know you, and your assurances mean nothing," Claude cut her off. Without another word, both heads disappeared behind the wall. The door remained stubbornly shut in the dwindling autumn sunshine. But Claude's reaction at least gave her more insight into what had happened to her in Marckolsheim.

If the German Witches Council was attempting to seed their members in the area to gather intelligence, just as the French Council was, then it made sense that people would lose trust in witches and be very angry. Lyse had been on the receiving end of the anger and betrayal in Marckolsheim.

She cursed beneath her breath. What could she do now? Perhaps if she went a little more west, she could find a place large enough to gather useful intelligence, far enough from the center of the German Empire that their witches hadn't spoiled it. Damn *them,* thought Lyse. Undoing all the good work to make mundane folk trust witches to curry favor with their mundane government. They spoiled things for all witches, not just themselves. With a grunt, Lyse hauled her clanking tool bag back up.

It was too late to make her way to any other town. She surveyed the countryside leading up to Dambach-la-Ville, looking for a place to spend the night. There was a small copse of trees a few yards down the road that would give her some shelter from the wind. She'd pull out the map and decide where to go in the morning.

Given that she was so close to a major town, even if they wouldn't let her in, Lyse built the largest fire she'd allowed herself in a long time. It still wasn't big enough to make her completely comfortable. She tucked Peldyn's last potato into the glowing coals after placing a weak shield around it to keep the ash from making the skin inedible. While she waited for the potato to cook, she sank her teeth into the last apple from her pack, licking the juices from her chin absently, deep in thought.

After her dinner of potato and apple, there would be nothing left for the morning save half a tin of loose tea. Perhaps some warm drink in her belly would trick it into thinking something solid followed. She prodded the potato with a stick, shifting it around. There were late vegetables growing in the plots near the wall. If she waited until the deep night, she could creep over and take some. Just one cabbage, a few carrots, and some potatoes would be enough to keep her heart and soul together until she reached the next town. But Lyse didn't like the thought of taking them with no payment. She'd never stolen anything in her life. Chewing the apple down to the pips, she tried to think of some way to pay the people of Dambach-la-Ville for a few meager vegetables before she went on her way, but her basic magic skills were too simplistic to accomplish any good for the town, and they would not trust her sufficiently for her to use her technomancy. Try as she might, she could think of no fair exchange. She continued to mull the issue when the sound of wings overhead caught her attention.

A Council crow glided to the ground inside the circle of her firelight. She gasped at the ribbon of office he wore around his throat. The Grande Dame's personal crow! A shiver of unease passed through Lyse. She and the crow exchanged silent nods of respect before he offered his leg for her to untie the message. As soon as Lyse had it, the crow hopped back and took flight, not waiting for a response.

Lyse unrolled the tiny bit of paper with trembling fingers. Anxiety gripped her belly as she read the short message, and fear slid cold down her spine. The Grande Dame made clear her displeasure with Lyse's failure in Marckolsheim. She went further to say the mission to Dambach-la-Ville must end in success, or consequences would be severe. Lyse tried to swallow, but it felt like an invisible hand clenched her throat. To have the attention of the Grande Dame… one known for her… *creativity* in such matters. Lyse knew from experience that she rarely left a mark the naked eye could see.

She crumpled the paper and tossed it into the fire. Her circumstance seemed doomed from every direction. And, short of death, she could not avoid the matter. Running would prove but temporary escape. Even if she were not bound to the Council by blood magic with deadly consequences for betrayal, France produced the finest Guardian witches in the world. Talented and well-trained, but most of all, tireless. A French Guardian always brought home her prey.

Despite her worry, Lyse's belly grumbled as the scent of roasted potato rose from the flames. Rolling her meager dinner out of the fire, she used her knife to cut it open to cool.

While she waited, she looked over her shoulder at the shadows of the stone walls around Dambach-la-Ville. It was success or nothing. There were no other options.

She ate her potato mechanically, her eyes staring out into the vague middle distance beyond the light of the fire. When she was done, she tidied her camp, moving slowly, deliberately, revealing no outward sign that she panicked within. Her task complete, she stirred up the fire for a bit more light. Time to take stock of her resources.

Lyse carefully examined each item as she pulled it out of her canvas sack, laying each one on the small drop cloth she carried for a workspace. Nothing matched; nothing went together. Gears, cogs, springs, twists of wire in a range of metals… Two convex lenses as big around as soup bowls reminded her of eyes. Two mismatched pistons attached to angled rods resembled elbows. Lyse drew in a soft breath. Perhaps… Her hands flew faster as she laid out other mismatched parts. It didn't have to look pretty. It just had to work.

She sat back on her heels when she was done. The most important part was already assembled—a computing mechanism about the size of a melon. She'd been working on it secretly for months. Her creation would be able to carry out her instructions, if not quite think independently. But the rest… She cursed under her breath. Her stores did not contain enough parts to complete the body.

Lyse dug back into her canvas bag to see if she might have left anything behind. There was only one thing, stuffed deep at the bottom, and it didn't suit the task at hand. Just before she went to her dorm room to pack for the mission, the dorm mother handed her a package. It had been overlooked in a bin in the mailroom for months. The package was from the Archivist of the French Witches Council. What could the old, dusty Archivist want with her? Of course, maybe this was something of a solution to her problem. The Grande Dame and the Archivist got along well. Perhaps she'd allow the Archivist to take Lyse on as an apprentice or a pet; Lyse really didn't care as long as it saved her hide.

Lyse yanked the knot out of the twine and carefully unfolded the rough brown paper to reveal an intricate soapstone box about six inches square. Someone had carved the surface in interlocking sacred geometric shapes. The weight of intent radiated off the curio. On top lay a missive from the Archivist herself apologizing for taking so long to return her inheritance. The last active witch of the family, an earth witch with a talent for stone work, had left it with the Archive to be delivered to the next witch in her line. It had gotten lost over the decades, languishing in storage. She turned the antique in her hands. Her foremother hadn't carved this with something as unwieldy as mundane tools. She'd altered the rock with her magic. With careful fingers and no small measure of awe, Lyse worked off the lid and peered inside to discover a flat, heart-shaped stone. Lyse lifted it out, her fingers trembling. She could feel the soul of her great-great-grand-mere in the piece of red shale. The hope she held for her line of daughters. The joy for when this stone would find another of her blood. The supreme confidence that any daughter of her line would make her way in the world and do remarkable things.

Lyse's heart soared. She would find a way. Dambach-la-Ville would not confound her. Somehow, she would procure the parts she needed. She was a stone witch's daughter; she had the fortitude of mountains in her blood. She would endure.

The next morning dawned colder than the one before, just as Lyse expected. Still buoyed by the heart of stone, she rubbed the frost from her eyelashes without a worry and set to work.

Lyse squatted next to her parts, now arranged as efficiently as she could across the ground. She was so engrossed in her work that she didn't hear the goats, or the young boy who herded them, come down the road.

"What are you doing?" the boy asked.

Lyse lost her balance. She windmilled her arms but still fell over backward. The boy apologized profusely as he helped her up while the goats nibbled at the scrubby grass at the edges of the road. Snatching up her tea to give herself a moment to think, Lyse grimaced. She needed to tell the boy something reasonable, or he might come back with Claude and the others to force her on her way.

I am a stone witch's daughter. I am a technomancer. The heart of the mountain beats in me, Lyse thought.

"I'm building a mechanical golem," Lyse said brightly.

The boy cast a suspicious eye over the random parts strewn over the ground. "What would it do?"

"Oh, protect me from any German soldiers wandering around, of course." Inspiration kindled in Lyse, and she held her breath to see if the boy would take the bait.

The boy perked up. "Really? You can build something like that?"

"Easily, I have everything I need. Why I could even build enough to protect all of Dambach-la-Ville if I had enough parts. Sadly, I only have enough for myself." Lyse sighed dramatically. "I do wish I had enough parts. I would so loathe for German soldiers to cause any more harm."

"A whole army of mechanical golems?" the boy whispered, his eyes widening in wonder.

"Well, that would take some time to build, and I certainly couldn't do it out here in the wild." Lyse wrapped her arms around herself, making sure to shiver a little more dramatically. "If only I had a few more parts, I could make my golem nicer."

"So, you can't really make even the one golem?" The boy sounded skeptical.

"Oh no, of course, I can make the golem. It just won't look very nice because the parts are mismatched. If I just had one or two nicer things, my golem might be impressive enough that your mayor would let me in. And then, since I'd have a warm, safe place to be, I could make that army."

"What do you need?"

Lyse kept her face calm even though she leapt for joy inside. "Oh, just some nice brass or bronze, in small sheets, for its feet. Something I could mold to give it hooves," she said as she flicked a glance at the boy's goats. "It will be more stable that way."

The boy nodded. "I'll see what I can do," the boy said. "My older brother is a blacksmith. He may have some useful scraps."

"That would be lovely!" Lyse bit the inside of her lip to keep herself from urging the boy to go straight back into town to his brother to fetch whatever he could find. Surely the goats had eaten enough grass while the two had stood talking.

Alas, the boy called a farewell and herded the goats further down the road to more open pastures. Lyse waved him off with a smile.

"My cousin has a small boiler that ruptured. Would that be any use?"

Lyse turned to see the older man who had pleaded for her yesterday evening. He held a lidded crock of something that smelled delicious and a small loaf of bread wrapped in a linen towel.

"That would be very useful, Monsieur…?"

"Durand. I am Lucian Durand, at your service." Monsieur Durand managed a small, awkward bow with the food in his arms. He thrust the crock and the bread out to Lyse. "I felt badly that I caused Claude to turn you away, so I brought you some food. My wife made it."

Lyse inhaled appreciatively. "It smells like you are a lucky man, Monsieur Durand." She took the food from him. Her cheeks colored as she surveyed her spartan campsite. "I'm afraid I don't have anywhere to invite you to sit, but I could make you a cup of tea."

Lucien chuckled. "Think nothing of it. Eat, eat! I shall go fetch the ruptured boiler for you."

Lyse waved cheerfully as he hiked back up the hill to town, but she settled in front of the fire as soon as possible. She crouched over the crock like an animal and shoveled the stew into her mouth. It was well-seasoned rabbit in a thick, savory broth with tender chunks of potato and carrot. The bread was both crusty and light, delicious on its own but even better for wiping the sides of the crock to catch every tiny scrap of rabbit and broth. One inner voice chided her over her manners; another reminded the first that at least she used a spoon instead of her hands.

The stew and the bread were long gone by the time Monsieur Durand returned with a small brass boiler, split neatly along the seam. And that was not all he'd brought. "My wife insisted," he said with a smile as he handed her a small basket. "And I thought you could use this." He handed her a thick gray wool blanket.

"Monsieur!" Lyse cried. "You are too generous!"

Lucien waved away her protests. "Not generous enough. My daughters may be married and far away now, but I will always pray for someone to help them in their need."

Lyse's shoulders relaxed. "Thank you, Monsieur Durand. Your kindness is deeply appreciated."

The boy from earlier called to them as he herded his goats back up the road. Lyse and Lucien smiled and waved back. "I'll bring what I can tomorrow!" he said as he passed with his griping herd.

"Thank you!" Lyse called after him.

"I should go, too," Lucien said as he tugged on his cap. "I'll see if there is anything else I can bring tomorrow." He turned and hurried to catch up with the boy, disappearing within the walls.

Lyse blinked away the tears gathering in the corners of her eyes. She made a pad of the new blanket to lay under her, shielding her from the cold ground, and settled in to investigate the riches Madame Durand sent her. The basket revealed a sandwich with thick slices of ham and creamy muenster cheese, several sausages, some sweet rolls with raisins and almonds that looked perfect for breakfast, a few apples, a jar of honey for her tea, and a bottle of the wine that made the village famous.

Lyse allowed her tears of gratitude to flow free.

The young goat herd held true to his word, bringing Lyse some slightly bent pieces of brass sheeting along with a few horseshoes his brother had made for the promised hooves. They were laughing together as the boy mimicked prancing steps, when Monsieur Durand brought her more food. And a pillow, just because there was an extra in the house.

The day after, a woman who said she was Claude's wife came to apologize for her husband's boorish behavior. She brought Lyse some screws and gears, along with jam and butter. She said she knew Madame Durand would not think to send such things. Lyse sensed an edge of competition in her voice. Before Claude's wife even left, another man arrived with spare cogs and pistons and a jar of grease. And so, it continued throughout the week, citizens of Dambach-la-Ville creeping out of the gate to bring her food, parts, and small comforts to make her camp cozy. At one point, even Claude had wandered by with a tangle of copper wire.

Seven days after the task began, Lyse stepped back to survey her work. Her creation stood just over six feet tall, with the girth of a burly wrestler.

The witches of Paris would be horrified. Even so, Lyse wiped the sweat from her brow and smiled. Nothing on the metal golem standing before her matched. It was like the soup her Maman made when she was a girl. Leftover scraps of meat and vegetables tossed together with whatever broth and herbs were available, never the same but always delicious.

Once patched, the ruptured boiler served well enough as a head to house the delicate workings that served as the creature's brain, with her convex lenses, indeed, serving as eyes, though she'd nothing to give it a nose or mouth. A patchwork metal shell protected the inner workings of the trunk of the body, and the blacksmith's cast-off tongs made rather formidable pincer hands for her guardian golem. Spare rods and bars came together for legs that bent back, like a goat's, tipped with brass hooves gleaming in the fading sunset. In tribute to the little goat herd, she'd shod them with the iron shoes his brother made. She grinned in satisfaction at the result. Tomorrow, she'd take their guardian for a trial run.

Lyse stirred in her nest of blankets as a sense of unease roused her from slumber. She strained her ears, but the night held only the normal sounds she'd come to expect. Stretching out her magical senses, she tried to determine what was amiss.

Malevolence hung in the air.

Cursing silently, she rolled out of her nest and went to investigate. A tickle of intuition told her to grab the shale heart, so she did.

Lyse crept out of her tent and past the banked coals in her fire circle. Staying very still, she strained her senses but garnered nothing more than the general feeling of malevolence she'd felt on waking.

Then she sniffed, her nose twitching at the acrid scent of smoke wafting from behind her.

Lyse jerked her head around. A flicker of orange light danced among the grapevines. She cursed aloud this time. Only one group would want to burn down the vineyards of Dambach-la-Ville – the German Empire. They would do anything to bring the headstrong town to heel.

Lyse grounded herself and gathered all the magical strength she could. Crying out in the near-silent night, she called every owl she could to fly over the walls and wake the citizens, warning them of the danger in their fields.

She looked at her golem, hesitant to wake it. Instinct had guided her hand more than knowledge. Would it work? Would it obey? She didn't know. There were no instructions for what she had done, repurposing spells and inventing new ones. She had promised a guardian, with no certainty she could provide one. She'd made a promise to Dambach-la-Ville, and they gave her everything they could spare.

This required strong magic, and strong magic required sacrifice. She pushed up her sleeve. Reaching into her pocket, she drew out the red shale heart. With care, she ran the sharp knapped edge across her skin and opened a wide gash in her forearm. She turned and rolled the stone in her blood until it was covered.

Pressing the bloody shale heart against the golem's chest, she poured every shred of magical energy in her body through it into the golem. An electric tingle of magic trilled down her nerves as she felt the stone sink into the metal and fuse itself to the golem. She kept her words simple.

"Follow me. Protect me."

The lenses forming the golem's eyes began to glow. As she took a reflexive step back, her construct took a step forward. Turning, Lyse ran for the vineyards. Already drained from the spell-working, her breath sawed painfully in and out of her lungs. Her legs weighed her like granite. But she ran. She heard the clanking steps of the golem close behind her.

Stumbling and weak, she finally made it across the fields to the vineyards. She found exactly what she thought she would find. German soldiers dressed head to toe in black held torches to the famed vines of Dambach-la-Ville. Lyse screeched as she threw herself at the nearest soldier. As she expected, he swatted her away with a brutal backhand. She flew to the ground, blood streaming from a split lip. She levered herself up, screaming at the soldiers to stop. One cursed at her and kicked her back to the ground.

The golem waded in.

The soldier who kicked her shrieked. Lyse could not tell why. Her head swam, and darkness gathered at the edges of her vision. She struggled to draw air. As she faded, realization dawned. Spell sickness. Lyse rolled to her side, her body numb. She had poured so much of herself into the golem; there was nothing left to keep her heart beating. She hoped her guardian would keep functioning after her death and continue to safeguard Dambach-la-Ville. Just before she lost consciousness, she thought she heard the hoots of owls and someone calling her name.

Lyse woke, aching and confused, in an actual bed for the first time in… well, she could scarcely remember. She tried to sit up, but her body screamed in protest until she reclined once more.

"Ah, there you are! Finally!" A friendly but unfamiliar woman leaned over her, smiling.

"Where…?" Lyse croaked.

"You are in Dambach-la-Ville, my dear," the woman said. "You saved us!"

"Who…?"

"I am Madame Durand, but please, call me Violette." She patted Lyse's hand. "You just rest. The owls came just in time to warn us. That metal golem had already dealt with the soldiers by the time we got there, but we still had to put the fire out. Just rest. You are safe."

Lyse let her muscles ease and relaxed into the soft feather bed. There was a mountain close. There were people who cared for her. She was home.

About the Authors

James Chambers received the Bram Stoker Award® for the graphic novel, *Kolchak the Night Stalker: The Forgotten Lore of Edgar Allan Poe* and is a four-time Bram Stoker Award nominee. He is the author of the short story collections *On the Night Border* and *On the Hierophant Road*, which received a starred review from *Booklist*, which called it "…satisfyingly unsettling"; and the novella collection, *The Engines of Sacrifice*, described as "…chillingly evocative…" in a *Publisher's Weekly* starred review. He has written the novellas, *Three Chords of Chaos, Kolchak and the Night Stalkers: The Faceless God*, and many others, including the Corpse Fauna cycle: *The Dead Bear Witness, Tears of Blood, The Dead in Their Masses*, and *The Eyes of the Dead*. He also writes the Machinations Sundry series of steampunk stories. He edited the Bram Stoker Award-nominated anthology, *Under Twin Suns: Alternate Histories of the Yellow Sign* and co-edited *A New York State of Fright* and *Even in the Grave*, an anthology of ghost stories. His website is: www.jameschambersonline.com.

Jeff Young is a bookseller first and a writer second—although he wouldn't mind a reversal of fortune.

He is an award-winning author who has contributed to the anthologies: *Afterpunk, In an Iron Cage: The Magic of Steampunk, Clockwork Chaos, Gaslight and Grimm, Phantasmical Contraptions and other Errors, By Any Means, Best Laid Plans, Dogs of War, Man and Machine, If We Had Known, Fantastic Futures 13, The Society for the Preservation of C.J. Henderson, Eccentric Orbits 2 & 3, Writers of the Future V.26, TV Gods* and *TV Gods: Summer Programming*. Jeff's own fiction is collected in *Spirit Seeker, Written in Light* and TOI *Special Edition 2 – Diversiforms*. He has also edited the *Drunken Comic Book Monkey* line, *TV Gods* and *TV Gods – Summer Programming* and is the managing editor for the magazine, *Mendie the Post-Apocalyptic Flower Scout*. He has led the Watch the Skies SF&F Discussion Group of Camp Hill and Harrisburg for twenty-two years. Jeff is also the proprietor of Helm Haven, the online Etsy and Ebay shops, costuming resources for Renaissance and Steampunk.

Much to his embarrassment, **Bernie Mojzes** has outlived Lord Byron, Percy Shelley, Janice Joplin and the Red Baron, without even once having been shot down over Morlancourt Ridge. Having failed to achieve a glorious martyrdom, he has instead turned his hand to the penning of paltry prose (a rather wretched example of which you currently hold in your hands), in the pathetic hope that he shall here find the notoriety that has thus far proven elusive. His work has appeared in a number of anthologies and magazines, including *Bad-Ass Faeries II* and *III*, *Gaslight & Grimm, Betwixt Magazine, Daily Science Fiction*, and *What Lies Beneath*. In his copious free time, he published and co-edited *Unlikely Story* (www.unlikely-story.com) and the ever-timely *Clowns: The Unlikely Coulrophobia Remix*, as well as editing *The Flesh Made Word* for Circlet Press. Should Pity or perhaps a Perverse Curiosity move you to seek him out, he can be found at http://www.kappamaki.com.

David Lee Summers became a steampunk in 1987 when he used a nineteenth century telescope on Nantucket to examine the evolution of distant pulsating stars. Since that time, he has published a dozen novels and numerous short stories and poems spanning a wide range of the imagination. *Owl Dance, Lightning Wolves, The Brazen Shark*, and *Owl Riders* comprise the Clockwork Legion steampunk series. His other novels include *The Astronomer's Crypt, Vampires of the Scarlet Order* and *Firebrandt's Legacy*. His latest novella is a World War II-era cryptid tale called *Breaking the Code*.

David's short stories have appeared in such magazines and anthologies as *Realms of Fantasy, Cemetery Dance, Straight Outta Tombstone, Gaslight and Grimm*, and *After Punk*. He's been twice nominated for the Science Fiction Poetry Association's Rhysling Award.

In addition to writing, David has edited the science fiction anthologies: *A Kepler's Dozen, Kepler's Cowboys*, and *Maximum Velocity: The Best of the Full-Throttle Space Tales*. When not working with the written word, David operates telescopes at Kitt Peak National Observatory. Learn more about David at www.davidleesummers.com.

There's been a debate among certain obscure and drunken literary scholars about whether **Patrick Thomas** was raised by Cthulhu or a leprechaun in a Manhattan bar. What there is no arguing about is that Patrick is the award-winning author of 50+ books including the beloved fantasy humor *Murphy's Lore* series, the darkly hilarious *Dear Cthulhu* advice empire, as well as the *Bikini Jones* books, the *Mystic Investigators* series, and the creator of the *Agents of the Abyss*. His other books include the *Hexcraft* and the *Terrorbelle* series, *Exile & Entrance*, *Cryptid Fight Club*, and the mystery *Assassins' Ball* co-written with John L. French.

Dear Cthulhu has expanded from magazines and books to broadcast monthly on the radio show *Destinies: The Voice of Science Fiction*. Over 100 of his stories have been published in magazines and anthologies. A number of his books were part of the props department of the *CSI* television show and *Nightcaps* was even thrown at a suspect's head. His urban fantasy *Fairy With A Gun* at one point had been optioned for film and TV by Laurence Fishburne's Cinema Gypsy Productions. Top Men Productions has turned his Soul For Hire Story, *Act of Contrition*, into a short film.

As Patrick T. Fibbs, he writes middle readers including the *Babe B. Bear Mysteries*, The *Undead Kid Diaries*, *Joy Reaper Checks Out*, the YA *Emotional Support Nightmare*, and the *Ughabooz* books for younger kids.

Visit him at www.patthomas.net and www.patricktfibbs.com.

Cynthia Radthorne is an author and illustrator residing in the Pacific Northwest. Her characters, both honorable and devious, populate her series of Asian-themed fantasy novels, The Tales of Tonogato. Her illustrations have appeared on book covers, web sites, trading card games, and at art show displays at science fiction and fantasy conventions. At Cynthia's website, www.CynthiaRadthorne.com, one can peruse a sample from one of her books and view her art gallery.

Once Upon a Time, **Christine Norris** thought she wanted to be an archaeologist but hates sand and bugs, so instead, she became a writer. She is the author of several speculative fiction works for children and adults, including *The Library of Athena* series, *A Curse of Ash and Iron*, and contributions to *Gaslight and Grimm* and *Grimm Machinations*. She is kept busy on a daily basis by her day job as a school librarian in New Jersey. She may or may not have a secret library in her basement, and she absolutely believes in fairies.

Gordon Linzner is the founder and former editor of *Space and Time Magazine* and the author of three published novels and dozens of short stories appearing in *Fantasy & Science Fiction*, *Twilight Zone*, *Sherlock Holmes Mystery Magazine*, and numerous other magazines and anthologies. He is also a copy editor, a licensed New York City tour guide, a sound technician, and the lead singer for the Saboteur Tiger Blues band, among other odd jobs. He is a full member of the Horror Writers Association and a lifetime member of the Science Fiction & Fantasy Writers Association.

Award-winning author, editor, and publisher **Danielle Ackley-McPhail** has worked both sides of the publishing industry for longer than she cares to admit. In 2014 she joined forces with Mike McPhail and Greg Schauer to form eSpec Books.

Her published works include eight novels, *Yesterday's Dreams, Tomorrow's Memories, Today's Promise, The Halfling's Court, The Redcaps' Queen, Daire's Devils, The Play of Light,* and *Baba Ali and the Clockwork Djinn,* written with Day Al-Mohamed. She is also the author of the solo collections *Eternal Wanderings, A Legacy of Stars, Consigned to the Sea, Flash in the Can, Transcendence, The Kindly Ones, Dawns a New Day, The Fox's Fire, Between Darkness and Light,* and the non-fiction writers' guides *The Literary Handyman, More Tips from the Handyman,* and *LH: Build-A-Book Workshop.* She is the senior editor of the *Bad-Ass Faeries* anthology series, *Gaslight & Grimm, Side of Good/Side of Evil, After Punk,* and *Footprints in the Stars.* Her short stories are included in numerous other anthologies and collections. She is a full member of the Science Fiction and Fantasy Writers Association.

In addition to her literary acclaim, she crafts and sells original costume horns under the moniker The Hornie Lady Custom Costume Horns, and homemade flavor-infused candied ginger under the brand of Ginger KICK! at literary conventions, on commission, and wholesale.

Danielle lives in New Jersey with husband and fellow writer Mike McPhail and four extremely spoiled cats.

Michelle D. Sonnier writes dark urban fantasy, steampunk, and anything else that lets her combine the weird and the fantastic in unexpected ways. She even writes horror, although it took her a long time to admit that since she prefers the existential scare over blood and gore. She is the author of *The Clockwork Witch, The Clockwork Solution,* and *Death's Embrace* and has published short stories in a variety of print and online venues. You can find her on Facebook (Michelle D. Sonnier, The Author). She lives in Maryland with her husband, son, and a variable number of cats.

Friends of the Faerie Tale

A. L. Kaplan
Alicia M Rabb
Allison E. Kaese
Alp Beck
Andee Bowden
Andrew Hatchell
Andrew Kaplan
Anonymous Readers
Anthony R. Cardno
Aramanth
Ashley Grant
Asp Zelazny
Barb Moermond
Becky B
Bess Turner
Beth Kee
Beth Lobdell
Beth Rimmels
Beth Sparks-Jacques
Bill Kohn
Bodge Inglee Richards
Brendan Lonehawk
Brian D Lambert
Brooks Moses
Brynn
Buddy Deal
C.A. Rowland
Carl W Bishop
Carol J. Guess
Carol Mammano
Chad Bowden
Charissa D. Jones
Charity Myhre
Charlee Roth

Cheri Kannarr
Christine Norris
Christopher Hykes
Christopher J. Burke
Cindy Joy
CJ Frost
Colleen Feeney
Craig & René Arnush
Cristov Russell
Cynthia Radthorne
Dale A Russell
Dana Fraedrich
Danielle Ackley-McPhail
David Goldstein
David Zurek
Dayton Shaw
Deborah A. Flores
Debra Lieven
Doc Coleman
Don Crossman
Donna Marie Hogg
Doug Williams
Douglas G. Yeager
Douglas Yeager
Ef Deal
Elaine Tindill-Rohr
Elaine Yang
Ellery Rhodes
Elyse M Grasso
Emma Lombard
Eric Schumacher
Eron Wyngarde
Gary Phillips
Gavin

Gayle Homes Martin
Ginger Devaney
Greg Levick
Hadrosaur Productions
Heather L.P. Estep
Heidi B Pilewski
Helen Walter
Hiram G Wells
Ian Harvey
Isaac 'Will It Work' Dansicker
Jaap van Poelgeest
Jack Deal
Jacob H Joseph
Janet Worley
Janito V. F. Filho
Jason
Jeanne Talbourdet
Jeff Young
Jenn Long
Jennifer Eaton
Jennifer L. Pierce
Jeremy Bottroff
Jess
Jessa Willson
Jessi Sindel
Jessica Lewis
Joanne Burrows
Joe Monson
John L. French
John Shrek Walters
John Stuart
John Wilson
Jon W. Quigley
Jonathan Mendonca
Jonathan Roth
Jordan G Ritchie
Josh McGinnis
Julian White
June L. Chase
June L. Chase
Kal Powell

Kat James
Kathryn Black
Katie French
Kelly A. Durkee-Erwin
Kelly Pierce
Kerry aka Trouble
Kestrel von Nerdenheimer
Kierin Fox
Krinsky
Kristiina Mannermaa
Krystal Bohannan
KT Magrowski
Kurt Beyerl
Kyro Dean
Larien
Laura Pesula
Linda Pierce
Lisa Kruse
Lloyd Lively
Lorraine J. Anderson
Louise Lowenspets
Lynda McCann
Mad Madeline
Madame Askew
Madeleine Holly-Rosing
maileguy
Margaret Bumby
Margaret M. St. John
Mari Hersh-Tudor
Maria V. Arnold
Marie Devey
Marilyn Bennett
Marissa C.
Mark Carter
Mark Newman
Martin Oe.
Mary-Michelle Moore
Matt & Liz Aronoff
Maureen Lewis
Mel Follmer
Melody Huckins

Michael Barbour
Michael Fedrowitz
Michele Hall
Michelle LaCrosse
Mike Smith
Morgan Hazelwood
Museworthy Inc.
Natasha Hubbard
Neil Ottenstein
Nellie B
No Name
Oliver James Minall
Otter Libris
Patrick Thomas
Paul Mojzes
Paul Ryan
Paul van Oven
Phil Huffsmith
Phil Pearson
pjk
prophet
PunkARTchick "Ruthenia"
Rachel
Raphael Bressel
Rhonda Goodman-Gaghan
Rich Walker
Richard Novak
Richard O'Shea
RKBookman
Robert C Flipse
Robert Claney
Robert Dahlen
Robin Schwarz
Russell Dennis Trimble
Sally W
Sanan Kolva

Sara E. Ontiveros
Sarah Olliso Flores
Scantrontb
Scott Schaper
Sebastian Ernst
Shawnee M
Shervyn
Sheryl R. Hayes
Sioux McGill
Sonya Mota
Stace Johnson
Stacy K Waddington
Steph Parker
Stephanie Lucas
Stephen Ballentine
Stephen Buchanan
Stuart Chaplin
Susan J. Voss
Susan R Grossman
Tasha Turner
Taylor Hunter
tchwrtr
Tess DeGroot
The Creative Fund by BackerKit
Thomas Karwacki
Tim DuBois
Timothy Ryan Scully
Tina M Noe Good
Tom Tiernan
Tracy 'Rayhne" Fretwell
Valerie Bello
Vicki Hsu
Walter J. Montie
white beard geek
William J. Jackson

9 781956 463255